ON THE
BLACK HILL

Also by Bruce Chatwin

IN PATAGONIA

THE VICEROY OF OUIDAH

ON THE BLACK HILL

BRUCE CHATWIN

THE VIKING PRESS

NEW YORK

Published in 1983 by The Viking Press
625 Madison Avenue, New York, N.Y.

LIBRARY OF CONGRESS CATALOGING IN PUBLICATION DATA
Chatwin, Bruce, 1942 –
On the black hill.
I. Title.
PR6053.H39505   1983   823'.914   82-10923
ISBN 0-670-52492-1

Grateful acknowledgment is made to New Directions Publish-
ing Corporation for permission to reprint a selection from
Personae by Ezra Pound. Copyright 1926 by Ezra Pound.

Printed in the United States of America
Set in Bembo

FOR FRANCIS WYNDHAM
AND FOR DIANA MELLY

'*Since we stay not here, being people but of a dayes abode, and our age is like that of a flie, and contemporary with a gourd, we must look some where else for an abiding city, a place in another countrey to fix our house in...*'

Jeremy Taylor

ON THE
BLACK HILL

I

FOR FORTY-TWO YEARS, Lewis and Benjamin Jones slept side by side, in their parents' bed, at their farm which was known as 'The Vision'.

The bedstead, an oak four-poster, came from their mother's home at Bryn-Draenog when she married in 1899. Its faded cretonne hangings, printed with a design of larkspur and roses, shut out the mosquitoes of summer, and the draughts in winter. Calloused heels had worn holes in the linen sheets, and parts of the patchwork quilt had frayed. Under the goose-feather mattress, there was a second mattress, of horsehair, and this had sunk into two troughs, leaving a ridge between the sleepers.

The room was always dark and smelled of lavender and mothballs.

The smell of mothballs came from a pyramid of hatboxes piled up beside the washstand. On the bed-table lay a pin-cushion still stuck with Mrs Jones's hatpins; and on the end wall hung an engraving of Holman Hunt's 'Light of the World', enclosed in an ebonized frame.

One of the windows looked out over the green fields of England: the other looked back into Wales, past a clump of larches, at the Black Hill.

Both the brothers' hair was even whiter than the pillow-cases.

Every morning their alarm went off at six. They listened to the farmers' broadcast as they shaved and dressed. Down-stairs, they tapped the barometer, lit the fire and boiled a kettle for tea. Then they did the milking and foddering before coming back for breakfast.

The house had roughcast walls and a roof of mossy stone tiles and stood at the far end of the farmyard in the shade of an old Scots pine. Below the cowshed there was an orchard of wind-stunted apple-trees, and then the fields slanted down to the dingle, and there were birches and alders along the stream.

Long ago, the place had been called Ty-Cradoc — and Caractacus is still a name in these parts — but in 1737 an ailing girl called Alice Morgan saw the Virgin hovering over a patch of rhubarb, and ran back to the kitchen, cured. To celebrate the miracle, her father renamed his farm 'The Vision' and carved the initials A.M. with the date and a cross on the lintel above the porch. The border of Radnor and Hereford was said to run right through the middle of the staircase.

The brothers were identical twins.

As boys, only their mother could tell them apart: now age and accidents had weathered them in different ways.

Lewis was tall and stringy, with shoulders set square and a steady long-limbed stride. Even at eighty he could walk over the hills all day, or wield an axe all day, and not get tired.

He gave off a strong smell. His eyes — grey, dreamy and astygmatic — were set well back into the skull, and capped with thick round lenses in white metal frames. He bore the scar of a cycling accident on his nose and, ever since, its tip had curved downwards and turned purple in cold weather.

His head would wobble as he spoke: unless he was fumbling with his watch-chain, he had no idea what to do with his hands. In company he always wore a puzzled look; and if anyone made a statement of fact, he'd say, 'Thank you!' or 'Very kind of you!' Everyone agreed he had a wonderful way with sheepdogs.

Benjamin was shorter, pinker, neater and sharper-tongued. His chin fell into his neck, but he still possessed the full stretch of his nose, which he would use in conversation as a weapon. He had less hair.

He did all the cooking, the darning and the ironing; and he kept the accounts. No one could be fiercer in a haggle over stock-prices and he would go on, arguing for hours, until the dealer threw up his hands and said, 'Come off, you old skinflint!' and he'd smile and say, 'What can you mean by that?'

For miles around the twins had the reputation of being incredibly stingy — but this was not always so.

They refused, for example, to make a penny out of hay. Hay, they said, was God's gift to the farmer; and providing The Vision had hay to spare, their poorer neighbours were welcome to what they needed. Even in the foul days of January, old Miss Fifield the Tump had only to send a message with the postman, and Lewis would drive the tractor over with a load of bales.

Benjamin's favourite occupation was delivering lambs. All the long winter, he waited for the end of March, when the curlews started calling and the lambing began. It was he, not Lewis, who stayed awake to watch the ewes. It was he who would pull a lamb at a difficult birth. Sometimes, he had to thrust his forearm into the womb to disentangle a pair of twins; and afterwards, he would sit by the fireside, unwashed and contented, and let the cat lick the afterbirth off his hands.

In winter and summer, the brothers went to work in striped flannel shirts with copper studs to fasten them at the neck. Their jackets and waistcoats were made of brown whipcord, and their trousers were of darker corduroy. They wore their moleskin hats with the brims turned down; but since Lewis had the habit of lifting his to every stranger, his fingers had rubbed the nap off the peak.

From time to time, with a show of mock solemnity, they consulted their silver watches — not to tell the hour but to see whose watch was beating faster. On Saturday nights they took turns to have a hip-bath in front of the fire; and they lived for the memory of their mother.

Because they knew each other's thoughts, they even quarrelled without speaking. And sometimes — perhaps after one of these silent quarrels, when they needed their mother to unite them — they would stand over her patchwork quilt and peer at the black velvet stars and the hexagons of printed calico that had once been her dresses. And without saying a word they could see her again — in pink, walking through the oatfield with a jug of draught cider for the reapers. Or in green, at a sheep-shearers' lunch. Or in a blue-striped apron bending over the fire. But the black stars brought back a memory of their father's coffin, laid out on the kitchen table, and the chalk-faced women, crying.

Nothing in the kitchen had changed since the day of his funeral. The wallpaper, with its pattern of Iceland poppies and russet fern, had darkened over with smoke-resin; and though the brass knobs shone as brightly as ever, the brown paint had chipped from the doors and skirting.

The twins never thought of renewing these threadbare decorations for fear of cancelling out the memory of that bright spring morning, over seventy years before, when they had helped their mother stir a bucket of flour-and-water paste, and watched the whitewash caking on her scarf.

Benjamin kept her flagstones scrubbed, the iron grate gleaming with black lead polish, and a copper kettle always hissing on the hob.

Friday was his baking day — as it had once been hers — and on Friday afternoons he would roll up his sleeves to make Welsh cakes or cottage loaves, pummelling the dough so vigorously that the cornflowers on the oilcloth cover had almost worn away.

On the mantelpiece stood a pair of Staffordshire spaniels, five brass candlesticks, a ship-in-a-bottle and a tea-caddy painted with a Chinese lady. A glass-fronted cabinet — one pane repaired with Scotch tape — contained china ornaments, silver-plated teapots, and mugs from every Coronation and Jubilee. A flitch of bacon was rammed into a rack in the rafters. The Georgian pianoforte was proof of idler days and past accomplishments.

Lewis kept a twelve-bore shotgun propped up beside the grandfather clock: both the brothers were terrified of thieves and antique-dealers.

Their father's only hobby — in fact, his only interest apart from farming and the Bible — had been to carve wooden frames for the pictures and family photographs that covered every spare stretch of wall. To Mrs Jones it had been a miracle that a man of her husband's temper and clumsy hands should have had the patience for such intricate work. Yet, from the moment he took up his chisels, from the moment the tiny white shavings flew, all the meanness went out of him.

He had carved a 'gothic' frame for the religious colour print 'The Broad and Narrow Path'. He had invented some 'biblical' motifs for the watercolour of the Pool of Bethesda; and when his brother sent an oleograph from Canada, he smeared the surface with linseed oil to make it look like an Old Master, and spent a whole winter working up a surround of maple leaves.

And it was this picture, with its Red Indian, its birchbark, its pines and a crimson sky — to say nothing of its association with the legendary Uncle Eddie — that first awoke in Lewis a yearning for far-off places.

Apart from a holiday at the seaside in 1910, neither of the twins had ever strayed further than Hereford. Yet these restricted horizons merely inflamed Lewis's passion for geography. He would pester visitors for their opinions on 'them savages in Africky'; for news of Siberia, Salonika or Sri Lanka; and when someone spoke of President Carter's failure to rescue the Teheran hostages, he folded his arms and said, decisively, 'Him should'a gone to get 'em through Odessa.'

His image of the outside world derived from a Bartholomew's atlas of 1925 when the two great colonial empires were coloured pink and mauve, and the Soviet Union was a dull sage green. And it offended his sense of order to find that the planet was now full of bickering little countries with unpronounceable names. So, as if to suggest that real journeys only existed in the imagination — and perhaps to show off — he would close his eyes and chant the lines his mother taught him:

Westward, westward, Hiawatha
Sailed into the fiery sunset
Sailed into the purple vapours
Sailed into the dusk of evening.

Too often the twins had fretted at the thought of dying childless — yet they had only to glance at their wall of photographs to get rid of the gloomiest thoughts. They knew the names of all the sitters and never tired of finding likenesses between people born a hundred years apart.

Hanging to the left of their parents' wedding group was a picture of themselves at the age of six, gaping like baby barn-owls and dressed in identical page-boy collars for the fête

13

in Lurkenhope Park. But the one that gave them most pleasure was a colour snapshot of their great-nephew Kevin, also aged six, and got up in a wash-towel turban, as Joseph in a nativity play.

Since then, fourteen years had passed and Kevin had grown into a tall, black-haired young man with bushy eyebrows that met in the middle, and slaty grey-blue eyes. In a few months the farm would be his.

So now, when they looked at that faded wedding picture; when they saw their father's face framed in fiery red sideburns (even in a sepia photo you could tell he had bright red hair); when they saw the leg-o'-mutton sleeves of their mother's dress, the roses in her hat, and the ox-eye daisies in her bouquet; and when they compared her sweet smile with Kevin's, they knew that their lives had not been wasted and that time, in its healing circle, had wiped away the pain and the anger, the shame and the sterility, and had broken into the future with the promise of new things.

II

OF ALL THE PEOPLE who posed outside the Red Dragon at Rhulen, that sweltering afternoon in August 1899, none had better reason for looking pleased with himself than Amos Jones, the bridegroom. In one week, he had achieved two of his three ambitions: he had married a beautiful wife, and had signed the lease of a farm.

His father, a garrulous old cider-drinker, known round the pubs of Radnorshire as Sam the Waggon, had started life as a drover; had failed to make a living as a carter; and now lived, cooped up with his wife, in a tiny cottage on Rhulen Hill.

Hannah Jones was not an agreeable woman. As a young bride, she had loved her husband to distraction; had put up with his absences and infidelities, and, thanks to a monumental meanness, had always managed to thwart the bailiffs.

Then came the catastrophes that hardened her into a mould of unrelieved bitterness and left her mouth as sharp and twisted as a leaf of holly.

Of her five children, a daughter had died of consumption; another married a Catholic; the eldest son was killed in a Rhondda coalpit; her favourite, Eddie, stole her savings and skipped to Canada — and that left only Amos to support her old age.

Because he was her final fledgling, she coddled him more carefully than the others, and sent him to Sunday School to learn letters and fear of the Lord. He was not a stupid boy, but, by the age of fifteen, he had disappointed her hopes for his education; and she booted him from the house and sent him to earn his own keep.

Twice a year, in May and November, he hung round the Rhulen Fair, waiting for a farmer to hire him, with a wisp of sheep's wool in his cap and a clean Sunday smock folded over his arm.

He found work on several farms in Radnorshire and Montgomery, where he learned to handle a plough; to sow, reap and shear; to butcher hogs and dig the sheep out of snowdrifts. When his boots fell apart, he had to bind his feet with strips of felt. He would come back in the evenings, aching at every joint, to a supper of bacon broth and potatoes, and a few stale crusts. The owners were far too mean to provide a cup of tea.

He slept on bales of hay, in the granary or stable-loft, and would lie awake on winter nights, shivering under a damp blanket: there was no fire to dry his clothes. One Monday morning, his employer horsewhipped him for stealing some slices of cold mutton while the family was out at Chapel — a crime of which the cat, not he, was guilty.

He ran away three times and three times forfeited his wages. And yet he walked with a swagger, wore his cap at a rakish angle, and, hoping to attract a pretty farmer's daughter, spent his spare pennies on brightly coloured handkerchiefs.

His first attempt at seduction failed.

To wake the girl he threw a twig against her bedroom window, and she slipped him the key. Then, tiptoeing through the kitchen, his shin caught on a stool, and he tripped. A copper pot crashed to the floor; the dog barked, and a man's deep voice called out: her father was on the staircase as he bolted from the house.

At twenty-eight, he spoke of emigrating to Argentina where there were rumours of land and horses – at which his mother panicked and found him a bride.

She was a plain, dull-witted woman, ten years older than he, who sat all day staring at her hands and was already a burden on her family.

Hannah haggled for three days until the bride's father agreed that Amos should take her, as well as thirty breeding ewes, the lease of a smallholding called Cwmcoynant, and grazing rights on Rhulen Hill.

But the land was sour. It lay on a sunless slope and, at the snowmelt, streams of icy water came pouring through the cottage. Yet by renting a patch of ground here, another patch there; by buying stock in shares with other farmers, Amos managed to make a living and hope for better times.

There were no joys in that marriage.

Rachel Jones obeyed her husband with the passive movements of an automaton. She mucked out the pigsties in a torn tweed coat tied up with a bit of twine. She never smiled. She never cried when he hit her. She replied to his questions with grunts or monosyllables; and even in the agony of childbirth, she clenched her mouth so tightly that she uttered not a sound.

The baby was a boy. Having no milk, she sent him away to nurse, and he died. In November 1898, she stopped eating and set her face against the living world. There were snowdrops in the graveyard when they buried her.

From that day Amos Jones was a regular churchgoer.

III

ONE SUNDAY MATINS, not a month after the funeral, the vicar of Rhulen announced that he had to attend a service in Llandaff Cathedral and that, next Sunday, the rector of Bryn-Draenog would preach the sermon.

This was the Reverend Latimer, an Old Testament scholar, who had retired from mission work in India and settled in this remote hill parish to be alone with his daughter and his books.

From time to time, Amos Jones had seen him on the mountain — a hollow-chested figure with white hair blowing about like cotton-grass, striding over the heather and shouting to himself so loudly that he frightened off the sheep. He had not seen the daughter, who was said to be sad and beautiful. He took his seat at the end of the pew.

On the way, the Latimers had to shelter from a cloudburst and, by the time their dog-cart drew up outside the church, they were twenty minutes late. While the rector changed in the vestry, Miss Latimer walked towards the choir-stalls, lowering her eyes to the strip of wine-red carpet, and avoiding the stares of the congregation. She brushed against Amos Jones's shoulder, and she stopped. She took half a step backwards, another step sideways, and then sat down, one pew in front of him, but across the aisle.

Drops of water sparkled on her black beaver hat, and her chignon of chestnut hair. Her grey serge coat was also streaked with rain.

On one of the stained-glass windows was a figure of the Prophet Elijah and his raven. Outside, on the sill, a pair of pigeons were billing and cooing and pecking at the pane.

The first hymn was 'Guide Me, O Thou Great Redeemer' and as the voices swelled in chorus, Amos caught her clear, quavering soprano while she felt his baritone murmuring like a bumblebee round the nape of her neck. All through the Lord's Prayer he stared at her long, white, tapering fingers. After the Second Lesson she risked a sidelong glance and saw his red hands on the red buckram binding of his prayerbook.

She blushed in confusion and slipped on her gloves.

Then her father was in the pulpit, twisting his mouth:

' "Though your sins be as scarlet, they shall be as white as snow; though they be red like crimson, they shall be as wool. If ye be willing and obedient..." '

She gazed at her hassock and felt her heart was breaking. After the service Amos passed her in the lych-gate, but she flashed her eyes and turned her back and peered into the boughs of a yew.

He forgot her – he tried to forget her – until one Thursday in April, he went to Rhulen market to sell some hoggets and exchange the news.

Along the length of Broad Street the farmers who had driven in from the country were tethering their ponies, and chatting in groups. Carts stood empty with their shafts in the air. From the bakery came the smell of freshly baked bread. In front of the Town Hall there were booths with red-striped awnings, and black hats bobbing round them. In Castle Street the crowds were even thicker as people jostled forward to inspect the lots of Welsh and Hereford cattle. The sheep and pigs were penned behind hurdles. There was a nip in the air, and clouds of steam rose up off the animals' flanks.

Outside the Red Dragon two greybeards were drinking cider and moaning about 'them bloomin' rogues in Parliament'. A nasal voice called out the price of wicker chairs, and a purple-faced stock-dealer pumped the hand of a thin man in a brown derby.

'And 'ow's you?'

'Middling.'

'And the wife?'

'Poor.'

Two blue farm waggons, strewn with straw and piled with dressed poultry, were parked beside the municipal clock; and their owners, a pair of women in plaid shawls, were gossiping away, trying hard to feign indifference to the Birmingham buyer, who circled around them, twirling his malacca cane.

As Amos passed, he heard one of them say: 'And the poor thing! To think she's alone in the world!'

On the Saturday, a shepherd riding on the hill had found

the Reverend Latimer's body, face downward in a pool. He had slipped in the peat bog and drowned. They had buried him at Bryn-Draenog on the Tuesday.

Amos sold his hoggets for what they would fetch and, as he put the coins into his waistcoat pocket, he saw that his hand was shaking.

Next morning, after foddering, he took a stick and walked the nine miles to Bryn-Draenog Hill. On reaching the line of rocks that crown the summit, he sat down out of the wind and retied a bootlace. Overhead, puffy clouds were streaming out of Wales, their shadows plunging down the slopes of gorse and heather, slowing up as they moved across the fields of winter wheat.

He felt light-headed, almost happy, as if his life, too, would begin afresh.

To the east was the River Wye, a silver ribbon snaking through water-meadows, and the whole countryside dotted with white or red-brick farmhouses. A thatched roof made a little patch of yellow in a foam of apple-blossom, and there were gloomy stands of conifers that shrouded the homes of the gentry.

A few hundred yards below, the sun caught the slates of Bryn-Draenog rectory and reflected back to the hill-top a parallelogram of open sky. Two buzzards were wheeling and falling in the blue air, and there were lambs and crows in a bright green field.

In the graveyard, a woman in black was moving in and out among the headstones. Then she passed through the wicket gate and walked up the overgrown garden. She was halfway across the lawn when a little dog came bounding out to greet her, yapping and pawing at her skirt. She threw a stick into the shrubbery and the dog raced off and came back, without the stick, and pawed again at her skirt. Something seemed to stop her from entering the house.

He raced downhill, his heel-irons clattering over the loose stones. Then he leaned over the garden fence, panting to catch his breath, and she was still standing, motionless among the laurels, with the dog lying quietly at her feet.

'Oh! It's you!' she said as she turned to face him.

'Your father,' he stammered. 'I'm sorry, Miss——'

'I know,' she stopped him. 'Do please come inside.'

He made an excuse for the mud on his boots.

'Mud!' she laughed. 'Mud can't dirty this house. And besides, I have to leave it.'

She showed him into her father's study. The room was dusty and lined with books. Outside the window, the bracts of a monkey-puzzle blocked out the sunlight. Tufts of horsehair spilled from the sofa on to a worn Turkey carpet. The desk was littered with yellowing papers and, on a revolving stand, there were Bibles and Commentaries on the Bible. On the black marble mantelpiece lay a few flint axeheads, and some bits of Roman pottery.

She went up to the piano, snatched the contents of a vase, and threw them in the grate.

'What horrible things they are!' she said. 'How I hate everlasting flowers!'

She eyed him as he looked at a watercolour – of white arches, a date palm, and women with pitchers.

'It's the Pool of Bethesda,' she said. 'We went there. We went all over the Holy Land on our way back from India. We saw Nazareth and Bethlehem and the Sea of Galilee. We saw Jerusalem. It was my father's dream.'

'I'd like some water,' he said.

She led the way down a passage to the kitchen. The table was scrubbed and bare; and there was not a sign of food.

She said, 'To think I can't even offer you a cup of tea!'

Outside again in the sunlight, he saw that her hair was streaked with grey, and there were crow's-feet spreading to her cheekbones. But he liked her smile, and the brown eyes shining between long black lashes. Around her waist there curled a tight black patent leather belt. His breeder's eye meandered from her shoulders to her hips.

'And I don't even know your name,' she said, and stretched out her hand.

'But Amos Jones is a wonderful name,' she continued, strolling beside him to the garden gate. Then she waved and ran back to the house. The last he saw of her, she was standing in the study. The black tentacles of the monkey-puzzle, reflected in the window, seemed to hold her white face prisoner as she pressed it to the pane.

He climbed the hill, then bounded from one grassy hummock to the next, shouting at the top of his voice: 'Mary Latimer! Mary Jones! Mary Latimer! Mary Jones! Mary!...Mary!...Mary...!

Two days later he was back at the rectory with the present of a chicken he had plucked and drawn himself.

She was waiting on the porch, in a long blue wool dress, a Kashmiri shawl round her shoulders and a cameo, of Minerva, on a brown velvet ribbon round her neck.

'I missed to come yesterday,' he said.

'But I knew you'd come today.'

She threw back her head and laughed, and the dog caught a whiff of the chicken and jumped up and down, and scratched its paws on Amos's trousers. He pulled the chicken from his knapsack. She saw the cold pimply flesh. The smile fell from her face, and she stood rooted to the doorstep, shuddering.

They tried to talk in the hall, but she wrung her hands and stared at the red-tiled floor, while he shifted from foot to foot and felt himself colouring from his neck to his ears.

Both were bursting with things to say to each other. Both felt, at that moment, there was nothing more to say; that nothing would come of their meeting; that their two accents would never make one whole voice; and that they would both creep back to their shells — as if the flash of recognition in church were a trick of fate, or a temptation of the Devil to ruin them. They stammered on, and gradually their words spaced themselves into silence: their eyes did not meet as he edged out backwards and ran for the hill.

She was hungry. That evening, she roasted the chicken and tried to force herself to eat it. After the first mouthful, she dropped her knife and fork, set the dish down for the dog and rushed upstairs to her room.

She lay, face down on the narrow bed, sobbing into the pillow with the blue dress spread round her and the wind howling through the chimney-pots.

Towards midnight, she thought she heard the crunch of footsteps on gravel. 'He's come back,' she cried out loud, gasping with happiness, only to realize it was a rambler rose, scratching its barbs against the window. She tried counting sheep over a fence but instead of sending her to sleep the silly animals awoke another memory — of her other love, in a dusty town in India.

He was an Anglo-Indian — a streak of a man with syrupy eyes and a mouth full of apologies. She saw him first in the telegraph office where he worked as a clerk. Then, when the cholera took her mother and his young wife, they exchanged condolences at the Anglican Cemetery. After that, they used to meet in the evenings and take a stroll beside the sluggish river. He took her to his house and gave her tea with buffalo milk and too much sugar. He recited speeches from Shakespeare. He spoke, hopefully, of Platonic love. His little girl wore golden earrings, and her nostrils were bunged up with mucus.

'Strumpet!' her father had bellowed when the postmaster warned him of his daughter's 'indiscretion'. For three weeks he shut her in a stifling room, till she repented, on a diet of bread and water.

Around two in the morning, the wind changed direction and whined in a different key. She heard a branch breaking — cra-ack! — and at the sound of splitting wood, she sat up, suddenly:

'Oh my God! He's choked on a chicken bone!'

She groped her way downstairs. A draught blew out the candle as she opened the kitchen door. She stood shivering in the darkness. Above the screaming wind she could hear the little dog snoring steadily in his basket.

At dawn, she looked beyond the bedrail and brooded on the Holman Hunt engraving. 'Knock, and it shall be opened unto you,' He had said. And had she not knocked and waved her lantern outside the cottage door? Yet, at the moment when sleep did, finally, come, the tunnel down which she had wandered seemed longer and darker than ever.

IV

AMOS HID HIS ANGER. All that summer, he lost himself in
work, as if to wipe away the memory of the contemptuous woman who had raised his hopes and ruined them.
Often, at the thought of her grey kid gloves, he banged his fist
on the lonely table.

In the hay-making season, he went to help a farmer on the
Black Hill, and met a girl called Liza Bevan.

They would meet in the dingle, and lie under the alders. She
plastered his forehead with kisses and ran her stubby fingers
through his hair. But nothing he could do — or she could
do — could rub away the image of Mary Latimer, puckering
her eyebrows in a pained reproach. At nights — awake, alone
— how he longed for her smooth white body between himself
and the wall!

One day, at the summer pony fair in Rhulen, he struck up a
conversation with the shepherd who had found the rector's
body.

'And the daughter?' he asked, making a show of shrugging
his shoulders.

'Be leaving,' the man said. 'Packing up the house and all.'

It began to rain next morning as Amos reached Bryn-
Draenog. The rain washed down his cheeks and pattered on
the leaves of the laurels. In the beeches round the rectory
young rooks were learning to flex their wings, and their
parents were flying round and round, cawing calls of en-
couragement. On the carriage-drive stood a tilbury. The
groom waved his curry-comb at the red-headed stranger who
strode into the house.

She was in the study with a ravaged, scant-haired gentleman
in pince-nez, who was leafing through a leather-bound book.

'Professor Gethyn-Jones,' she introduced him without a
flicker of surprise. 'And this is plain Mr Jones who has come to
take me for a walk. Do please excuse us! Do go on with your
reading!'

The professor slurred some words through his teeth. His
handshake was dry and leathery. Grey veins ran round his

knuckles like roots over rocks, and his breath was foul.

She went out and came back, her cheeks flushed, in wellington boots and an oiled drabbet cape.

'A friend of Father's,' she whispered once they were out of earshot. 'Now you see what I've suffered. And he wants me to give him the books – for nothing!'

'Sell them,' Amos said.

They walked up a sheeptrack, in the rain. The hill was in cloud and tassels of white water came streaming out of the cloud-bank. He walked ahead, brushing aside the gorse and the bracken, and she planted her footsteps in his.

They rested by the rocks, and then followed the old drove-road, arm in arm, talking with the ease of childhood friends. Sometimes, she strained to catch a word of his Radnor dialect. Sometimes, he asked her to repeat a phrase. But both knew, now, that the barrier between them was down.

He spoke of his ambitions and she spoke about her fears.

He wanted a wife and a farm, and sons to inherit the farm. She dreaded being dependent on her relatives, or having to go into service. She had been happy in India before her mother died. She told him about the Mission, and of the terrible days before the monsoon broke:

'The heat! How we nearly died of heat!'

'And I,' he said, 'I'd not a fire all winter but the fire in the pub where they hired me.'

'Perhaps I should go back to India?' she said, but in a tone of such uncertainty that he knew that was not what she wanted.

The clouds broke and columns of brassy light slanted downward on to the peat bog.

'Look!' he called, pointing to a skylark above their heads, spiralling higher and higher, as if to greet the sun. 'Lark'll have a nest hereabouts.'

She heard a soft crack and saw a yellow smear on the toe of her boot.

'Oh no!' she cried. 'Now look what I've done!'

Her foot had crushed the nestful of eggs. She sat down on a tuft of grass. The tears stained her cheeks and she only stopped crying when he folded his arm around her shoulders.

At the Mawn Pool they played ducks-and-drakes on the dark

water. Black-headed gulls flew up from the reed-beds, filling the air with mournful cries. When he lifted her across a patch of bog, she felt as light and insubstantial as the drifting mist.

Back at the rectory — as though to quieten her father's shade — they addressed one another in cold, terse phrases. They did not disturb the professor, who was buried in the books.

'Sell them!' said Amos, as he left her on the porch.

She nodded. She did not wave. She knew now when, and for what, he would be coming.

He came on the Saturday afternoon, on a Welsh bay cob. At the end of a lead-rein he held a piebald gelding with a side-saddle. She called from the bedroom the second she heard the sound of hoofs. He shouted, 'Hurry now! There's a farm for rent on the Black Hill.'

'I am hurrying,' she called back, and flew down the banisters in a riding habit of dove-grey Indian cotton. Her straw hat was crowned with roses, and a pink satin ribbon tied under her chin.

He had dipped into his savings to buy a new pair of boots, and she said, 'My! What boots!'

The scents of summer had clotted in the lanes. In the hedgerows, the honeysuckle had tangled with the dog-rose; and there were cloud-blue crane's-bills and purple foxgloves. In the farmyards, ducks waddled out of their way; sheepdogs barked, and ganders hissed and craned their necks. He broke off a branch of elder to whisk away the horseflies.

They passed a cottage with hollyhocks round the porch and a border ablaze with nasturtiums. An old woman in a goffered cap looked up from her knitting and croaked a few words to the travellers.

'Old Mary Prosser,' he whispered, and, when they were out of earshot, 'them do say as she's a witch.'

They crossed the Hereford road at Fiddler's Elbow; crossed the railway line, and then climbed the quarrymen's track that zigzags up the scarp of Cefn Hill.

At the edge of the pine plantation, they paused to rest the

horses and looked back down over the town of Rhulen – at the jumble of slate roofs, the broken walls of the castle, the spire of the Bickerton Memorial, and the church weathercock glinting in a watery sun. A bonfire was burning in the vicarage garden, and a scarf of grey woodsmoke floated over the chimneys and streamed away along the river valley.

It was cold and dark among the pines. The horses scuffed the dead pine-needles. Midges whined, and there were frills of yellow fungus on the fallen branches. She shuddered as she looked along the long aisles of pine-trunks and said, 'It's dead in here.'

They rode to the edge of the wood and they rode on in the sunlight, out onto an open slope and, when the horses felt the grass underfoot, they broke into a canter and kicked up crescents of turf that flew out behind them, like swallows.

They cantered over the hill and trotted down into a valley of scattered farms, down through lines of late-flowering hawthorns, to the Lurkenhope lane. Each time they passed a gate, Amos made some comment on the owner: 'Morgan the Bailey. Very tidy person.' 'Williams the Vron, as married his cousin.' Or 'Griffiths Cwm Cringlyn what the father died of drink.'

In one field, boys were gathering hay into cocks and, by the roadside, a red-faced man was whetting his scythe, his shirt-front open to the navel.

'Nice mate o' yours!' he winked at Amos as they went by.

They watered the horses in the brook; and then they stood on the bridge and watched the waterweeds wavering in the current, and the brown trout darting upstream. Half a mile further, Amos opened a mossy gate. Beyond it, a cart-track wound uphill to a house in a clump of larches.

'Them do call it "The Vision",' he said. 'And there be a hundred and twenty acre, and half gone to fern.'

V

THE VISION WAS an outlying farm on the Lurkenhope Estate, whose owners, the Bickertons, were an old Catholic family made rich by the West India trade.

The tenant had died in 1896, leaving an old unmarried sister who had carried on alone until they fetched her to a madhouse. In the yard, a young ash-tree reared its trunk through the boards of a hay-waggon. The roofs of the buildings were yellow with stonecrop; and the dungheap was overgrown with grass. At the end of the garden stood a brick-built privy. Amos slashed down the nettles to clear a path to the porch.

A broken hinge prevented the door from opening properly and, as he lifted it, a gust of fetid air flew in their faces.

They went into the kitchen and saw a bundle of the old woman's possessions, rotting away in a corner. The plaster was flaking and the flagstones had grown a film of slime. Twigs from a jackdaw's nest up the chimney were choking the grate. The table was still laid, with two places, for tea; but the cups were covered with spiders' webs, and the cloth was in shreds.

Amos took a napkin and flicked away the mouse-droppings.

'And rats!' said Mary cheerfully, as they heard the scuttle of feet in the rafters. 'But I'm used to rats. In India you have to get used to rats.'

In one of the bedrooms she found an old rag doll and handed it to him, laughing. He made a move to chuck it from the window; but she stayed his hand and said, 'No, I shall keep it.'

They went outside to inspect the buildings and the orchard. There'd be a good crop of damsons, he said, but the apple-trees would have to be replanted. Peering through the brambles, she saw a row of mouldering beehives.

'And I', she said, 'shall learn the secrets of the bee.'

He helped her over a stile and they walked uphill across two fields overgrown with gorse and blackthorn. The sun had dropped behind the escarpment, and swirls of coppery cloud were trailing over the rim. The thorns bit her ankles and tiny beads of blood burst through the white of her stockings. She said, 'I can manage,' when he offered to carry her.

The moon was up by the time they came back to the horses. The moonlight caught the curve of her neck, and a nightingale flung liquid notes into the darkness. He slipped an arm around her waist and said, 'Could you live in this?'

'I could,' she said, turning to face him, as he knotted his hands in the small of her back.

Next morning, she called on the vicar of Rhulen and asked him to publish the banns: on her finger she wore a ring of plaited grass stems.

The clergyman, who was having breakfast, spilled egg down his cassock and stuttered, 'It would not have been your father's wish.' He advised her to wait six months before deciding — at which she pursed her lips and answered, 'Winter is coming. We have no time to lose.'

Later in the day, a group of townswomen watched Amos helping her into his trap. The draper's wife squinted angrily, as if eyeing the eye of a needle, and pronounced her 'four months gone'. Another woman said, 'For shame!' — and all of them wondered what Amos Jones could see in 'that hussy'.

At dawn on the Monday, long before anyone was about, Mary stood outside the Lurkenhope Estate Office, waiting for the Bickertons' land-agent to discuss the terms of the lease. She was alone. Amos had little control of his manners when confronted with the presence of the gentry.

The agent was a jowly, wine-faced man, a distant cousin of the family, who had been cashiered from the Indian Army, and had lost his pension. They paid him a wretched salary; but since he had a head for figures and a method for dealing with 'uppity' tenants, they allowed him to shoot their pheasants and drink their port.

He prided himself on his humour and, when Mary explained her visit, he rammed his thumbs into his waistcoat and roared with laughter:

'So you're thinking of joining the peasants? Ha! I wouldn't!'

She blushed. High on the wall, there was a moth-eaten fox's

mask, snarling. He drummed his fingers on the leather top of his desk.

'The Vision!' he said abruptly. 'Can't say I've ever been to The Vision. Can't even think where The Vision is! Let's look it up on the map!'

He heaved himself to his feet and led her by the hand to the estate map that covered one end of the room. His fingernails were stained with nicotine.

He stood beside her, breathing hoarsely: 'Rather cold up there on the mountain, what?'

'Safer than on the plain,' she said, disentangling her fingers from his.

He sat down again. He did not motion her to a chair. He muttered of 'other applicants on the list' and told her to wait four months for Colonel Bickerton's reply.

'Too late, I'm afraid,' she smiled, and slipped away.

She walked back to the North Lodge and asked the keeper's wife for a sheet of paper. She penned a note to Mrs Bickerton, whom she had met once with her father. The agent was furious to learn that a manservant had driven down from the castle inviting Mary to tea that same afternoon.

Mrs Bickerton was a frail, fair-skinned woman in her late thirties. As a girl, she had devoted herself to painting, and had lived in Florence. Then, when her talent seemed to desert her, she married a handsome but brainless cavalry officer, possibly for his collection of Old Masters, possibly to annoy her artist friends.

The Colonel had recently resigned his commission without ever having fired at an enemy. They had a son called Reggie, and two daughters – Nancy and Isobel. The butler showed Mary through the rose-garden gate.

Mrs Bickerton was sheltering from the hot sun, beside a bamboo tea-table, in the shade of a cedar of Lebanon. Pink rambler roses tumbled over the south front, but holland-blinds were drawn in all the windows, and the castle looked uninhabited. It was a 'fake' castle, built in the 1820s. From another lawn came the knock of croquet balls and the noise of young, moneyed laughter.

'China or Indian?' Mrs Bickerton had to repeat the question.

Three ropes of pearls fell into the ruffles of her grey chiffon blouse.

'India,' her guest replied vaguely; and as the older woman poured from the silver teapot, Mary heard her say, 'Are you sure it's the right thing?'

'I am sure,' she said, and bit her lip.

'I like the Welsh,' Mrs Bickerton went on. 'But they do seem to get so angry, later. It must be to do with the climate.'

'No,' repeated Mary. 'I am sure.'

Mrs Bickerton's face was sad and drawn, and her hand was trembling. She tried to offer Mary the post of governess to her children: it was useless to argue.

'I shall speak to my husband,' she said. 'You can count on the farm.'

As the gate swung open, Mary wondered if the same pink roses would flower so freely, high up on her side of the mountain. Before the month was out, she and Amos had made plans to last the rest of their lives.

Her father's library contained a number of rare volumes; and these, sold to an antiquarian bookseller from Oxford, paid for two years' rent, a pair of draught horses, four milch cows, twenty fattening cattle, a plough and a second-hand chaff-cutter. The lease was signed. The house was scrubbed and whitewashed, and the front door painted brown. Amos hung up a branch of rowan to 'keep off the bad eyes' and bought a flock of white pigeons for the dovecote.

One day, he and his father carted the piano and four-poster from Bryn-Draenog. They had the 'Devil's job' getting the bed upstairs; and, afterwards in the pub, Old Sam bragged to his cronies that The Vision was 'God's own little love-nest'.

The bride had one anxiety: that her sister might come from Cheltenham and ruin the wedding. She sighed with relief to read the letter of refusal and, when she came to the words 'beneath you', burst into a fit of uncontrollable laughter and tossed it in the fire with the last of her father's papers.

By the time of the first frosts, the new Mrs Jones was pregnant.

VI

SHE SPENT the first months of her marriage making improvements to the house.

The winter was hard. From January to April the snow never melted off the hill and the frozen leaves of foxgloves drooped like dead donkeys' ears. Every morning she peered from the bedroom window to see if the larches were black or crisped with rime. The animals were silent in the deep cold, and the chatter of her sewing machine could be heard as far as the lambing paddock.

She made cretonne curtains for the four-poster and green plush curtains for the parlour. She cut up an old red flannel petticoat and made a rag rug, of roses, to go in the kitchen hearth. After supper, she would sit on the upright settle, her knees covered in crochet-work, while he gazed in adoration at his clever little spider.

He worked in all weathers – ploughing, fencing, ditching, laying drainage pipes, or building a drystone wall. At six in the evening, dog-tired and dirty, he came back to a mug of hot tea and a pair of warmed carpet slippers. Sometimes, he came back soaked to the skin and clouds of steam would billow upwards to the rafters.

She never knew how tough he really was.

'Do take off those clothes,' she'd scold him. 'You'll catch your death of pneumonia.'

'I expect,' he'd smile, and puff rings of tobacco smoke in her face.

He treated her as a fragile object that had come by chance into his possession and might easily break in his hands. He was terrified of hurting her, or of letting his hot blood carry him away. The sight of her whalebone corset was enough to unman him completely.

Before his marriage, he had doused himself once a week in the wash-house. Now, for fear of upsetting her sensibilities, he insisted on having hot water in the bedroom.

A Minton jug and basin, stencilled with a trellis of ivy

leaves, stood on the wash-stand under the Holman Hunt engraving. And before putting on his nightshirt, he would strip to the waist and lather his chest and armpits. A candle stood beside the soap-dish; and Mary would lie back on the pillow watching the candlelight as it flickered red through his sideburns, threw a golden rim around his shoulders, and cast a big, dark shadow on the ceiling.

Yet he felt so awkward when washing, that if ever he sensed her eyeing him through the bed-curtains, he would wring out the sponge and snuff the candle, and bring to bed both the smell of animals and the scent of lavender soap.

On Sunday mornings, they drove down to Lurkenhope to take Holy Communion in the parish church. Reverently, she let the wafer moisten on her tongue: 'The Body of Our Lord Jesus Christ which is given for you...' Reverently, she raised the chalice to her lips: 'The Blood of Our Lord Jesus Christ which is shed for you...' Then, lifting her gaze to the brass cross on the altar, she tried to concentrate on the Passion, but her thoughts would wander to the hard, breathing body beside her.

As for their neighbours, most of them were Chapel-folk whose mistrust of the English went back, centuries before Non-Conformism, to the days of the Border Barons. The women especially were suspicious of Mary; but she soon won them over.

Her housekeeping was the envy of the valley; and at teatime on Sundays, providing the lanes were clear of ice, four or five pony traps would drive up to The Vision yard. The Reuben Joneses were regulars, as were Ruth and Dai Morgan the Bailey; young Haines of Red Daren, and Watkins the Coffin, a despairing pox-pitted fellow, who despite his club-foot would hobble over the mountain from Craig-y-Fedw.

The guests came in with solemn faces and Bibles under their arms: their piety soon vanished as they tucked into Mary's fruitcake, or the fingers of cinnamon toast, or the scones with thick fresh cream and strawberry jam.

Presiding over these tea-parties, Mary felt that she had been a farmer's wife for years, and that her daily activities – of churning milk, drenching calves, or feeding poultry – were

32

not things she had learned but had come as second nature. Gaily, she would chatter away about scab, or colic, or laminitis. 'Really,' she'd say, 'I can't think why the mangolds are so small this year.' Or 'There's so little hay, I don't know how we'll last the winter through.'

Up at the end of the table, Amos would be terribly embarrassed. He hated to hear his clever wife making a fool of herself. And if she saw him bridling with annoyance, she would change the subject and amuse her guests with the watercolours in her Indian sketchbook.

She showed them the Taj Mahal, the Burning Ghats and the naked yogis who sat on beds of nails.

'And 'ow big's them elephants?' asked Watkins the Coffin.

'About three times the size of a carthorse,' she said, and the cripple creased with laughter at the absurdity of the idea.

India was too far, too big and too confused to appeal to the Welshmen's imagination. Yet — as Amos never tired of reminding them — her feet had trodden in the steps of His Feet; she, too, had seen the real Rose of Sharon; and for her, Carmel, Tabor, Hebron and Galilee were as real as, say, Rhulen, or Glascwm, or Llanfihangel-nant-Melan.

Most Radnorshire farmers knew chapter and verse of the Bible, preferring the Old Testament to the New, because in the Old Testament there were many more stories about sheep-farming. And Mary had such a talent for describing the Holy Land that all their favourite characters seemed to float before their eyes: Ruth in the cornfield; Jacob and Esau; Joseph in his patchwork coat; or Hagar, the Rejected One, gasping for water in the shade of a thornbush.

Not everyone, of course, believed her — least of all her mother-in-law, Hannah Jones.

She and Sam had the habit of turning up uninvited; and she would brood over the table, wrapped in a fringed black shawl, gobbling up the sandwiches and making everyone feel uncomfortable.

One Sunday, she interrupted Mary to ask whether 'by any chance' she'd been to Babylon.

'No, Mother. Babylon is not in the Holy Land.'

33

'No,' echoed Haines of Red Daren. 'It be not in the Holy Land.'

No matter how hard Mary tried to be pleasant, the old woman had hated her son's new wife on sight. She ruined the wedding-breakfast by calling her 'Your Ladyship!' to her face. The first family lunch ended in tears when she crooked her finger and sneered, 'Past the age of childbearing, I would have said.'

She never set foot in The Vision without finding something to scorn: the napkins folded like waterlilies, the marmalade pot, or the caper sauce for mutton. And when she ridiculed the silver toast-rack, Amos warned his wife to put it away 'or you'll have us the laughing-stock'.

He dreaded his mother's visits. Once, she jabbed Mary's terrier with the ferrule of her umbrella and, from that day, the little dog would bare its teeth, and try to scuttle under her skirt and nip her ankle.

The final break came when she snatched some butter from her daughter-in-law's hand and screamed, 'You don't waste good butter on pastry!' — and Mary, whose nerves were on edge, screamed back, 'Well, what do you waste it on? You, I suppose?'

Though he loved his wife, though he knew she was in the right, Amos flew to his mother's defence. 'Mother means well,' he'd say. Or 'She's had a hard life.' And when Hannah took him aside to complain of Mary's extravagance and 'stuck-up' ways, he let her finish her diatribe and — in spite of himself — agreed with it.

The truth was that Mary's 'improvements' made him more, not less, uncomfortable. Her spotless flagstones were a barrier to be crossed. Her damask table-cloths were a reproach to his table-manners. He was bored by the novels she read aloud after supper — and her food was, frankly, uneatable.

As a wedding present, Mrs Bickerton had sent a copy of *Mrs Beeton's Book of Household Management* — and though its recipes were quite unsuited to a farmhouse kitchen, Mary read it from cover to cover, and took to planning menus in advance.

So, instead of the predictable round of boiled bacon, dumplings and potatoes, she served up dishes he'd never even heard of — a fricassee of chicken or a jugged hare, or mutton with rowanberry sauce. When he complained of constipation, she said, 'That means we must grow green vegetables,' and made out a list of seeds to order for the garden. But when she suggested planting an asparagus bed, he flew into a towering rage. Who did she think she was? Did she think she'd married into the gentry?

The crisis came when she experimented with a mild Indian curry. He took one mouthful and spat it out. 'I want none of your filthy Indian food,' he snarled, and smashed the serving dish on the floor.

She did not pick up the bits. She ran upstairs and buried her face in the pillow. He did not join her. He did not, in the morning, make amends. He took to sleeping rough and went for long walks at night with a bottle in his pocket. One wet night, he came home drunk and sat staring savagely at the table-cloth, clenching and unclenching his fists. Then he got to his feet and lurched towards her.

She cringed and raised her elbow.

'Don't hit me,' she cried.

'I won't hit you,' he roared, and rushed out into the dark.

At the end of April there were pink buds in the orchard, and a vizor of cloud above the mountain.

Mary shivered by the grate and listened to the tireless lapping of the rain. The house absorbed the damp like a sponge. Mouldy rings disfigured the whitewash, and the wallpaper bulged.

There were days when it occurred to her that she had sat for years in the same damp, dark room, in the same trap, living with the same bad-tempered man. She looked at her chapped and blistered hands, and felt she would grow old and coarse and ugly before her time. She even lost the memory of having a father and mother. The colours of India had faded; and she began to identify herself with the one, wind-battered thornbush that she could see from her window, silhouetted on the lip of the escarpment.

VII

THEN CAME the fine weather.

On the 18th of May — even though it was not a Sunday — they heard the peal of church bells on the far side of the hill. Amos harnessed the pony and they drove down to Rhulen, where Union Jacks were fluttering from every window to celebrate the Relief of Mafeking. A brass band was playing and a parade of schoolchildren passed down Broad Street with pictures of the Queen and Baden-Powell. Even the dogs wore patriotic ribbons tied to their collars.

As the procession passed, she nudged him in the ribs, and he smiled.

'Be the winter as makes me mad.' He appeared to be pleading with her. 'Some winters seem as they'll never end.'

'Well, next winter', she said, 'we shall have someone else to think about.'

He planted a kiss on her forehead, and she threw her arms around his neck.

When she woke next morning, a breeze was ruffling the net curtains; a thrush sang in the pear-tree; pigeons were burbling on the roof, and patches of white light wandered over the bed-cover. Amos was asleep in his calico nightshirt. The buttons had come undone, and his chest was bare. Squinting sideways, she glanced at the heaving ribcage, the red hairs round his nipples, the pink dimple left by his shirtstud, and the line where the sunburned neck met the milky thorax.

She cupped her hand over his biceps muscle, and withdrew it.

36

'To think I might have left him' – she held the words within her teeth and, blushing, turned her face to the wall.

As for Amos, he now thought of nothing but his baby boy – and, in his imagination, pictured a brawny little fellow who would muck out the cowshed.

Mary also hoped for a boy, and already had plans for his career. Somehow, she would send him to boarding-school. He'd win scholarships. He'd grow up to be a states-man or a lawyer or a surgeon who would save people's lives.

Walking down the lane one day, she absent-mindedly tugged at the branch of an ash-tree; and as she looked at the tiny transparent leaves breaking from the smoky black buds, she was reminded that he, too, was reaching for the sun-light.

Her one close friend was Ruth Morgan the Bailey, a small homely woman with a face of great simplicity and flaxen hair tied up in a coif. She was the best midwife in the valley, and she assisted Mary to prepare the layette.

On sunny days, they sat on wicker chairs in the front garden, sewing flannels and binders; trimming vests, petti-coats and bonnets; or knitting blue wool bootees that tied with satin ribbon.

Sometimes, to exercise her stiff hands, Mary played Chopin waltzes on the piano that badly needed tuning. Her fingers ran up and down the keyboard, and a flight of jangling chords flew out of the window, and up among the pigeons. Ruth Morgan heaved with emotion and said it was the loveliest music in the world.

Only when the layette was finished did they spread it out for Amos to admire:

'But them's not for a boy,' he said, indignantly.

'Oh yes!' they cried in unison. 'For a boy!'

Two weeks later, Sam the Waggon came to lend a hand with the shearing and, rather than go back home, stayed on to help in the kitchen-garden. He sowed and hoed. He pricked out lettuce seedlings, and cut pea-sticks and bean-poles. One

37

day, he and Mary dressed up a scarecrow in one of the missionary's tropical suits.

Sam had the face of a sad old clown. Fifty years of fisticuffs had flattened his nose. A lonely incisor lingered in his lower jaw. Nets of red string covered his eyeballs and his eyelids seemed to rustle as he blinked. The presence of an attractive woman drove him to acts of reckless flirtation.

Mary liked his gallantries and laughed at his yarns – for he, too, had 'run about the world'. Every morning he picked her a bouquet from her own front flower-bed; and every night, as Amos passed him on the way upstairs, he'd rub his hands and cackle, 'Lucky dog! Ooh! If I were a younger man...!'

He still owned an ancient fiddle – a relic of his droving days – and when he took it from its case, he would caress the gleaming wood as if it were a woman's body. He knew how to knit his eyebrows like a concert violinist and to make the instrument quaver and sob – though when he hit the high notes, Mary's terrier would raise its snout and howl.

Occasionally, if Amos was away, they practised duets – 'Lord Thomas and Fair Eleanor' or 'The Unquiet Grave'; and once he caught them polka-ing on the flagstones.

'Stop that!' he shouted. 'Will ye hurt the baby?'

Sam's behaviour made Hannah so angry that she fell ill.

Before Mary's appearance, she had only to call out, 'Sam!' for her husband to hang his head, mutter 'Aye, m'dear!' and shuffle off on some trivial errand. Now, the people of Rhulen saw her storming down to the Red Dragon, filling the street with deep-throated cries, 'Saa-am!...Saa-am!' – but Sam would be out on the hillside gathering mushrooms for his daughter-in-law.

One muggy evening – it was the first week in July – a clatter of wheel rims sounded in the lane, and Hughes the Carter drove up with Hannah and a pair of bundles. Amos was screwing a new hinge to the stable-door. He dropped the screwdriver and asked why she had come.

She answered gloomily, 'I belong by the bedside.'

A day or two later, Mary woke with an attack of nausea and throbbing pains that raced up and down her spine. As Amos left the bedroom, she clung to his arm and pleaded, 'Please ask her to go. I'd feel better if she'd go. I beg you. Or I'll——'

'No,' he said, lifting the latch. 'Mother belongs here. She must stay.'

All that month there was a heatwave. The wind blew from the east and the sky was a hard and cloudless blue. The pump ran dry. The mud cracked. Swarms of horseflies buzzed about the nettles, and the pains in Mary's spine grew worse. Night after night, she dreamed the same dream — of blood and nasturtiums.

She felt that her strength was draining away. She felt that something had snapped inside; that the baby would be born deformed, or born dead, or that she herself would die. She wished she had died in India, for the poor. Propped up on pillows, she prayed to the Redeemer to take her life but — Lord! Lord! — to let him live.

Old Hannah spent the heat of the day in the kitchen, shivering under a black shawl, knitting — knitting very slowly — a pair of long white woollen socks. When Amos beat to death an adder that had been sunning itself by the porch, she curled her lip and said, 'That means a death in the family!'

The 15th of July was Mary's birthday; and because she was feeling a little better, she came downstairs and tried to make conversation with her mother-in-law. Hannah hooded her eyes and said, 'Read to me!'

'What shall I read, Mother?'

'The floral tributes.'

So Mary turned to the funeral columns of the *Hereford Times* and began:

' "The funeral of Miss Violet Gooch who died tragically last Thursday at the age of seventeen was held at St Asaph's Church——" '

'I said the floral tributes.'

'Yes, Mother,' she corrected herself, and began again:

' "Wreath of arum lilies from Auntie Vi and Uncle Arthur. 'Nevermore!'...Wreath of yellow roses. 'With ever loving memory from Poppet, Winnie and Stanley...' Artificial wreath in glass case. 'With kind remembrance from the Hooson Emporium...' Bouquet of Gloire de Dijon roses.

'Sleep softly, my dearest. From Auntie Mavis, Mostyn Hotel, Llandrindod...' Bouquet of wild flowers. 'Only good-night, Belovèd, not farewell! Your loving sister, Cissie...' " '

'Well, go on!' Hannah had opened an eyelid. 'What's the matter with you? Go on! Finish it!'

'Yes, Mother...'"The coffin, of beautifully polished oak with brass fittings, was made by Messrs Lloyd and Lloyd of Presteigne with the following inscription on the lid: 'A harp! A magnificent harp! With a broken string!' " '

'Ah!' the old woman said.

The preparations for Mary's confinement made Sam so jittery anyone would have thought that he, not his son, were the father. He was always thinking of ways to please her: indeed, his was the one face that made her smile. He spent the last of his savings commissioning a rocking cradle from Watkins the Coffin. It was painted red, with blue and white stripes, and had four carved finials in the form of songbirds.

'Father, you shouldn't have...' Mary clapped her hands, as he tried it out on the kitchen flags.

And it's a coffin, not a cradle, she'll be needing,' Hannah mumbled, and went on with her knitting.

For over fifty years she had kept, from her bridal trousseau, a single unlaundered white cotton nightdress to wear with the white socks when they laid her out as a corpse. On August 1st, she turned the heel of the second sock and, from then on, knitted slower and slower, sighing between the stitches and croaking, 'Not long now!'

Her skin, papery at the best of times, appeared to be transparent. Her breath came in cracked bursts, and she had difficulty moving her tongue. It was obvious to everyone but Amos that she had come to The Vision to die.

On the 8th of August the weather broke. Stacks of smoky, silver-lidded clouds piled up behind the hill. At six in the evening, Amos and Dai Morgan were scything the last of the oats. All the birds were silent in the stillness that precedes a storm. Thistledown floated upwards, and a shriek tore out across the valley.

The labour pains had begun. Upstairs in the bedroom, Mary lay writhing, moaning, kicking off the sheets and biting the pillow. Ruth Morgan tried to calm her. Sam was in the kitchen, boiling water. Hannah sat on the settle, and counted her stitches.

Amos saddled the cob and cantered over the hill, helter-skelter down the quarrymen's track to Rhulen.

'Courage, man!' said Dr Bulmer, as he divided his forceps and slid each half down one of his riding-boots. Then, shoving a flask of ergot into one pocket, a bottle of chloroform into the other, he buttoned the collar of his mackintosh cape, and both men set their faces to the storm.

The rainwater hissed on the rooftiles as they tethered their horses to the garden fence.

Amos attempted to follow upstairs. The doctor pushed him back, and he dropped on to the rocking-chair as if he'd been hit on the chest.

'Please God it be a boy,' he moaned. 'An' I'll never touch her again.' He grabbed at Ruth Morgan's apron as she went by with a water-jug. 'Be she all right?' he pleaded, but she shook him off and told him not to be silly.

Twenty minutes later, the bedroom door opened and a voice boomed out:

'Any more newspaper? An oilskin? Anything'll do!'

'Be it a boy?'

'Two of them.'

That night, Hannah rounded off the toe of her second sock and, three days later, died.

VIII

THE TWINS' FIRST MEMORY — a shared memory which both remembered equally well — was of the day they were stung by the wasp.

They were perched on high-chairs at the tea-table. It must

41

have been teatime because the sun was streaming in from the west, bouncing off the table-cloth and making them blink. It must have been late in the year, perhaps as late as October, when wasps are drowsy. Outside the window, a magpie hung from the sky, and bunches of red rowanberries thrashed in the gale. Inside, the slabs of bread-and-butter glistened the colour of primroses. Mary was spooning egg-yolk into Lewis's mouth and Benjamin, in a fit of jealousy, was waving his hands to attract attention when his left hand hit the wasp, and was stung.

Mary rummaged in the medicine cupboard for cotton-wool and ammonia, dabbed the hand and, as it swelled and turned scarlet, said soothingly, 'Be brave, little man! Be brave!'

But Benjamin did not cry. He simply pursed his mouth and turned his sad grey eyes on his brother. For it was Lewis, not he, who was whimpering with pain, and stroking his own left hand as if it were a wounded bird. He went on snivelling till bedtime. Only when they were locked in each other's arms did the twins doze off – and from then on, they associated eggs with wasps and mistrusted anything yellow.

This was the first time Lewis demonstrated his power to draw the pain from his brother, and take it on himself.

He was the stronger twin, and the firstborn.

To show he was the firstborn, Dr Bulmer nicked a cross on his wrist; and even in the cradle he was the stronger. He was unafraid of the dark and of strangers. He loved to rough-and-tumble with the sheepdogs. One day, when nobody was about, he squeezed through the door of the beast-house, where Mary found him, several hours later, gabbling away to the bull.

By contrast, Benjamin was a terrible coward who sucked his thumb, screamed if separated from his brother, and was always having nightmares – of getting caught in a chaff-cutter, or trampled by carthorses. Yet whenever he really did get hurt – if he fell in the nettles or walloped his shin – it was, Lewis who cried instead.

They slept in a truckle bed, in a low-beamed room along the landing, where, in another early memory, they woke one morning to find that the ceiling was an unusual shade of grey.

42

Peering out, they saw the snow on the larches, and the snowflakes spiralling down.

When Mary came in to dress them, they were curled, head to toe, in a heap at the bottom of the bed.

'Don't be silly,' she said. 'It's only snow.'

'No, Mama,' came two muffled voices from under the blankets. 'God's spitting.'

Apart from Sunday drives to Lurkenhope, their first excursion into the outside world was a visit to the Flower Show of 1903 when the pony shied at a dead hedgehog in the lane, and their mother won First Prize for runner beans.

They had never seen such a crowd and were bewildered by the shouts, the laughter, the flapping canvas and jingling harness, and the strangers who gave them pickaback rides round the exhibits.

They were wearing sailor-suits; and with their grave grey eyes and black hair cut in a fringe, they soon attracted a circle of admirers. Even Colonel Bickerton came up:

'Ho! Ho! My Jolly Jack Tars!' he said, and chucked them under the chin.

Later, he took them for a spin in his phaeton; and when he asked their names, Lewis answered Benjamin and Benjamin answered Lewis.

Then they got lost.

At four o'clock, Amos went off to pull for Rhulen in the tug-of-war; and since Mary had entered for the Ladies' Egg-and-Spoon Race, she left the twins in charge of Mrs Griffiths Cwm Cringlyn.

Mrs Griffiths was a big, bossy, shiny-faced woman, who had twin nieces of her own and prided herself as an expert. Lining the boys up side by side, she scrutinized them all over until she found a tiny mole behind Benjamin's right ear.

'There now!' she called out loud. 'I found a difference!' — whereupon Benjamin shot a despairing glance at his brother, who grabbed his hand, and they both dived through the spectators' legs and hid in the marquee.

They hid under a cloth-covered trestle, under the prize-winning vegetable marrows, and so much enjoyed the view of ladies' and gentlemen's feet that they went on hiding until they heard their mother's voice calling and calling in a voice more cracked and anxious than a bleating ewe.

On the way home, huddled in the back of the dog-cart, they discussed their adventure in their own secret language. And when Amos bawled out, 'Stop that nonsense, will ye?' Lewis piped up, 'It's not nonsense, Papa. It's the language of the angels. We were born with it.'

Mary tried to drill into their heads the difference between 'yours' and 'mine'. She bought them Sunday suits – a grey tweed for Lewis and blue serge for Benjamin. They wore them for half an hour, then sneaked off and came back wearing each other's jackets. They persisted in sharing everything. They even split their sandwiches in two, and swapped the halves.

One Christmas, their presents were a fluffy teddy-bear and a felt Humpty-Dumpty, but on the afternoon of Boxing Day, they decided to sacrifice the teddy on a bonfire, and concentrate their love on 'The Dump'.

The Dump slept on their pillow, and they took him for walks. In March, however – on a grey blustery day with catkins on the branches and slush in the lane – they decided that he, too, had come between them. So the moment Mary's back was turned, they sat him on the bridge, and tipped him in the brook.

'Look, Mama!' they cried, two stony faces peeping over the parapet at the black thing bobbing downstream.

Mary saw The Dump get caught in an eddy and stick on a branch.

'Stay there!' she called and rushed to the rescue, only to miss her footing and almost fall into the scummy brown flood-water. Pale and dishevelled, she ran to the twins and hugged them.

'Never mind, Mama,' they said. 'We never liked The Dump.'

Nor, in the following autumn, did they like their new baby sister, Rebecca.

———

They had pestered their mother to give them a baby sister; and when, at last, she arrived, they climbed up to the bedroom, each carrying a coppery chrysanthemum in an egg-cup full of water. They saw an angry pink creature biting Mary's breast. They dropped their offerings on the floor, and dashed downstairs.

'Send her away,' they sobbed. For a whole month, they lapsed into their private language and it took them a year to tolerate her presence. One day, when Mrs Griffiths Cwm Cringlyn came to call, she found them writhing convulsively on the kitchen floor.

'What's up with the twins?' she asked in alarm.

'Take absolutely no notice,' said Mary. 'They're playing at having babies.'

By the age of five, they were helping with the housework, to knead the bread dough, shape the butter-pats, and spread the sugar icing on a sponge cake. Before bedtime, Mary would reward them with a story from the Brothers Grimm or Hans Christian Andersen: their favourite was the story of the mermaid who went to live in the Mer-King's palace at the bottom of the sea.

By six, they were reading on their own.

Amos Jones mistrusted book-learning and would growl at Mary not to 'mollycoddle the kids'.

He gave them bird-scarers and left them alone in the oatfield to shoo away the woodpigeons. He made them mix the chicken-mash, and pluck and dress the birds for market. Fine weather or foul, he would sit them on his pony, one in front and one behind, and ride around the hill-flock. In autumn, they watched the ewes being tupped: five months later, they witnessed the birth of the lambs.

They had always recognized their affinity with twin lambs. Like lambs, too, they played the 'I'm the King of the Castle' game; and one breezy morning, as Mary was pegging up her laundry, they slipped under her apron, butted their heads against her thighs, and made noises as if suckling an udder.

'None of that, you two,' she laughed, and pushed them away. 'Go and find your grandfather!'

IX

OLD SAM had come to live at The Vision, and slipped into second childhood.

He wore a moleskin waistcoat, a floppy black cap, and went around everywhere with a buckthorn stick. He slept in a cobwebby attic no bigger than a cupboard, surrounded by the few possessions he had bothered to keep: the fiddle, a pipe, a tobacco-box and a porcelain statuette picked up somewhere on his travels – of a portly gentleman with a portmanteau and an inscription round the base reading, 'I shall start on a long journey.'

His principal occupation was to look after Amos's pigs. Pigs, he said, 'was more intelligent than persons'; and certainly all his six sows adored him, snorted when he rattled their swill-pail and answered, each one, to their names.

His favourite was a Large Black called Hannah; and while Hannah rootled for grubs under the apple-trees, he would scratch behind her ears and recall the more agreeable moments of his marriage.

Hannah, however, was hopeless as a mother. She crushed her first litter to death. The second time, having swelled to a colossal size, she produced a solitary male piglet, whom the twins called Hoggage and adopted as their own.

One day, when Hoggage was three months old, they decided it was time to baptize him.

'I'll be vicar,' said Lewis.

'I bags be vicar,' said Benjamin.

'All right! Be the vicar, then!'

It was a boiling hot day in June. The dogs lay panting in the shade of the barn. Flies were zooming and zizzing. Black cows were grazing below the farmhouse. The hawthorns were in flower. The whole field was black and white and green.

The twins stole out of the kitchen with an apron to wear as a surplice and a stripy towel for the christening robe. After a mad chase round the orchard, they cornered Hoggage by the hen-house and carried him squealing to the dingle. Lewis held him, while Benjamin wetted his finger and planted a cross above his snout.

But though they dosed Hoggage with worm-powders, though they stuffed him with stolen cake, and though Hoggage made up for his smallness with an amenable personality — to the extent of letting the twins take rides on his back — Hoggage remained a runt; and Amos had no use for runts.

One morning in November, Sam went to the meal-shed for barley and found his son sharpening the blade of a meat-cleaver. He tried to protest, but Amos scowled and ground his whetstone even harder.

'No sense to keep a runt,' he said.

'But not Hoggage?' Sam stammered.

'I said, no sense to keep a runt.'

To get them out of earshot, the old man took his grandsons mushrooming on the hill. When they came home at dusk, Benjamin saw the pool of blood beside the meal-shed door and, through a chink, saw Hoggage's carcass hanging from a hook.

Both boys held back their tears until bedtime; and then they soaked their pillow through.

Later, Mary came to believe they never forgave their father for the murder. They acted dumb if he taught them some job on the farm. They cringed when he tried to pet them; and when he petted their sister Rebecca, they hated him even more. They planned to run away. They spoke in low, conspiratorial whispers behind his back. Finally, even Mary lost patience and pleaded, 'Please be nice to Papa.' But their eyes spat venom and they said, 'He killed our Hoggage.'

X

THE TWINS LOVED to go on walks with their grandfather, and had two particular favourites – a 'Welsh walk' up the mountain, and an 'English walk' to Lurkenhope Park.

The 'Welsh walk' was only practical in fine weather. Often, they would set out in sunshine, only to come home soaked to the skin. And equally often, when walking down to Lurkenhope, they would look back at the veil of grey rain to the west while, overhead, the clouds broke into blue and butterflies fluttered over the sunlit cow-parsley.

Half a mile before the village, they passed the mill of Maesyfelin and the Congregational Chapel beside it. Then came two ranks of estate workers' cottages, with leggy redbrick chimneys and gardens full of cabbages and lupins. Across the village green a second, Baptist Chapel squinted at the church, the vicarage and the Bannut Tree Inn. There was a screen of ancient yews around the Anglican graveyard: the half-timbering of the belfry was said to represent the Three Crosses of Golgotha.

Sam always stopped at the pub for a pint of cider and a game of skittles with Mr Godber the publican. And sometimes, if the game dragged on, old Mrs Godber would come out with mugs of lemonade for the twins. She made them bawl into her ear-trumpet and, if she liked what they said, she'd give them each a threepenny bit and tell them not to spend it on sweeties – whereupon they would race to the Post Office, and race back again, their chins smudged over with chocolate.

Another five minutes' walk brought them to the West Lodge of the park. From there, a carriage-drive looped downhill through stands of oaks and chestnuts. Fallow deer browsed under the branches, flicking their tails at the flies, their bellies shining silvery in the deep pools of shade. The sound of human voices scared them, and their white scuts bobbed away through the bracken.

The twins had a friend in Mr Earnshaw, the head-gardener, a short, sinewy man with china-blue eyes, who was a frequent guest at Mary's tea-parties. They usually found him in the potting-shed, in a leather apron, with crescents of black loam under his fingernails.

They loved to inhale the balmy tropical air of the hothouse; to stroke the bloom on white peaches, or peer at orchids with faces like monkeys in picture books. They never came away without a present — a cineraria or a waxy red begonia — and even seventy years later, Benjamin could point to a pink geranium and say, 'That's from a cutting we had off of Earnshaw.'

The lawns of the castle fell away in terraces towards the lake. On the shore stood a boathouse built of pine-logs and, one day, hiding in the rhododendrons, the twins saw the boat!

Its varnished hull came whispering towards them through the waterlilies. Combs of water fell from the oars. The oarsman was a boy in a red-striped blazer; and in the stern, half-hidden under a white parasol, sat a girl in a lilac dress. Her fair hair hung in thick tresses, and she trailed her fingers through the lapping green wavelets.

Back at The Vision, the twins rushed up to Mary:

'We've seen Miss Bickerton,' they clamoured in unison. As she kissed them goodnight, Lewis whispered, 'Mama, when I grow up I'm going to marry Miss Bickerton,' and Benjamin burst into tears.

To go on the 'Welsh walk' they used to tramp over the fields to Cock-a-loftie, a shepherd's cottage left derelict since the land-enclosures. Then they crossed a stone stile on to the moor, and followed a pony-trail northwards, with the screes of the mountain rising steeply on the left. Beyond a spinney of birches, they came to a barn and longhouse, standing amid heaps of broken wall. A jet of smoke streamed sideways from the chimney. There were a few contorted ash-trees, a few pussy-willows, and the rim of the muddy pond was covered with bits of goose fluff.

This was the homestead of the Watkins family, Craig-y-Fedw, 'The Rock of the Birches' — better known locally as 'The Rock'.

On the twins' first visit, sheepdogs barked and yanked at
their chains; a scrawny red-haired boy ran for the house; and
Aggie Watkins came out, blocking the doorway in a long
black skirt and an apron made of gunny-sack.

She blinked into the sun but on recognizing the walkers she
smiled.

'Oh! It's thee, Sam,' she said. 'An' you'll stay and have a cup
of tea.'

She was a thin, stooped woman with wens on her face, a
bluish complexion and strands of loose, lichenous hair that
blew about in the breeze.

Outside the door were the stacks of planks that Tom
Watkins used for making his coffins.

'An' it's a pity you missed Old Tom,' she went on. 'Him
and the mule be gone with a coffin for poor Mrs Williams
Cringoed as died of her lungs.'

Tom Watkins made the cheapest coffins in the county, and
sold them to people who were too mean or too poor to pay for
a proper funeral.

'And them be the twins!' she said, folding her arms.
'Church-folk, same as Amos and Mary?'

'Church,' said Sam.

'And the Lord have mercy! Bring 'em in!'

The kitchen wall had been freshly whitewashed, but the
rafters were black with soot and the dirt floor was scabbed
with dried fowl-droppings. Ash-grey bantams strutted in and
out, pecking up the scraps that had fallen from the table. In the
room beyond, a box-bed was piled with blankets and overcoats; and above it hung a framed text: 'The Voice of One
Crying in the Wilderness. Prepare Ye the Way of the Lord,
make His Paths straight...'

In another room – in what had once been the parlour – two
heifers were munching hay; and an acrid smell oozed round
the kitchen door and mingled with the smell of peat and curds.
Aggie Watkins wiped her hands on her apron before putting a
pinch of tea in the pot:

'An' the weather,' she said. 'Bloomin' freezing for June!'

'Freezing!' said Sam.

Lewis and Benjamin sat on the edge of a chair, while the

red-haired boy crouched over a kettle and fanned the flames with a goose's wing.

The boy's name was Jim. He stuck out his tongue and spat.

'Aagh! The devil!' Aggie Watkins raised her fist and sent him scampering for the door. 'Take ye no notice,' she said, unfolding a clean white linen table-cloth; for, no matter how hard the times, she always spread a clean white linen cloth for tea.

She was a good woman who hoped the world was not as bad as everyone said. She had a bad heart brought on by poverty and overwork. Sometimes, she took her spinning-wheel up the mountain and spun the wisps of sheep's wool that had caught in the gorse and heather.

She never forgot an insult and she never forgot a kindness. Once, when she was laid up, Mary sent Sam over with some oranges and a packet of Smyrna figs. Aggie had never tasted figs before and, to her, they were like manna from Heaven.

From that day, she never let Sam go back without a present in return. 'Take her a pot of blackberry jam,' she'd say. Or 'What about some Welsh cakes? I know she likes Welsh cakes.' Or 'Would she have some duck eggs this time?' And when her one scraggy lilac was in bloom, she heaped him with branches as if hers were the only lilac in creation.

The Watkinses were Chapel-folk and they were childless.

Perhaps it was because they were childless that they were always looking for souls to save. After the Great War, Aggie managed to 'save' several children; and if anyone said, 'He was raised at The Rock,' or 'She was reared at The Rock,' you knew for sure the child was illegitimate or loony. But in those days the Watkinses had only 'saved' the boy Jim and a girl called Ethel — a big girl of ten or so, who would spread her thighs and stare at the twins with glum fascination, covering one eye, then the other, as if she were seeing double.

From The Rock a drovers' trail wound up the north shoulder of the Black Hill, in places so sharply that the old man had to pause and catch his breath.

51

Lewis and Benjamin gambolled ahead, put up grouse, played finger-football with rabbit-droppings, peered over the precipice onto the backs of kestrels and ravens and, every now and then, crept off into the bracken, and hid.

They liked to pretend they were lost in a forest, like the Twins in Grimms' fairy-tale, and that each stalk of bracken was the trunk of a forest tree. Everything was calm and damp and cool in the green shade. Toadstools reared their caps through the dross of last year's growth; and the wind whistled far above their heads.

They lay on their backs and gazed at the clouds that crossed the fretted patches of sky; at the zig-zagging dots which were flies; and, way above, the other black dots which were the swallows wheeling.

Or they would dribble their saliva onto a gob of cuckoo-spit; and when their mouths ran dry, they would press their foreheads together, each twin losing himself in the other's grey eye, until their grandfather roused them from their reverie. Then they bounded out along the path and pretended to have been there all the time.

On fine summer evenings, Sam walked them as far as the Eagle Stone — a menhir of grey granite, splotched with orange lichen, which, in the raking light, resembled a perching eagle.

Sam said there was an 'Old 'Un' buried there. Or else it was a horses' grave, or a place where the 'Pharisees' danced. His father had once seen the fairies — 'Them as 'ad wings like dragonflies' — but he could never remember where.

Lifting the boys onto the stone, Sam would point out farms and chapels and Father Ambrosius's monastery nestling in the valley below. Some evenings, the valley was shrouded in mist; but beyond rose the Radnor Hills, their humped outlines receding grey on grey towards the end of the world.

Sam knew all their names: the Whimble, the Bach and the Black Mixen — 'and that be the Smatcher nearby where I was born'. He told them stories of Prince Llewellyn and his dog, or more shadowy figures like Arthur or Merlin or the Black Vaughan; by some stretch of the imagination, he had got William the Conqueror mixed up with Napoleon Bonaparte.

The twins looked on the path to the Eagle Stone as their own private property. 'It's Our Path!' they'd shout, if they happened to meet a party of hikers. The sight of a bootprint in the mud was enough to put them in a towering rage, and they'd try to rub it out with a stick.

One sunset, as they came over the crest of the hill, instead of the familiar silhouette, they saw a pair of boaters. Two young ladies, arms akimbo, sat perched on top of the stone; a few paces off, a young man in grey flannels was bending behind a camera tripod.

'Keep still,' he called out from under the flapping black cloth. 'Smile when I say so! One...Two...Three...Smile!'

Suddenly, before Sam could stop him, Lewis had grabbed his stick and walloped the photographer behind the knees.

The tripod lurched, the camera fell, and the girls, convulsed with giggles, almost fell off the stone.

Reggie Bickerton, however – it was he who was the cameraman – turned crimson in the face and chased Lewis through the heather, shouting, 'I'll skin the blighter!' And though his sisters called out, 'No, Reggie! No! No! Don't hurt him!' he bent the little boy over his knee and spanked him.

On the way home, Sam taught his grandsons the Welsh for 'dirty Saxon', but Mary was crestfallen at the news.

She felt crushed and ashamed – ashamed of her boys and ashamed of being ashamed of them. She tried to write a note of apology to Mrs Bickerton but the nib scratched and the words would not come.

XI

THAT AUTUMN, already wearied by the weight of the on-coming winter, Mary went on frequent visits to the vicar.

The Reverend Thomas Tuke was a classical scholar of private means, who had chosen the living of Lurkenhope because the squire was a Catholic, and because the vicarage garden lay on greensand — a soil that was perfect for growing rare Himalayan shrubs.

A tall, bony man with a mass of snowy curls, he had the habit of fixing his parishioners with an amber stare before offering them the glory of his profile.

His rooms bore witness to a well-ordered mind and, since his housekeeper was stone-deaf, he was under no obligation to speak to her. The shelves of his library were lined with sets of the classics. He knew the whole of Homer by heart: each morning, between a cold bath and breakfast, he would compose a few hexameters of his own. On the wall of the staircase was a fan-shaped arrangement of oars — he had been a Cambridge rowing blue — and in the front hall, ranked like a colony of penguins, were several pairs of riding boots, for he was also Joint Master of the Rhulen Vale Hunt.

To the villagers their vicar was a mystery. Most of the women were in love with him — or transported by the timbre of his voice. But he was far too busy to attend to their spiritual needs, and his actions often outraged them.

One Sunday, before Holy Communion, some women in flowery hats were approaching the church door, their features reverently composed to receive the Sacrament. Suddenly, a window of the vicarage banged open; the vicar's voice bawled out, 'Mind your heads!' and he fired off a couple of barrels at the wood-pigeons crooning in the elms.

The shot fell pattering among the tombstones. 'Bloody heathen!' muttered Amos; and Mary hardly held back her giggles.

She liked the vicar's sense of the ridiculous, and his sharp turn of phrase. To him — and him alone — she confessed that farm life depressed her; that she was starved of conversation and ideas.

'You're not the only one,' he said, squeezing her hand. 'So we'd better make the best of it.'

He lent her books. Shakespeare or Euripides, the Upanishads or Zola — her mind ranged freely over the length and breadth of literature. Never, he said, had he met a more intelligent woman, as if this in itself were a contradiction in terms.

He spoke with regret of his youthful decision to take Holy Orders. He even regretted the Bible — to the extent of distributing translations of the *Odyssey* round the village:

'And who, after all, were the Israelites? Sheep-thieves, my dear! A tribe of wandering sheep-thieves!'

His hobby was bee-keeping; and in a corner of his garden he had planted a border of pollen-bearing flowers.

'There you are!' he'd exclaim as he opened a hive. 'The Athens of the Insect World!' Then, gesturing to the architecture of honey-cells, he would hold forth on the essential nature of civilization, its rulers and ruled, its wars and conquests, its cities and suburbs, and the relays of workers, on which the cities lived.

'And the drones,' he'd say. 'How well we know the drones!'

'Yes,' said Mary. 'I have known drones.'

He encouraged her to replace her own hives. Halfway through the first season, one of them was attacked by wax-moth, and the bees swarmed.

Amos ambled into the kitchen and, with an amused grin, said, 'Your bees is all knit up on the damsons.'

His offer of help was worse than useless. Mary posted the boys to keep watch in case the swarm flew off, and hurried to Lurkenhope to fetch the vicar: Benjamin would never forget the sight of the old man descending the ladder, his arms, his chest and neck enveloped in a buzzing brown mass of bees.

'Aren't you afraid?' he asked, as the vicar scooped them up in handfuls and put them in a sack.

'Certainly not! Bees only sting cowards!'

In another corner of his garden, the vicar had made a rockery for the flowering bulbs he had collected on his travels in

Greece. In March there were crocuses and scillas; in April, cyclamen, tulips and dog's-tooth violets; and there was a huge dark purple arum that stank of old meat.

Mary loved to picture these flowers growing wild, in sheets of colour, on the mountains; and she pitied them, exiled on the rockery.

One blustery afternoon, as the boys were booting a football round the lawn, the vicar took her to see a fritillary from the slopes of Mount Ida in Crete.

'Very rare in cultivation,' he said. 'Had to send half my bulbs to Kew!'

Suddenly, Lewis lobbed the ball in the air; a gust carried it sideways, and it landed on the rockery where it smashed the fragile bell-flower.

Mary dropped to her knees and tried to straighten the stem, stifling a sob, not so much for the flower as for the future of her sons.

'Yokels!' she said, bitterly. 'That's what they'll grow up to be! That's if their father has his way!'

'Not if I have my way,' said the vicar, and lifted her to her feet.

After Matins that Sunday, he stood by the south porch shaking hands with his parishioners and, when Amos's turn came, said: 'Wait for me a minute, would you, Jones? I only want a word or two.'

'Yes, sir!' said Amos, and paced around the font, shooting nervous glances up at the bell-ropes.

The vicar beckoned him into the vestry. 'It's about your boys,' he said, pulling the surplice over his head. 'Bright boys, both of them! High time they were in school!'

'Yes, sir!' Amos stammered. He had not meant to say 'Yes!' or 'Sir!' The vicar's tone had caught him off his guard.

'There's a good man! So that settles it! Term begins on Monday.'

'Yes, sir!' he had said it again, this time in irony, or as a reflection of his rage. He rammed on his hat and strode out among the sunwashed tombstones.

Jackdaws were wheeling round the belfry, and the elm-trees were creaking in the wind. Mary and the children had already mounted the trap. Amos cracked his whip over the pony's back, and they lurched up the street, swerving and scattering some Baptists.

Little Rebecca yelled with fright.

'Why must you drive so fast?' Mary tugged at his sleeve.

'Because you make me mad!'

After a silent lunch, he went out walking on the hill. He would have liked to work, but it was the Sabbath. So he walked alone, over and round the Black Hill. It was dark when he came home and he was still cursing Mary and the vicar.

XII

ALL THE SAME, the twins went off to school.

At seven in the morning, they set off in black Norfolk jackets and knickerbockers, and starched Eton collars that chafed their necks and were tied with grosgrain bows. On the damp days Mary dosed them with cod-liver oil and made them wrap up in scarves. She packed their sandwiches in greaseproof paper, and slipped them in their satchels, along with their books.

They sat in a draughty classroom where a black clock hammered out the hours and Mr Birds taught geography, history and English; and Miss Clifton taught mathematics, science and scripture.

They did not like Mr Birds.

His purple face, the veins on his temples, his bad breath and his habit of spitting into a snuff handkerchief — all made a most disagreeable impression, and they cringed whenever he came near.

For all that, they learned to recite Shelley's 'Ode to a Skylark'; to spell Titicaca and Popocatepetl; that the British Empire was the best of all possible empires; that the French were cowards, the Americans traitors; and that Spaniards burned little Protestant boys on bonfires.

On the other hand they went with pleasure to the classes of Miss Clifton, a buxom woman with milky skin and hair the colour of lemon peel.

Benjamin was her favourite. No one knew how she told the difference; but he was, most certainly, her favourite and, as she bent forward to correct his sums, he would inhale her warm motherly smell and snuggle his head between her velvet bodice and the dangling gold chain of her crucifix. She flushed with pleasure when he brought her a bunch of sweet-williams, and, during elevenses, took the twins to her room and told them they were 'proper little gentlemen'.

Her favouritism did not make them popular. The school bully, a bailiff's son called George Mudge, sensed a challenge to his authority and was always trying to part them.

He made them play football on opposite teams. Yet, in the middle of the game, their eyes would meet, their lips part in pleasure; and they would dribble the ball down the pitch, passing it from one to the other, heedless of all the other players, and the catcalls.

Sometimes, in class, they set down identical answers. They made the same mistake over a verse of 'The Lady of Shalott', and Mr Birds accused them of cheating. Summoning them to the blackboard, he made them down their breeches, flexed his birch, and placed on each of their backsides six symmetrical welts.

'It's not fair,' they whimpered as Mary lulled them to sleep with a story.

'No, my darlings, it isn't fair.' She pinched out the candle, and tiptoed to the door.

Shortly afterwards Mr Birds was dismissed from his post for reasons that were 'not to be talked about'.

A fortnight before Christmas, a parcel came from Uncle Eddie in Canada containing the oleograph of the Red Indian.

Having started out as a lumberjack, Amos's brother had fallen on his feet and was now the manager of a trading company at Moose Jaw, Saskatchewan. A photo of himself, in a fur hat and with his foot on a dead grizzly, drove the twins wild with excitement. Mary gave them her copy of Long-fellow, and they could soon recite from memory the lives of Hiawatha and Minnehaha.

With the other children they played Comanches and Apaches in the spinney behind the schoolhouse. Lewis took the name of 'Little Raven' and beat out the Comanche war-song on an old tin bucket: it was Benjamin's duty to guard the Apache wigwams. Both crossed their hearts and hoped to die and swore to be enemies for ever.

One lunch-break, however, George Mudge, the Apache Chief, found the pair having a powwow in the brambles, and barked out, 'Traitor!'

He summoned his henchmen, who tried to haul Benjamin off for 'nettle-torture' but found Lewis blocking their path. In the fight that followed, the Apaches ran off, leaving their chief to the mercy of the twins, who twisted his arm and pushed his face in the mud.

'We skinned him alive,' crowed Benjamin, as they stormed into the kitchen.

'Did you?' sighed Mary, disgusted at the sight of their clothes.

But this time, Amos was delighted: 'That's my boys! Show me where ye hit him! Ouch! Aye! Proper little fighters both! Again now! Aye! Aye! An' ye twisted his arm? Ouch! That's a way to git him...!'

A photo, taken at the hay-making of 1909, shows a happy, smiling group in front of a horse-drawn cart. Amos has a scythe slung over his shoulder. Old Sam is in his moleskin waistcoat. Mary, in a gingham dress, is holding a hay-rake. And the children — together with young Jim the Rock, who had come to earn a few pennies — are all sitting cross-legged on the ground.

The twins are as yet indistinguishable: but years later, Lewis recalled it was he who held the sheepdog, while Benjamin tried to stop his sister wriggling — in vain, for Rebecca appears in the picture as a whitish blur.

Later that summer Amos broke in a couple of mountain ponies, and the boys went riding round the countryside, often as far as the Lurkenhope lumber-mill.

This was a red-brick building standing on a strip of level ground between the mill-race and the wall of a gorge. The slates had blown off the roof; ferns grew out of the gutters; but the waterwheel still turned the saw-bench and, outside the door, there were mounds of resinous sawdust and stacks of yellow planks.

The twins liked to watch Bobbie Fifield, the sawyer, as he guided the tree-trunks on to the whining blade. But the real attraction was his daughter, Rosie, an impish girl of ten with an insolent way of tossing her head of blonde curls. Her mother dressed her in cherry-red frocks and told her she was 'pretty as a picture'.

Rosie took them to secret hideouts in the wood. No one could fool her into mistaking which twin was which. She preferred to be with Lewis, and would sidle up and purr sweet nonsense in his ear.

Pulling off the petals of a daisy, she would call out, 'He loves me! He loves me not! He loves me! He loves me not!' — always reserving the final petal for 'He loves me not!'

'But I do love you, Rosie!'

'Prove it!'

'How?'

'Walk through those nettles and I'll let you kiss my hand.'

One afternoon, she cupped her hands around his ear and whispered, 'I know where there's an evening primrose. Let's leave Benjamin behind.'

'Let's,' he said.

She threaded her way through the hazels and they came into a sunlit clearing. Then she unhooked her dress and let it fall round her waist.

'You may touch them,' she said.

Gingerly, Lewis pressed two fingers against her left nipple — then she darted off again, a flash of red and gold, seen and half-seen through the flickering leaves.

'Catch me!' she called. 'Catch me! You can't catch me!'

Lewis ran, and stumbled over a root, and picked himself up, and ran on:

'Rosie!'

'Rosie!'

'Rosie!'

His shouts echoed through the wood. He saw her. He lost her. He stumbled again and fell flat. A stitch burned in his side and, from far below, Benjamin's plaintive wailing reined him back.

'She's a pig,' said Benjamin, later, narrowing his eyes in wounded love.

'She's not a pig. Pigs are nice.'

'Well, she's a toad.'

The twins had their own hideout, in the dingle below Craig-y-Fedw – a hollow hidden among rowans and birches, where water whispered over a rock and there was a bank of grass cropped close by sheep.

They made a dam of turf and branches and, on the hot days, would pile their clothes on the bank and slide into the icy pool. The brown water washed over their narrow white bodies, and clusters of scarlet rowanberries were reflected on the surface.

They were lying on the grass to dry, without a word between them, only the currents that ebbed and flowed through their touching ankles. Suddenly the branches behind them parted, and they sat up:

'I can see you.'

It was Rosie Fifield.

They grabbed their clothes but she ran off, and the last they saw of her was the head of blonde curls hurtling downhill

through the fern fronds.
'She'll tell,' said Lewis.
'She won't dare.'
'She will,' he said, gloomily. 'She's a toad.'

XIII

AFTER THE HARVEST FESTIVAL, the seagulls flew inland and
Jim Watkins the Rock came to work as a farm boy at The
Vision.

He was a thin wiry boy with unusually strong hands and
ears that stuck out under his cap, like dock-leaves. He was
fourteen. He had the moustache of a fourteen-year-old, and a
lot of blackheads on his nose. He was glad to get work away
from home, and he had just been baptized.

Amos taught him to handle a plough. It worried Mary that
the horses were so big and Jim was so very small, but he soon
learned to turn at the hedgerow and draw a straight furrow
down the field. Though he was very smart for his age, he was
a laggard when it came to cleaning tack, and Amos called him
a 'lazy runt'.

He slept in the hay-loft, on a bed of straw.

Amos said, 'I slept in the loft when I were a lad, and that's
where he sleeps.'

Jim's favourite pastime was catching moles – 'oonts' as he
called them in Radnor dialect (molehills are 'oontitumps')
– and when the twins left, smartened up for school, he'd lean
over the gate and leer, 'Ya! Ha! Slick as oonts, ain't they?'

He took the twins on scavenging expeditions.

One Saturday, they had gone to gather chestnuts in Lurkenhope Park when a whip hissed in the grey air and Miss
Nancy Bickerton rode up on a black hunter. They hid behind a
tree-trunk, and peered around. She rode so close they saw the

mesh of her hairnet over her golden bun. Then the mist closed over the horse's haunches, and all they found was a pile of steaming dung in the withered grass.

Benjamin often wondered why Jim smelled so nasty and finally plucked up courage to say, 'Trouble with you is you stink.'

'Be not I as stinks,' said Jim, adding mysteriously, 'another!'

He led the twins up the loft ladder, rummaged in the straw and took hold of a sack with something wriggling inside. He untied the string and a little pink nose popped out.

'Me ferret,' he said.

They promised to keep the ferret a secret and, at half-term, when Amos and Mary were at market, all three stole off to net a warren at Lower Brechfa. By the time they had caught three rabbits, they were far too excited to notice the black clouds roiling over the hill. The storm broke, and pelted hailstones. Soaked and shivering, the boys ran home and sat by the fireside.

'Idiots!' said Mary when she came in and saw their wet clothes. She dosed them with gruel and Dover's powders, and packed them off to bed.

Around midnight, she lit a candle and crept into the children's room. Little Rebecca was asleep with a doll on her pillow and thumb in mouth. In the bigger bed, the boys were snoring in perfect time.

'Are the youngsters fine?' Amos rolled over, as she climbed back in beside him.

'Fine,' she said. 'They're all fine.'

But in the morning Benjamin looked feverish and complained of pains in his chest.

By evening the pains were worse. Next day, he had convulsions and coughed up bits of hard, rusty-coloured mucus. Pale as a communion wafer, and with hectic spots on his cheekbones, he lay on the lumpy bed, listening only for the swish of his mother's skirt, or the tread of his twin on the stair: it was the first time the two had slept apart.

Dr Bulmer came and diagnosed pneumonia.

For two weeks Mary hardly left the bedside. She ladled liquorice and elderberry down his throat and, at the least sign of a rally, she fed him spoonfuls of egg-custard and slips of buttered toast.

He would cry out, 'When am I going to die, Mama?'

'I'll tell you when,' she'd say. 'And it'll be a long while yet.'

'Yes, Mama,' he'd murmur, and drift off to sleep.

Sometimes, Old Sam came up and pleaded to be allowed to die instead.

Then, without warning, on December 1st, Benjamin sat up and said he was very, very hungry. By Christmas he had come back to life – though not without a change in his personality.

'Oh, we know Benjamin,' the neighbours would say. 'The one as looks so poor.' For his shoulders had slumped, his ribs stuck out like a concertina, and there were dark rings under his eyes. He fainted twice in church. He was obsessed by death.

With the warmer weather he would tour the hedgerows, picking up dead birds and animals to give them a Christian burial. He made a miniature cemetery on the far side of the cabbage patch, and marked each grave with a cross of twigs.

He preferred now not to walk beside Lewis, but one step behind; to tread in his footsteps, to breathe the air that he had breathed. On days when he was too sick for school he would lie on Lewis's half of the mattress, laying his head on the imprint left by Lewis on the pillow.

One drizzly morning, the house was unusually quiet and, when Mary heard the creak of a floorboard overhead, she went upstairs. Opening the door of her bedroom, she saw her favourite son, up to his armpits in her green velvet skirt, her wedding hat half-covering his face.

'Psst! For Heaven's sake,' she whispered. 'Don't let your father see you!' She had heard the sound of hobnails on the kitchen floor. 'Take them off! Quickly now!' – and with a sponge and water, she washed off the smell of cologne.

'Promise you'll never do that again.'

'I promise,' he said, and asked if he could bake a cake for Lewis's tea.

He creamed the butter, beat the eggs, sifted the flour, and watched the brown crust rise. Then, after filling the two layers with raspberry jam, he dusted the top with icing sugar and, when Lewis came back ravenous from school, he carried it, proudly, to the table.

He held his breath as Lewis took the first mouthful.

'It's good,' said Lewis. 'It's a very good cake.'

Mary saw in Benjamin's illness the chance of giving him a better education, and decided to tutor him herself. They read Shakespeare and Dickens; and since she had a little Latin, she borrowed a grammar and dictionary from the vicar and a few of the easier texts — Caesar and Tacitus, Cicero and Virgil — although the *Odes* of Horace were beyond them.

When Amos tried to object she cut him short: 'Come now: surely you can allow one bookworm in the family?' But he shrugged and said, 'No good'll come of it.' Education as such, he did not mind. What annoyed him was the thought of his sons growing up with educated accents, and wanting to leave the farm.

To keep the peace, Mary often scolded her pupil: 'Benjamin, go at once and help your father!' Secretly, she swelled with pride when, without looking up, he'd say, 'Mama, please! Can't you see I'm reading?' It came as a wonderful surprise when the vicar tested his knowledge and said, 'I do believe we have a scholar on our hands.'

None of them, however, had bargained for Lewis's reaction. He sulked, skimped his jobs; and once, in the small hours of the morning, Mary heard a noise in the kitchen and found him, red-eyed by candlelight, trying to extract the sense from one of his brother's books. Worse, the twins began to bicker over money.

They kept their savings in a pottery pig. And though there was no question but that the coins in its belly belonged to both of them, when Lewis wanted to break the pig open, Benjamin shook his head.

A few months earlier, at the start of a football match, Lewis had confided his pocket-money into his brother's safe-keeping — the game was too rough for the invalid — and from then on, it was Benjamin who controlled his money; Benjamin who refused to let him buy a water-pistol; who seldom let him spend so much as a farthing.

Then, unexpectedly, Lewis found an interest in aviation. To her science class, Miss Clifton had explained the flight of Monsieur Blériot across the English Channel, but from her drawing on the blackboard the twins pictured his monoplane as a kind of mechanical dragonfly.

One Monday, in June of 1910, a boy called Alfie Bufton came back from the weekend with a sensational piece of news: on the Saturday, his parents had taken him to an air-display at the Worcester and Hereford Agricultural Show, where not only had he seen a Blériot monoplane, he had seen one crash.

All week, Lewis waited impatiently for the next issue of the *Hereford Times*, but was forbidden to open its pages until his father had read them first. This Amos did, aloud, after supper: it seemed an age before he came to the crash.

The aviator's first attempt had been a fiasco. The machine rose a few feet, and sank to the ground. The crowds scoffed and clamoured for their money back – whereupon the aviator, a Captain Diabolo, harangued the police to clear the course and took off a second time. Again the machine rose, higher this time; then it veered to the right and crash-landed not far from the Flower Tent.

'The propeller,' Amos continued, with dramatic pauses, 'capable of 2,700 revolutions per minute, dealt blows to the right and left.' Several spectators had been wounded, and a Mrs Pitt of Hindlip had died of her injuries in the Worcester Infirmary.

'Remarkable to state' – he pitched his voice an octave lower – 'about three-quarters of an hour after the disaster, a swan flew low across the showground. His graceful flight seemed to reduce the aviator's unfortunate attempts to mockery.'

Another week had to pass before Lewis was allowed to snip out the article – with its spindly line engraving – and paste it in his scrapbook, a scrapbook that would, eventually, be devoted to air disasters; that went on growing, volume by volume, until the months before his death; and if anyone mentioned the Comet crashes of the Fifties, or the Jumbo collision in the Canaries, he would shake his head and murmur, darkly, 'But I remember the Worcester Catastrophe.'

The other memorable event of 1910 was their trip to the seaside.

XIV

ALL SPRING AND SUMMER, Benjamin continued to cough green phlegm and, when he coughed a few streaks of blood, Dr Bulmer recommended a change of air.

The Reverend Tuke had a sister with a house at St David's in Pembrokeshire. And since the time had come for his annual sketching holiday, he asked if he could take his two young friends along.

Amos bridled when Mary broached the subject: 'I know your kind. All fancy talk and holidays by the seaside!'

'So?' she said. 'I suppose you want your son to catch consumption.'

'Hm!' He scratched the creases of his neck.

'Well then?'

On August 5th, Mr Fogarty the curate drove the party down to the train at Rhulen. The station had been given a coat of fresh brown paint and between each pillar of the platform hung a wire basket planted with trailing geraniums. The station-master was having a spot of bother with a drunk.

The man was a Welshman who had not paid his fare on the incoming train. He had taken a swipe at the porter. The porter had socked him on the jaw, and he now lay, face down on the paving, in a torn tweed coat. Blood leaked from his mouth. His watch-glass had shattered; and the jeering spectators ground the splinters under their boot-heels.

The porter put his mouth to the drunk's ear and bellowed, 'Get up, Taffy!'

'Atcha! A-atch!' the injured man grunted.

'Mama, why are they hurting him?' Benjamin piped up, as he peered through the circle of shiny brown gaiters.

The drunk attempted to stand, only to crumple again at the knees; and this time, two porters grabbed him under the armpits and heaved him to his feet. His face was grey. His pupils rolled back into his skull, and the whites of his eyes were red.

'But what's he done?' Benjamin insisted.

'What I done?' the man croaked. 'H'ain't done nought!' and, opening his maw, he let fly a string of obscenities.

The crowd recoiled. Someone shouted, 'Call a constable!' The porter socked his face again, and a fresh flow gushed down his chin.

'Dirty Saxons,' Benjamin shrilled. 'Dirty Sax——' but Mary clamped her hand over his mouth and hissed, 'One squeak out of you and you're going home.'

She dragged the twins to the end of the platform where they could watch the engine stop. It was a hot day and the sky was a very dark shade of blue. The railway tracks glittered as they rounded the edge of the pine wood. It was the first time they had ridden in a train.

'But I want to know what he done,' Benjamin jumped up and down.

'Sshh, will you?' And at that moment, the signal went down — *clonk!* — and the train came steaming round the bend. The engine had red wheels and the piston moved in and out, slower and slower, till it came to a panting halt.

Mary and Mr Fogarty helped the clergyman hump the bags into the compartment. The whistle blew, the door slammed and the twins stood at the window, waving. Mary waved a handkerchief, smiling and crying at the thought of Benjamin's bravery.

The train passed along winding valleys with whitewashed farms on the hills. They watched the telegraph wires dancing up and down the window, crossing and criss-crossing, and then whizzing over the roof. Stations went by, tunnels, bridges, churches, gas-works and aqueducts. The seats in the compartment reminded them of the texture of bullrushes.

They saw a heron low over a river.

Because they were running late, they missed the connection at Carmarthen, and missed the last omnibus from Haverfordwest to St David's. Fortunately, the vicar found a farmer who offered to take them in his waggonette.

It was dark as they came over the crest of Keeston Hill. One of the traces slipped and, while the driver climbed down to hitch it up, the twins stood and stared at St Bride's Bay.

A soft seawind brushed their faces. The full moon scintillated on the black water. A fishing boat glided by, on bat-wings, and vanished. They heard the wash of waves on the beach, and a bell-buoy moaning. Two lighthouses, one on Skomer, the other on Ramsay Island, flashed their beams. The streets of St David's were deserted as the wagonette rumbled over the cobbles, past the Cathedral, and halted by a big white gate.

For the first few days, the twins were in awe of the ladies who lived there, and of the 'artistic' style of the house.

Miss Catharine Tuke was the artist—a pretty, brittle woman with a fringe of cloud-grey hair, who drifted from room to room in a flowery kimono, and was rarely seen to smile. Her eyes were the colour of her Russian Blue cat; and in her studio she had made an arrangement of driftwood and sea-holly.

Miss Catharine spent her winters in the Bay of Naples where she painted a great many views of Vesuvius, and scenes from classical mythology. In summer, she painted seascapes and copied the Old Masters. Sometimes, in the middle of a meal, she'd say, 'Ah!' and slip away to work on a picture. The canvas that fascinated Benjamin showed a beautiful young man, naked against a blue sky, pierced through and through with arrows, and smiling.

Miss Catharine's companion was called Miss Adela Hart.

She was a much larger, sorrowful lady, with a very nervous temperament. She spent most of her day in the kitchen, cooking the dishes she had learned in Italy. She always wore the same heliotrope costume that was halfway between a dress and a shawl. She wore a necklace of amber beads and she cried a lot.

She cried in the kitchen and she cried at mealtimes. She kept snivelling into a lace handkerchief and calling her friend 'Beloved!' or 'My Pussy!' or 'Poppens!' – and Miss Catharine would frown, as if to say, 'Not in front of visitors!' But that only made it worse; for then she broke into a real flood: 'I can't help it,' she'd cry. 'I can't!' And Miss Catharine would purse her lips and say, 'Please go to your room.'

'Why does she call her Pussy?' Benjamin asked the vicar. 'I don't know.'

'Miss Hart should be called Pussy. She's got whiskers.'

'Don't be unkind about Miss Hart.'

'She hates us.'

'She doesn't hate you. She's not used to having little boys in the house.'

'Well, I wouldn't like anyone to call me Pussy.'

'No one's going to call you Pussy,' said Lewis.

They were walking along a white road to the sea. There were whitecaps in the bay and the golden ears of barley swished this way and that way, in the wind. The clergyman clung to his panama and easel. Benjamin carried the paintbox, and Lewis, dragging the handle of the shrimp-net behind him, left a trail in the dust like a grass-snake's.

On reaching the cove, the old man set up the easel and the twins scampered off to play in rock-pools.

They caught shrimps and blennies, poked their fingers into sea-anemones, and stroked the sea-grass that felt like slimy fleece. One by one, the swells flopped on to the pebbly beach, where some lobstermen were caulking their boat.

At low tide, oyster-catchers flew in, needling for shellfish with beaks of flame. Stranded by the entrance was the hulk of a clipper-bowed schooner, her timbers festooned with seaweed and encrusted with mussels and barnacles.

The twins made friends with one of the lobstermen, who lived in a white-roofed cottage, and had once been a member of her crew.

As a young man, he had sailed on the Cape Horners. He had seen the Giant Patagonians and the girls of Tahiti. Listening to his stories, Lewis's jaw would drop with wonder, and he would go off alone to daydream.

70

He pictured himself on the crow's-nest of a full-rigged ship, scanning the horizon for a palm-fringed shore. Or he would lie among the sea-pinks, stretching his eye to the skerries where seagulls wandered like patches of sunlight, while green rollers thumped on to the rocks below, and sent up curtains of spray.

On a calm day, the old sailor took them mackerel-fishing in his lugger. They sailed out beyond the Guillemot Rock; and no sooner had they let down the spinner than they felt a buzz on the line and saw a glint of silver in the wake. The sailor's fingers were blooded when he came to take the fish off the hook.

By mid-morning, the bilges were full of fish – flapping, flouncing, iridescent in their death-agony: their scarlet gills reminded the boys of the carnations in Mr Earnshaw's greenhouse. Miss Hart cooked the mackerel for supper; and from then on, they were all good friends.

On the day of their departure, the sailor gave them a ship-in-a-bottle with yardarms made of matchsticks and sails from a handkerchief. And when the train drew into Rhulen Station, Benjamin raced down the platform shouting: 'Look-what-we've-got! A ship-in-a-bottle!'

Mary could hardly believe that this smiling sunburned boy was the sick son she had sent away. Neither she nor Amos took much notice of Lewis, who came up with the shrimp-net and said, quietly and emphatically, 'When I grow up, I'm going to be a sailor.'

XV

THE AUTUMN WAS CRUEL. On Guy Fawkes' Day, Mary gazed at the gloomy yellow light over the hill and said, 'It looks like snow.'

'Too early for snow yet,' said Amos; but it was snow.

The snow fell in the night, and melted, leaving long white smears on the screes. Then it fell again, a heavy fall this time; and though they dug a great many sheep from the drifts, the ravens had a feast when it thawed.

And Sam was sick.

At first, there was something the matter with his eyes. He woke with a crust of discharge over his eyelids and Mary had to bathe them open with warm water. His mind began to wander. He kept repeating the same story, about a girl in the cider-house in Rosgoch, and how he had hidden a horn cup in a niche beside the fireplace.

'I'd like that cup,' he said.

'I'm sure it's still there,' she said. 'And one day we'll go and find it.'

It was towards the end of November that they started losing chickens.

Lewis had a pet pullet that would peck the grains of corn from his hand; but one morning, on opening the hatch of the hen-house, he found that she had vanished. A week later, Mary counted six birds missing. Two more went in the night. She searched for clues and found, neither blood nor feathers, but the imprint of a boy's boot in the mud.

'Oh dear,' she sighed, as she wiped the eggs and arranged them in the egg-rack, 'I'm afraid we've got a human fox.' But she kept her suspicions from Amos until she had proof. He was already in a very ugly mood.

After the snowfall, he had driven half the flock off the mountain and set them to graze the oat-stubble. A strip of thicket, choked with brambles and riddled with badger sets, ran along the top of the oatfield; and on the far side there was a ragged hedge, which was the boundary between The Vision and The Rock. One afternoon, Mary went to pick sloes and came back with the news that Watkins's sheep had broken through and were in among their own.

Infuriated, less by the loss of feed than the risk of scab – for Watkins seldom bothered to dip – Amos sorted out the strays and told young Jim to drive them back along the lane.

'Be a good lad,' he said. 'Get your father to keep his beasts in.'

A week went by, and the sheep broke through again. But this time, when Amos inspected the thicket, he saw from the fresh white cuts that someone had hacked a passage through.

'That settles it,' he said.

He took an axe and two billhooks and, calling the twins, set off to pleach the hedge himself.

The ground was hard. The sky was blue. Strewn over the creamy stubble were heaps of orange mangolds, half-eaten, and the grimy white sheep clustered round them. A smokescreen of old man's beard stretched away over the brambles. They had hardly felled the first thornbush when Watkins himself came limping down the pasture with a shotgun in his hand.

Tongue-tied with rage, he stood with his back to the raking sunlight, his forefinger quivering round the trigger-guard.

'Get ye away, Amos Jones.' He had broken the silence. 'That land belongs to we' — and he launched into a tirade of abuse.

No, Amos answered. The land belonged to the Estate, and he had a map to prove it.

'No. No,' Watkins shouted. 'The land belongs to we.'

They went on shouting but Amos saw the dangers of provoking him further. He calmed him down, and the two men agreed to meet in Rhulen at the Red Dragon on market day.

In the tap-room of the Red Dragon it was a little too hot. Amos sat away from the fire, peering through dirty net curtains on to the street. The barman swabbed down the counter. A pair of horse-dealers in high spirits were swigging at their tankards, and shooting gobs of spit on to the sawdust-covered floor: from another table came the clack of dominoes and the noise of boozy laughter. Outside, the sky was grey and grainy, and it was freezing hard. The clock showed Watkins twenty minutes late. A hard black hat moved up and down the street, in front of the tap-room window.

'I'll give him ten more minutes.' Amos looked again at the clock.

Seven minutes later, the door swung open and Watkins pushed his way into the room. He nodded with the spiritually uplifted air of a man at a prayer-meeting. He did not take off the hat, or sit down.

'What's yours?' asked Amos.

'Nothing,' said Watkins, folding his arms and sucking in his cheeks so the skin over his cheekbones shone.

Amos pulled from his pocket a copy of his lease to The Vision. The beer glass had made a wet ring on the table. He wiped it with his sleeve before spreading out the map. His fingernail came to rest on a little pink tongue marked '$\frac{1}{2}$ acre'.

'There!' he said. 'Look!'

In law, plainly, the patch of scrubland belonged to the Lurkenhope Estate.

Watkins screwed up his eyes at the maze of lines, letters and numbers. The air whistled through his teeth. His whole frame shook as he scrunched up the map, and chucked it, across the room, into the grate.

'Stop him!' Amos shouted; but by the time he had rescued the singeing paper, Watkins had bolted through the door. That evening, young Jim, too, was missing.

Next morning, after foddering, Amos changed into his Sunday suit and called on the Bickertons' agent. The agent heard him out, resting his jowls on his fists and, occasionally, raising an eyebrow. The integrity of the Estate had been called into question: it was appropriate to act.

Four men were sent to build a wall between the two farms, and a police constable went to Craig-y-Fedw, warning the Watkinses not to touch a stone of it.

Every year at The Vision, the week before Christmas was set aside for 'feathering' ducks and geese.

Amos wrung their necks and tied them up, one after the other, by their webs to a beam in the barn. By evening the place was like a snowstorm. Little Rebecca went about sneezing as she stuffed the down into a sack. Lewis singed the carcasses with a taper; and Benjamin showed not a trace of squeamishness when it came to drawing the guts.

They stored the dressed birds in the dairy, which was said to be rat-proof. Amos lined the waggon with straw, and then sent everyone to bed — to be up at four in time to catch the Birmingham buyers.

The night was cloudless and the moonlight kept Mary awake. Some time after midnight, she thought she heard an animal in the yard. She tiptoed to the window, and peered out. The larches trailed their black hair over the moon. The figure of a small boy flitted into the shadow of the cowshed. A latch grated. The dogs did not bark.

'So,' she breathed. 'The fox.'

She woke her husband, who put on a coat and caught Jim in the dairy with five geese already in his sack. The carthorses whinnied at the sound of the screaming.

'I hope you didn't hurt him too much,' Mary said, as Amos climbed into bed.

'Dirty thieves!' he said, and rolled over.

It was starting to snow again, in Rhulen, at dusk on Christmas Eve. Outside the butcher's in Broad Street, strings of hares, turkeys and pheasants were swinging in the gusts. Snowflakes sparkled on wreaths of holly and ivy; and as the shoppers passed under the glare of the gaslights, a door would fling open, a band of brighter light fall across the pavement, and a cheerful voice call out, 'And a Merry Christmas to you! Come in for a glass of grog!'

A children's choir was singing carols: the snowflakes hissed as they hit their hurricane lamp.

'Look!' Benjamin nudged his mother. 'Mrs Watkins!'

Aggie Watkins was walking down the street, in a hat of black ribbons and a brown plaid shawl. Under her arm she carried a basket of eggs:

'Fresh eggs! Fresh eggs!'

Mary set down her own basket and walked towards her with a serious smile:

'Aggie, I am sorry about Jim, but——'

She jerked herself back as a stream of saliva shot from the old woman's mouth, and landed on the hem of her skirt.

'Fresh eggs! Fresh eggs!' Aggie's raucous voice increased in volume. She hobbled round the clock and back again: 'Fresh eggs! Fresh eggs!' A man stopped her, but she rolled her eyes glassily at the gaslights: 'Fresh eggs! Fresh eggs!' And when the Hereford buyer blocked her path—'Come on, Mother Watkins! It's Christmas! What'll I give you for the basket?' —she raised her arm in fury, as if he meant to steal her baby: 'Fresh eggs! Fresh eggs!' Then the snow flurries closed around her, and the night.

'Poor thing,' said Mary. She had climbed into the dog-cart and was spreading a rug over the children. 'I'm afraid she's a little touched.'

XVI

THREE YEARS LATER, with a big bruise over her left eye, Mary wrote to her sister in Cheltenham stating her reasons for leaving Amos Jones.

She did not make excuses. Nor did she ask for sympathy. She simply asked for shelter till she found herself a job. Yet, as she wrote, her tears made blotches on the notepaper, and she told herself that her marriage had not been doomed; that it could have worked; that they had both been in love and loved each other still; and that all of their troubles had begun with the fire.

Around eleven o'clock on the night of the 2nd of October 1911, Amos had put away his carving chisels and was watching his wife sew the final stitches of a sampler, when Lewis ran downstairs shouting, 'Fire! There's a fire!'

Parting the curtains, they saw a red glow above the line of the cowshed roof. At the same moment, a column of sparks and flame shot upwards into the darkness.

'It's the ricks,' said Amos, and rushed outside.

He had two ricks on a patch of level ground between the

buildings and the orchard.

The wind blew from the east and fanned the blaze. Wisps of burning hay flew up into the smokecloud, and fell. Frightened by the glare and the crackle, the animals panicked. The bull bellowed; horses stomped in their stalls; and the pigeons, pink in the flamelight, flew round and round in erratic circles.

Mary worked the pump-handle; and the twins carried the slopping pails to their father who was up a ladder, desperately trying to douse the thatch of the second rick. But the burning hay fell thicker and thicker, and that rick, too, was soon a crucible of flame.

The fire was seen for miles, and by the time Dai Morgan came up with his farm-servant, the sides of both ricks had caved in.

'Get out of my sight,' Amos snarled. He also shook off Mary as she tried to take his arm.

At dawn, a pall of grey smoke hung over the buildings, and Amos was nowhere to be seen. Stifled by the fumes, she called out fearfully, 'Amos? Amos? Answer me! Where are you?' — and found him, black in the face and beaten, slumped in the muck, against the pigsty wall.

'Do come inside,' she said. 'You must sleep now. There's nothing you can do.' He gritted his teeth and said, 'I'll kill him.'

Obviously, he believed it was arson. Obviously, he believed that Watkins was the arsonist. But Mr Hudson, the constable in charge of the case, was a bland, pink-faced fellow, who did not like interfering in a neighbour's quarrel. He suggested that the hay had been damp.

'Delayed combustion, most likely,' he said, doffing his cap and cocking his leg over his bicycle.

'I'll give him delayed combustion!' Amos reeled indoors, tramping mud over the kitchen floor. A teacup whizzed past Mary's head, smashed a pane of the china-cabinet and she knew that there were bad times on the way.

His hair fell out in handfuls. His cheeks became streaked with livid veins; and the blue eyes, once friendly, sank in their sockets and peered, as if down a tunnel, at a hostile world outside.

He never washed and seldom shaved — though that, in itself, was a relief; for when he whetted his razor, a look of such viciousness passed over his face that Mary held her breath and backed towards the door.

In bed, he used her roughly. To stifle her groans, he rammed his hand over her mouth. The boys, in their room along the landing, could hear her struggles and clung to one another.

He beat them for the smallest misdemeanour. He even beat them for speaking in a classy accent. They learned to rephrase their thoughts in the dialect of Radnorshire.

He only seemed to care, now, for his daughter — a wilful, mean-eyed child whose idea of fun was to pull the legs off daddy-long-legs. She had a head of flaming hair that licked downwards. He would dandle her on his knee and croon, 'You're the one as loves me. Ain't ye? Ain't ye?' And Rebecca, who sensed Mary's lack of affection, would glare at her mother and brothers as if they were tribal enemies.

Little by little, the war with The Rock flourished into a ritual of raid and counter-raid: to call in the law was beneath the dignity of either belligerent. Nor was there any premeditated pattern; but a flayed lamb here, a dead calf there, or a gander dangling from a tree — all served as reminders that the feud continued.

Mary had long grown used to her husband's rages that came and went with the seasons. She even welcomed them, like thunder, because after the thunder, their old love had the habit of returning.

In other years, they had an unspoken pact: that the storm would pass by Easter. All through Holy Week she would watch him struggling with his demons. On Holy Saturday, they would go out walking in the woods and come back with a basket of primroses and violets to make a floral cross for the altar of Lurkenhope Church.

After supper, she would spread the flowers on the table, and, setting aside the violets for the letters INRI, she would thread the stems of the primroses into a frame of copper wire. He would be standing behind her, caressing the nape of her neck. Then, with the final letter finished, he would lift her in

78

his arms and carry her to bed.

But that year – the year of the fire – he did not go out walking. He did not eat his supper. And when, anxiously, she laid out the primroses, he attacked them, beating them as if they were flies, and crushing them to a greenish pulp.

She gave a strangled cry and ran out into the night.

That was the summer when the hay rotted and the sheep went unshorn.

Amos prevented Mary from seeing the few friends she had. He hit her for putting a second pinch of tea in the pot. He forbade her to set foot in the Albion Drapery, in case she squandered money on embroidery silks. And when news came of the Reverend Tuke's death – from pneumonia, after falling in a salmon-pool – he stopped her sending flowers to the funeral.

'He was my friend,' she said.

'He was a heathen,' he said.

'I shall leave you,' she said, but had nowhere else to go – and her other friend, Sam, was dying.

All spring, he had complained of 'gatherings' down his left side, and was too weak to move from his garret. He lay under the greasy quilt, gaping at the cobwebs, or drifting off to sleep. Once when Benjamin came up with his food on a tray, he said:

'I'd like my cup. Be a good lad! Run over to Rosgoch and get her to give you the cup.'

By June, the pain of living was more than he could bear.

He suffered for Mary and, in a lucid interval, tried to reason with his son.

'Mind your own business,' said Amos. 'You stupid old fool!'

One market day, when they were alone in the house, Sam persuaded his daughter-in-law to pay a call on Aggie Watkins:

'Tell her goodbye from me! She's a good old girl. A nice tidy person as never meant no harm.'

Mary slipped on a pair of galoshes and squelched her way across the boggy pasture. The wind moved over the field. The grassheads flashed like shoals of minnows, and there were purple orchids and heads of red sorrel. A pair of plovers flew off, screaming, and the mother alighted by some reeds and stretched her 'broken' wing. Mary said a silent prayer as she untied the gate into Craig-y-Fedw.

The dogs howled and Aggie Watkins came to the door. Her face registered no emotion, and no expression. Bending forward, she unleashed a black mongrel tied up beside the water-butt.

'Git,' she said.

The dog crouched and bared its gums but, when Mary turned for the gate, it bounded forward and sank its teeth into her hand.

Amos saw the bandage and guessed the cause. He shrugged and said, 'Serves you right!'

By Sunday the wound had turned septic. On Monday she complained of a swollen gland in her armpit. Grudgingly, he offered to drive her to the evening surgery – along with little Rebecca, who had a sore throat.

The twins came back from school to find their father greasing the hubs of the trap. Mary, pale but smiling, was sitting in the kitchen with her arm in a sling.

'We've been waiting for you,' she said. 'Don't worry. Do your homework and keep an eye on Grandpa.'

By sunset, the twins were speechless with grief, and Old Sam had been two hours dead.

At five in the afternoon, the boys were scribbling their sums at the kitchen table when a creak on the landing made them stop. Their grandfather was groping his way down the stairs.

'Sshh!' said Benjamin, tugging his brother by the sleeve.

'He should be in bed,' Lewis said.

'Sshh!' he repeated, and dragged him into the back kitchen.

The old man hobbled across the kitchen and went outside. There was a high windy sky, and the mares'-tails seemed to dance with the larches. He was wearing his wedding-best – a frock coat and trousers, and shiny patent leather pumps. A red handkerchief, knotted round his neck, made him young again – and he carried the fiddle and bow.

The twins peeped round the curtains.

'He's got to go back to bed,' Lewis whispered.

'Quiet!' hissed Benjamin. 'He's going to play.'

A harsh croak burst from the ancient instrument. But the second note was sweeter, and the successive notes were sweeter still. His head was up. His chin stuck truculently out over the sound-box; and his feet shuffled over the flagstones in perfect time.

Then he coughed and the music stopped. One tread at a time, he heaved himself up the stairs. He coughed again, and again, and after that there was silence.

The boys found him stretched out on the quilt with his hands folded over the fiddle. His face, drained of colour, wore a look of amused condescension. A bumble-bee, trapped inside the window, was buzzing and bouncing against the pane.

'Don't cry, my darlings!' Mary stretched her good arm around them as they blubbed out the news. 'Please don't cry. He had to die some time. And it was a wonderful way to die.'

Amos spared no expense on the funeral and ordered a brass-bound coffin from Lloyd's of Presteigne.

The hearse was drawn by a pair of glistening black horses and, on all four corners of the roof, there were black urns full of yellow roses. The mourners walked behind, picking their steps through the puddles and cart-ruts. Mary wore a collar of jet droplets that she had inherited from an aunt.

Mr Earnshaw had sent a wreath of arums to lay on the lid of the coffin. But when the pall-bearers set it down in the chancel, there were mounds of other wreaths to heap around it.

Most of these were sent by people who were strangers to Mary, but who certainly knew Old Sam. She hardly recognized a soul. She looked round the church, wondering who, in Heaven's name, were all those old biddies snivelling into their handkerchiefs. Surely, she thought, he can't have had that many flames?

Amos stood Rebecca on the pew so she could see what was going on.

' "Death be not proud..." ' The new vicar began his address; and though the words were beautiful, though the vicar's voice was resonant and pleasant, Mary's mind kept wandering to the two boys sitting beside her.

How tall they'd grown! They'll soon have to shave, she thought. But how thin and tired they were! How tiring it was to come home from school, and then be put to work on the farm! And how awkward they looked in those threadbare suits! If only she had money, she'd buy them nice new suits! And boots! It was so unfair to make them go about in boots two sizes too small! Unfair, too, not to let them go again to the seaside! They'd been so well and happy last summer. And there now, Benjamin coughing again! She must knit him another muffler for the winter, but where would she get the wool?

' "Ashes to ashes, dust to dust..." ' The clods thumped on to the coffin-lid. She handed the sexton a sovereign and walked away with Amos to the lych-gate, where they stood and bade farewell to the mourners.

'Thank you for coming,' she said. 'Thank you...No. He died quite peacefully...It was a mercy...Yes, Mrs Williams, the Lord be praised! No. We shan't be coming this year. So much to do...' — nodding, sighing, smiling, and shaking hands with all these kind commiserating people, one after the other till her fingers ached.

And afterwards, at home, when she had taken out her hatpins and her hat lay like a slug on the kitchen table, she turned to Amos with a look of heartfelt longing, but he turned his back and sneered, 'I suppose you never had a father of your own.'

XVII

THAT OCTOBER, a new visitor made his appearance at The Vision.

Mr Owen Gomer Davies was a Congregational Minister who had recently removed from Bala to Rhulen and had taken charge of the Chapel at Maesyfelin. He lived with his sister, at Number 3, Jubilee Terrace, and had a bird-bath in his garden, and a yucca.

He was a bulky man, with unpleasantly white skin, a roll of fat round his collar, and facial features set in the form of a Greek cross. His sharp mouth grew even sharper if he happened to smile. His handshake was frigid, and he had a melodious singing voice.

One of his first acts, on coming into the county, had been to quarrel with Tom Watkins over the price of a coffin. That alone was enough to recommend him to Amos — though to Mary he was a grotesque.

His views on the Bible were childlike. The doctrine of Transubstantiation was far too abstruse for his literal mind; and from the sanctimonious gesture with which he dropped a saccharin -tablet into his teacup, she suspected him of a weakness for sticky cakes.

One teatime, he solemnly set his fists on the table and announced that Hell was 'hotter than Egylypt or Jamaico!' — and Mary, who had hardly smiled all week, had to cover her face with a napkin.

She provoked him by wearing an uncommon amount of jewellery. 'Ah!' he said. 'The sin of Jezebel!'

He made a point of wincing whenever she opened her mouth, as if her English accent alone condemned her to Eternal Damnation. He seemed intent on weaning away her husband — and Amos was easily led.

The feud with Watkins had preyed on his mind. He had called on God for guidance. Here, at last, a man of God was willing to take his side. He read, with furious concentration, the mounds of pamphlets that the preacher deposited on the tea-table. He left the Church of England, and took the twins away from school. He made Benjamin sleep apart from his brother, in the hay-loft; and when he caught the boy sneaking up the ladder with the ship-in-the-bottle, he confiscated it.

Ten hours, twelve hours, the twins had to work all day till they collapsed, except of course on Sundays when the family did nothing but worship.

The Chapel at Maesyfelin was one of the oldest Non-Conformist chapels in the country.

A long stone building, devoid of decoration but for a sundial over the door, it lay between the stream and the lane, encircled by a windbreak of Portuguese laurel. Alongside was the Chapel Hall, a corrugated structure painted green.

Inside, the walls of the chapel were whitewashed. There were oak box-pews and plain oak benches, and on the pulpit were written the names of all the former ministers — the Parrys, the Williamses, the Vaughans and Joneses — going back to the days of the Commonwealth. At the east end stood the communion table carved with the date of 1682.

In India, Mary had watched the ways of Non-Conformist missionaries, and for her the word 'Chapel' represented all that was harsh and cramped and intolerant. Yet she masked her feelings and consented to go. Mr Gomer Davies was so blatant a fraud, surely it was best to let him go on bamboozling Amos, who would, one day, come to his senses? She sent a note to the vicar explaining her absence. 'A passing phase,' she added as a postscript; for she was incapable of taking it seriously.

How to keep a straight face as Mrs Reuben Jones pounded out the hymns of William Williams on the wheezy harmonium? Or at the warbling voices and wobbly feather hats? Or the men — sensible farmers all week — now sweating and swaying and hooting 'Hallelujah!' and 'Amen!' and 'Yea, Lord! Yea!' And when, in the middle of the 150th Psalm, Mrs Griffiths Cwm Cringlyn reached for her handbag and pulled out a tambourine, again Mary had to close her eyes and suppress the temptation to giggle.

And surely the sermons were absolute rubbish?

One Sunday, Mr Gomer Davies enumerated all the animals

aboard the Ark and at evening service he excelled himself. He stationed five lighted candles on the rim of the pulpit so that, when he pointed his finger at the congregation, five separate shadows of his forearm were reflected onto the ceiling. Then, in a low, liturgical voice, he began, 'I see your sins as cats' eyes in the night...'

For all that, there came a time when it shamed her to think that she had mocked these austere ceremonies; times when the Holy Word seemed to set the walls a-tremble; and one particular time when a visiting preacher overwhelmed her with his eloquence:

'He is a Black Lamb, my beloved lamb, black as a raven and chief among the thousand. My beloved is a White Lamb, a ruddy lamb and chief among the ten thousand. He is a Red Lamb. Who is this that cometh out of Edom, his garments red, from Bozrah? Is this not a Wonderful Lamb, my brethren? O my brethren, strive to lay hold of this lamb! Strive! Strive to lay hold of a limb of this lamb...!'

After the sermon, the preacher called the worshippers to communion. They sat on benches, the husbands facing the wives. Along the length of the table stretched a runner of freshly laundered linen.

The preacher cut the loaf into chunks, blessed them and passed them round on a pewter plate. Then he blessed the wine in a pewter cup. Mary took the cup from her neighbour and, as her lips touched the rim, she knew, in a flash of revelation, this *was* the Lord's Feast; this *was* the Upper Room; and all the great cathedrals were built not so much for the glory of God as the vanity of Man; and Popes and bishops were Caesars and princes; and if, afterwards, anyone reproached her for deserting the Church of England, she stooped her head and said, simply, 'The Chapel gives me great comfort.'

But Amos went on raving and ranting and suffering from migraines and insomnia. Never—even among fakirs and flagellants—had Mary encountered such fanaticism. In the evenings, straining his eyes in the lamplight, he would comb the Bible for vindication of his rights. He read the Book of Job: ' "My bones are pierced in me in the night season: and my sinews take no rest..." '

He threatened to move away, to buy a farm in Carmarthenshire, in the heart of Wales. But his bank account was empty, and his thirst for vengeance rooted him to the spot.

In March of 1912, he caught Watkins in the act of hacking down a gate. There was a fight: he staggered home with a gash above his temple. A week later, the postman found the Watkinses' mule by the laneside, still breathing, with a pile of intestines spilling out on to the grass. On April Fool's Day, Amos woke to find his favourite dog dead on the muck-heap; and he broke down and blubbed like a baby.

Mary saw no end to the misery. She looked at herself in the mirror, at a face more grey and cracked than the mirror's pitted surface. She wanted to die, but knew she had to live for the twins. To distract herself, she read the novels she had loved as a girl – hiding them from Amos, who, in his present mood, would burn them. One wintry afternoon, drowsy from the fire, she dozed off with a copy of *Wuthering Heights* open on her lap. He came in, woke her roughly, and slammed the corner of the binding into her eye.

She jumped to her feet. She had had enough. Her fear had gone and she was strong again. She stiffened her back and said, 'You silly fool!'

He stood by the piano, shaking all over, with his lip hanging loose – and then he was gone.

There was one course open to her now – her sister in Cheltenham! Her sister who had a house and an income! From her writing-case she removed two sheets of notepaper. 'Nothing', she concluded the final paragraph, 'can be lonelier than the loneliness of marriage...'

Before breakfast next morning, Amos trundled the milk-churn from the dairy and saw her hand the envelope to the postman. He seemed to know each line of the letter. He tried to be pleasant to the twins, but they returned his advances with a steely stare.

As her black eye subsided and turned a yellowish purple, Mary felt more and more elated. The daffodils were in flower. She began to forgive him and, from his guilty glances, she knew he accepted her conditions. She resisted the temptation to gloat. The letter came from Cheltenham. He was terribly nervous as he watched her slit it open.

Her eyes danced over the spinsterish handwriting, and she threw back her head and laughed:

'...Father always said you were headstrong and impulsive...No one can say I didn't warn you...But wedlock is wedlock...a binding sacrament...and you must stick to your husband through thick and thin...'

She said, 'I'm not even going to tell you what's in it.' She blew him a kiss. Her lips trembled with tenderness as the letter flared up in the fire.

XVIII

SIX MONTHS LATER, Benjamin had shot up in height, and was three inches taller than Lewis.

First, he grew a wispy black moustache and the fuzz spread over his cheeks and chin. Then his whole face came up in pimples and he was not a pretty sight. He was ashamed and embarrassed to be so much bigger than his brother.

And Lewis was jealous — jealous of the broken voice, jealous even of the pimples, and worried he might never grow as tall. They avoided each other's eyes, and the meals went by in silence. On the morning of Benjamin's first shave, Lewis stamped out of the house.

Mary fetched a dressing mirror and set a basin of warm water on the kitchen table. Amos whetted the razor on its leather strop and showed him how to hold it. But Benjamin was so nervous, and his hand was so unsteady, that when he wiped away the lather, his face was covered with bleeding cuts.

Ten days later, he shaved again, alone.

Often, in the past, if either twin caught sight of himself — in a mirror, in a window, or even on the surface of water — he mistook his own reflection for his other half. So now, when Benjamin poised his razor at the ready and glanced up at the glass, he had the sensation of slitting Lewis's throat.

After that, he stubbornly refused to shave until Lewis had grown as tall, and grown a beard. Mary watched her sons and sensed that, one day, they would both slide back into the old, familiar pattern of dependence. In the meantime, Lewis was flirting with girls; and because he was limber and attractive, the girls egged him on.

He flirted with Rosie Fifield. They exchanged a breathless kiss behind a haystack and held hands for twenty minutes at a choral evening. One moonless night, strolling along the lane to Lurkenhope, he passed some girls in white dresses searching the hedgerow for glow-worms. He heard Rosie's laughter, rippling clear and cold in the darkness. He slipped his hand around her satin sash, and she slapped him:

'Get ye away, Lewis Jones! And take your big nose out of my face!'

Benjamin loved his mother and his brother, and he did not like girls. Whenever Lewis left the room, his eyes would linger in the doorway, and his irises cloud to a denser shade of grey: when Lewis came back, his pupils glistened.

They never went back to school. They worked on the farm, and providing they worked in tandem they could do the work of four. Left alone — to dig potatoes or pulp the swedes — Benjamin's energy began to fail, and he would wheeze and cough and feel faint. Their father saw this and, with a farmer's eye to efficiency, he knew it was useless to part them: it took the twins another ten years to work out a division of labour.

Lewis still dreamed of faraway voyages but his interest had shifted to airships. And when a picture of a Zeppelin appeared in the newspaper — or the mention of Count Zeppelin's name — he would cut out the article and paste it in his scrapbook.

Benjamin said that Zeppelins looked like cucumbers.

He never thought of abroad. He wanted to live with Lewis for ever and ever; to eat the same food; wear the same clothes; share a bed; and swing an axe in the same trajectory. There were four gates leading into The Vision; and, for him, they were the Four Gates of Paradise.

He loved the sheep, and the open air made him strong again. His eye was quick to spot a case of pulpy kidney or a prolapsed uterus. At lambing time he would walk round the flock with a crook on his arm, checking the ewes' teats to make sure the milk was flowing.

He was also very religious.

Crossing the pasture one evening, he watched the swallows glinting low over the dandelion clocks, and the sheep standing out against the sunset, each one ringed with an aureole of gold — and understood why the Lamb of God should have a halo.

He would spend long hours patterning his ideas of sin and retribution into a vast theological system that would, one day, save the world. Then, when the fine print tired his eyes — both the twins were a little astygmatic — he would pore over Amos's colour print of 'The Broad and Narrow Path'.

This was a gift from Mr Gomer Davis, and hung beside the fireplace in its frame of gothic niches.

On the left side, ladies and gentlemen were strolling in groups towards 'The Way of Perdition'. Flanking the gate were statues of Venus and the Drunken Bacchus; and, beyond them, there were more smart people — drinking, dancing, gambling, going to theatres, pawning their property and taking trains on Sundays.

Higher up the road, the same sort of people were seen robbing, murdering, enslaving and going to war. And finally, hovering over some blazing battlements — which looked a bit like Windsor Castle — the Devil's Attendants weighed the souls of sinners.

The right side of the picture was 'The Way of Salvation'; and here the buildings were, unmistakably, Welsh. In fact, the Chapel, the Sunday School and the Deaconesses' Institution — all with high-pitched gables and slate roofs — reminded Benjamin of an illustrated brochure for Llandrindod Wells.

Only the humbler classes were to be seen on this narrow and difficult road, performing any number of pious acts, until they, too, trudged up a mountainside that looked exactly like the Black Hill. And there, on the summit, was the City of New Jerusalem, and the Lamb of Zion, and the choirs of trumpeting angels...!

This was the image that haunted Benjamin's imagination. And he believed, seriously, that the Road to Hell was the road to Hereford, whereas the Road to Heaven led up to the Radnor Hills.

XIX

THEN THE WAR CAME.

For years, the tradesmen in Rhulen had said there was going to be war with Germany, though nobody knew what war would mean. There had been no real war since Waterloo, and everyone agreed that with railways and modern guns this war would either be very terrible, or over very quickly.

On the 7th of August 1914, Amos Jones and his sons were scything thistles when a man called over the hedge that the Germans had marched into Belgium, and rejected England's ultimatum. A recruiting office, he said, had opened in the Town Hall. About twenty local lads had joined.

'More fool them,' Amos shrugged, and glared downhill into Herefordshire.

All three went on with their scything, but the boys looked very jittery when they came in for supper.

Mary had been pickling beetroot, and her apron was streaked with purple stains.

'Don't worry,' she said. 'You're far too young to fight. Besides, it'll probably be over by Christmas.'

Winter came, and there was no end to the war. Mr Gomer Davies started preaching patriotic sermons and, one Friday, sent word to The Vision, bidding them to a lantern lecture, at five o'clock, in the Congregation Hall.

The sky was deepening from crimson to gunmetal. Two limousines were parked in the lane; and a crowd of farm boys, all in their Sunday best, were chatting to the chauffeurs or peering through the windows at the fur rugs and leather upholstery. The boys had never seen such automobiles at close quarters. In a nearby shed, an electric generator was purring.

Mr Gomer Davies stood in the vestibule, welcoming all comers with a handshake and muddy smile. The war, he said, was a Crusade for Christ.

Inside the Hall, a coke stove was burning and the windows had misted up. A line of electric bulbs spread a film of yellow light over the planked and varnished walls. There were plenty of Union Jacks strung up, and a picture of Lord Kitchener.

The magic lantern stood in the middle of the aisle. A white sheet had been tacked up to serve as a screen; and a khaki-clad Major, one arm in a sling, was confiding his box of glass slides to the lady projectionist.

Veiled in cigar smoke, the principal speaker, Colonel Bickerton, had already taken his seat on the stage and was having a jaw with a Boer War veteran. He extended his game leg to the audience. A silk hat sat on the green baize tablecloth, beside a water-carafe and a tumbler.

Various ministers of God—all of whom had sunk their differences in a blaze of patriotism—went up to pay their respects to the squire, and show concern for his comfort.

'No, I'm quite comfortable, thank you.' The Colonel enunciated every syllable to perfection. 'Thank you for looking after me so well. Pretty good turn-out, I see. Most encouraging, what?'

The hall was full. Lads with fresh, weatherbeaten faces crammed the benches or elbowed forward to get a better look at the Bickertons' daughter, Miss Isobel—a brunette with moist red lips and moist hazel eyes, who sat below the platform, composed and smiling, in a silver fox-fur cape. From her dainty hat there spurted a grey-pink glycerined ostrich plume. At her elbow crouched a young man with carroty hair and mouth agape.

It was Jim the Rock.

The Joneses took their seats on a bench at the back. Mary could feel her husband, tense and angry beside her. She was afraid he was going to make a scene.

The vicar of Rhulen opened the session by proposing a vote

of thanks to Mr Gomer Davies for the use of the Hall, and electricity.

Rumbles of 'Hear! Hear!' sounded round the room. He went on to sketch the origins of the war.

Few of the hill-farmers understood why the murder of an Archduke in the Balkans should have triggered off the invasion of Belgium; but when the vicar spoke of the 'peril to our belovèd Empire' people began to sit up.

'There can be no rest,' he raised his voice, 'until this cancer has been ripped out of European society. The Germans will squeal like every bully when cornered. But there must be no compromise, no shaking hands with the devil. It is useless to moralize with an alligator. Kill it!'

The audience clapped and the clergyman sat down.

Next in turn was the Major, who had been wounded, he said, at Mons. He began with a joke about 'making the Rhine whine' — whereupon the Colonel perked up and said, 'Never cared for Rhine wines myself. Too fruity, what?'

The Major then lifted his swagger stick.

'Lights!' he called, and the lights went off.

One by one, a sequence of blurred images flashed across the screen — of Tommies in camp, Tommies on parade, Tommies on the cross-Channel ferry; Tommies in a French café; Tommies in trenches; Tommies fixing bayonets, and Tommies 'going over the top'. Some of the slides were so fuzzy it was hard to tell which was the shadow of Miss Isobel's plume, and which were shell-bursts.

The last slide showed an absurd goggle-eyed visage with crows' wings on its upper lip and a whole golden eagle on its helmet.

'That', said the Major, 'is your enemy — Kaiser Wilhelm II of Germany.'

There were shouts of 'String 'im up' and 'Shoot 'im to bloody bits!' — and the Major, also, sat down.

Colonel Bickerton then eased himself to his feet and apologized for the indisposition of his wife.

His own son, he said, was fighting in Flanders. And after the stirring scenes they'd just witnessed, he hoped there'd be few shirkers in the district.

'When this war is over,' he said, 'there will be two classes of persons in this country. There will be those who were qualified to join the Armed Forces and refrained from doing so...'

'Shame!' shrilled a woman in a blue hat.

'I'm the Number One!' a young man shouted and stuck up his hand.

But the Colonel raised his cufflinks to the crowd, and the crowd fell silent:

'...and there will be those who were so qualified and came forward to do their duty to their King, their country...and their womenfolk...'

'Yes! Yes!' Again the hands arose with fluid grace and, again, the crowd fell silent:

'The last-mentioned class, I need not add, will be the aristocracy of this country — indeed, the only true aristocracy of this country — who, in the evening of their days, will have the consolation of knowing that they have done what England expects of every man: namely, to do his duty...'

'What about Wales?' A sing-song voice sounded to the right of Miss Bickerton; but Jim was drowned in the general hullabaloo.

Volunteers rushed forward to press their names on the Major. There were shouts of 'Hip! Hip! Hurrah!' Other voices broke into song, 'For they are jolly good fellows...' The woman in the blue hat slapped her son over the face, shrieking, 'Oh, yes, you will!' — and a look of childlike serenity had descended on the Colonel.

He continued, in thrilling tones: 'Now when Lord Kitchener says he needs you, he means YOU. For each one of you brave young fellows is unique and indispensable. A few moments ago, I heard a voice on my left calling, "What about Wales?"'

Suddenly, you could hear a pin drop.

'Believe you me, that cry, "What about Wales?" is a cry that goes straight to my heart. For in my veins Welsh blood and English blood course in equal quantities. And that...that is why my daughter and I have brought two automobiles here with us this evening. Those of you who wish to enlist in our beloved Herefordshire Regiment may drive with me... But

93

those of you, loyal Welshmen, who would prefer to join that other, most gallant regiment, the South Wales Borderers, may go with my daughter and Major Llewellyn-Smythe to Brecon...'

This was how Jim the Rock went to war—for the sake of leaving home, and for a lady with moist red lips and moist hazel-coloured eyes.

XX

IN INDIA, Mary had once seen the Lancers riding to the Frontier; and a bugle-call sent tingles up her spine. She believed in the Allied Cause. She believed in Victory, and in answer to Mrs Bickerton's 'appeal for knitted garments' she and Rebecca spent their spare time knitting gloves and balaclavas for the boys at the Front.

Amos hated the war and would have no truck with it.

He hid his horses from the Remount Officers. He ignored an order from the Ministry to plant wheat on a north-facing slope. It was a matter of pride, both as a man and as a Welshman, to stop his sons from fighting for the English.

He read into the Bible a confirmation of his views. Surely the war was God's visitation on the Cities of the Plain? Surely all the things you read in the papers — the shelling, the bombs, the U-boats and mustard gas — were they not the instruments of His Vengeance? Perhaps the Kaiser was another Nebuchadnezzar? Perhaps there'd be a Seventy Year Captivity for Englishmen? And perhaps there'd be a remnant who'd be spared—a remnant such as the Rechabites, who drank no wine, neither lived in cities, nor bowed before false idols, but obeyed the Living God?

He expounded these opinions to Mr Gomer Davies, who stared at him as if he were mad and accused him of being a traitor. He, in turn, accused the minister of glossing over the Sixth Commandment and discontinued his attendance at Chapel.

In January of 1916 — after the Conscription Act became law — he learned that a Rechabite Friendly Society held regular meetings in Rhulen, and so came into contact with Conscientious Objectors.

He took the twins to their sessions in a draughty loft over a cobbler's shop in South Street.

Most of the members were artisans or manual labourers, but there was a gentleman among them — a lanky young fellow with a big Adam's apple, who dressed in shabby tweeds and rewrote the minutes in elevated prose.

The Rechabites held that tea was a sinful stimulant: so refreshments were limited to a blackcurrant cordial and a plate of thin arrowroot biscuits. One by one, the speakers professed their faith in a peaceable world and pronounced on the fate of their comrades. Many were under sentence of court martial or in jail. And one of their number, a quarryman, had led a hunger strike in the Hereford Detention Barracks, when the sergeants tried to make him handle the regimental rum supply. He had died, from pneumonia, after forcible feeding. A mixture of milk and cocoa, syringed up his nostrils, had filtered down into his lungs.

'Poor Tom!' the cobbler said, and called for three minutes' silence.

The company stood — an arc of bald heads bowed in a pool of lamplight. Then all linked hands and sang a song, the words of which they knew, but not the tune:

> Nation with nation, land with land
> Unarmed shall live as comrades free
> In every heart and brain shall throb
> The pulse of one fraternity.

At first, Mary found it hard to reconcile her husband's violent temperament with his pacifism: after news of the Somme, she conceded he might be right.

Twice a week, she walked down to Lurkenhope to cook a meal for Betty Palmer, a poor widow, who had lost her only son in the battle, and lost the will to eat. Then, in May of 1917, she patched up her quarrel with Aggie Watkins.

She saw a lonely figure in black, dragging her feet round the market booths, drying her tears on her sleeve.

'It must be Jim,' she cried out loud.

Aggie's face was blotchy from crying, and her bonnet was awry. A light rain was falling and the street vendors were covering their wares, and taking shelter under the arches of the Town Hall.

'It be Jim,' Aggie sobbed. ' 'Im were in France and workin' with mules. An' now comes this card as says 'im's done for.'

She poked her arthritic fingers into her basket of eggs, pulled out a crumpled card, and passed it to Mary.

It was one of the Standard Field Service Postcards that front-line soldiers were allowed to send home after a battle.

Mary frowned as she tried to puzzle it out, and then relaxed into a smile.

'But he's not dead, Aggie. He's fine. Look! That's what the cross means. It says, "I'm quite well." '

A spasm shook the old woman's face. Glowering with disbelief, she grabbed the card. But when she saw Mary's open arms, and the tears in her eyes, she dropped her basket, and the two women flung their arms round each other's necks, and kissed.

'Now look what you've done,' Mary said, pointing to the egg-yolks smeared over the shiny wet cobbles.

'Eggs!' said Mrs Watkins, disdainfully.

'And look!' said Mary, recovering the card. 'It's got an address for parcels. Let's send him a cake!'

That afternoon, she baked a big fruitcake, full of raisins and nuts and glacé cherries. She wrote the name 'JIM THE ROCK' in blanched almonds on the crust, and left it on the table for Amos to see.

He shrugged and said, 'I'd like a cake like that.' A day or so later, he passed Tom Watkins in the lane. They nodded – and a truce was assumed to exist.

But the news from the Great War was worse than ever.

In cottage kitchens, mothers sat helplessly waiting for the postman's knock. When the letter came from the King, a black-bordered card would appear in one of the windows. In a cottage along the lane to Rhulen, Mary saw two cards fixed in front of the net curtains. After Passchendaele, a third card joined them.

'I can't bear it,' she choked, clutching Amos by the sleeve as they drove by. 'Not all three of them!' The twins would be eighteen in August, and liable to serve. All winter, she had the same recurring dream – of Benjamin standing under an apple-tree, with a red hole through his forehead, and a reproachful smile.

On the 21st of February – a date Mary shuddered to remember – Mr Arkwright, the Rhulen solicitor, drove up to The Vision in his motor. He was one of the five members of the local Military Service Tribunal. A dapper little man with arctic eyes and sandy waxed moustachios, he wore a grey Homburg and a grey serge topcoat; and on the passenger seat sat his red setter bitch.

He began by demanding why, in the name of God, the twins hadn't registered for their National Identity Cards. Did they, or did they not, realize they had broken the law? Then, taking great care not to muddy his spats or shoes, he jotted down particulars of the land, the numbers of stock, and the buildings, and wound up by pronouncing, with the solemnity of a judge passing sentence, that The Vision was too small a farm to warrant exemption for more than one son.

'Of course,' he added, 'none of us likes taking lads off the land. Food shortages and all that! But the law's the law!'

'Them be twins,' stammered Amos.

'I know they're twins. My dear good man, we can't start making exceptions...'

'Them'll die apart...'

'If you please! Healthy boys like them! Never heard such nonsense!... Maudie!... Maudie!' The red setter was barking at a rabbit-hole in the hedge. She lolloped back to her master, and sat down again in the passenger seat. Mr Arkwright revved the engine and released the handbrake. The tyres cracked the ice-puddles as the car slewed off down the yard.

'Tinpot tyrant!' Amos raised his fist, standing alone in a cloud of blue exhaust.

XXI

NEXT MARKET DAY, Amos approached the bailiff of a big farm near Rhydspence, who was said to be short of hands. The man agreed to take on Lewis as a ploughman, and sponsor him when his case came up before the Tribunal.

Benjamin almost fainted at the news.

'Don't worry,' Mary tried to console him. 'He'll be back when the war's over. Besides, it's only ten miles away, and he's bound to come and see us on Sundays.'

'You don't understand,' he said.

Lewis put on a brave face when the time came to leave. He tied a few clothes in a bundle, kissed his mother and brother, and jumped into the trap beside Amos. The wind ripped at Benjamin's coat-sleeves as he watched them disappearing down the lane.

He began to pine.

Though he ate his food, the thought of Lewis eating different food, off different plates, at a different table, made him sadder and sadder and he soon grew thin and weak. At nights, he would reach out to touch his brother, but his hand came to rest on a cold unrumpled pillow. He gave up washing for fear of reminding himself that — at that same moment — Lewis might be sharing someone else's towel.

'Do cheer up,' Mary said. She could see the separation was more than he could bear.

He revisited the places where they had played as children. Sometimes, he called the sheepdog, 'Mott! Mott! Come on, let's find the master! Where's he? Where's he?' And the dog would jump up and wag his tail, and they would clamber up the screes of the Black Hill, until the Wye came into view — all a-glitter in the winter sunshine — and the fresh brown plough around Rhydspence where Lewis might be ploughing.

At other times, he went alone to the dingle and watched the peaty water sluicing through their old bathing pool. Everywhere, he kept seeing Lewis's face — in a cattle-trough, in the milk-pail, even in puddles of liquid dung.

He hated Lewis for leaving and suspected him of stealing his soul. One day, staring into the shaving mirror, he watched his face grow fainter and fainter, as if the glass were eating his reflection until he vanished altogether in a crystalline mist.

This was the first time he thought of killing himself.

Lewis used to arrive for Sunday lunch, pink in the face after a ten-mile hike across country, his leggings coated with mud and his breeches with dead burrs.

He kept them all amused with stories of life on a big farm. He liked his job. He liked to tinker with the new-fangled machinery, and had driven a tractor. He liked looking after the pedigree Herefords. He liked the bailiff, who instructed him in the mysteries of the stud-book; and he had made friends with one of the dairy-maids. He loathed the Irish stock-man, who was a 'bloody drunken savage'.

One Wednesday, towards the end of April, the bailiff sent him by train to Hereford, along with some lots of store-cattle, which were due to be sold at auction. Since the lots came up at eleven, the rest of the day was free.

It was a very gloomy day and the clouds brushed low over the Cathedral tower. Lines of grey sleet smacked on to the pavements and rattled on the oilcloth hoods of the horse-cabs. In High Town, the poor cab-horses stood in line beside the swollen gutter; and under a green-painted canopy, some cabbies were warming their hands over a brazier.

'Come on in, laddie!' one of them beckoned, and Lewis joined them.

A military vehicle drove by, and a pair of sergeants strutted past in mackintosh capes.

'Bitter day for a funeral,' said a man with a cheesy complexion.

'Bitter,' agreed another.

'And what age are you, laddie?' the first man went on, rattling a poker in the coals.

'Seventeen,' said Lewis.

'And your birth-date?'

'August.'

'Watch it, laddie! Watch it, or they'll have you, for sure.'

Lewis fidgeted on the bench. When the sleet let up, he sauntered through the maze of lanes behind Watkins's Brewery. He stood in the entrance of a cooper's shop and saw the brand-new barrels amid heaps of yellow shavings. From another street, he heard a brass band playing, and walked towards it.

Outside the Green Dragon Hotel a knot of bystanders had gathered to watch the funeral procession go by.

The dead man was a Colonel of the Herefords, who had died of war wounds. The Guard of Honour marched with eyes fastened on the tips of their naked sword blades. The drummer wore a leopard skin. The march was the 'Dead March' in *Saul*.

The wheels of the gun-carriage grated on the macadam and the coffin, draped in a Union Jack, passed across the level-lidded gaze of the ladies. Four black automobiles followed, with the widow, the Lord Mayor and the mourners. Jackdaws spewed from the belfry as the bells began to toll. A woman in a fox-fur grabbed Lewis's arm and clamoured, shrilly:

'And you, young man, aren't you ashamed to be seen in civvies?'

He nipped off down an alley in the direction of the market.

An aroma of coffee beans caused him to halt before a bow-fronted window. On the shelves sat little wicker baskets heaped with conical mounds of tea: the names on the labels — Darjeeling, Keemun, Lapsang Souchong, Oolong — carried him away to a mysterious east. The coffees were on the lower shelves, and in each warm brown bean he saw the warm brown lips of a negress.

He was daydreaming of rattan huts and lazy seas, when a butcher's cart rolled by; the carter yelled, 'Watch it, mate!' and chutes of muddy water flew up and dirtied his breeches.

In Eign Street, he paused to admire a cap of houndstooth tweed displayed in the window of a Messrs Parberry and Williams, Gentlemen's Hosiers.

Mr Parberry himself stood in the doorway, a pendulous man with strands of oily black hair coiled around his skull.

'Come on in, my boy!' he said in a fluty voice. 'Costs you nothing to look round. And what takes your fancy this fine spring morning?'

'The cap,' said Lewis.

The shop smelled of oilskins and kerosene. Mr Parberry removed the cap from the window, fingered the label, priced it at five shillings and sixpence, and added, 'I'll knock the sixpence off!'

Lewis ran his thumbnail over the milled edges of the florins in his pocket. He had just been paid his wages. He had a pound's-worth of silver.

Mr Parberry cocked the cap on Lewis's head and turned him to face the pier-glass. It was the right size. It was a very smart cap.

'I'll take two of them,' Lewis said. 'One for my brother.'

'Good for you!' said Mr Parberry, and ordered his assistant to fetch down an oval hatbox. He spread the caps on the counter, but no two were identical; and when Lewis insisted, 'No, I must have two the same,' the man lost his temper and spluttered, 'Get out, you young whippersnapper! Get out and stop wasting my time!'

At one o'clock, Lewis looked in at the City and County Dining-Room to give himself a feed. The waitress said she'd have a table in a jiffy and told him to wait five minutes. From the menu-board, he chose a steak-and-kidney pudding, and a jam roly-poly for afters.

Stubble-jowled farmers were gorging great quantities of suet and black pudding; and a gentleman chaffed the waitress for failing to serve him. From time to time, the clatter of plates broke through the hubbub, and a volley of curses was heard through the kitchen hatch. Whiffs of frying-fat and tobacco filled the room. A tabby cat slipped in and out among the customers' legs and, on the floor, there were patches of beer-sodden sawdust.

The slatternly waitress came back, grinned, set her hands on her hips, said, 'Come on, pretty boy!' – and Lewis took to his heels.

He purchased a pasty from a street-vendor and, feeling very low, took shelter in the entrance of a ladies' fashion-house.

Models in tea-gowns stared with blue glass eyes on to the rainy street, and there was a picture of Clemenceau beside the King and Queen.

He was about to bite into the pasty when he started to shiver. He watched his fingertips, whitening. He knew his brother was in danger, and ran for the station.

The train for Rhulen was standing at Platform One.

It was hot and airless in the compartment, and the windows had misted up. His teeth went on chattering. He could feel the goose-pimples rubbing against his shirt.

A girl with glowing cheeks stepped in, set down her basket and sat in the far corner. She took off her homespun shawl and hat, and laid them on the seat. The afternoon was very dark. The lights were lit. The train moved off with a whistle and a jerk.

He wiped his sleeve over the misted window and looked out at the telegraph poles that flashed, one after the other, across the rosy reflection of the girl.

'You've got a fever,' she said.

'No,' he said. He did not turn round. 'My brother's freezing.'

He wiped the window again. The furrows of a ploughed field went whizzing by, like the spokes of a wheel. He saw the Cefn Hill plantation, and the Black Hill covered with snow. He was waiting with the door open, poised to jump, as the train pulled in to Rhulen.

'Can I help?' the girl called after him.

'No,' he called back, and raced down the platform.

It was after four by the time he reached The Vision and Rebecca was alone in the kitchen, distractedly darning a sock.

'Them've gone out looking for Benjamin,' she said.

'And I know where him do be,' Lewis said.

He went to the porch and changed his wet cape for a dry

one. He pulled a sou'wester over his face and walked out into the snow.

Around eleven that morning, Amos had looked towards the west and said, 'I don't like the look of them clouds. Better get the ewes off the hill.'

It was late in the lambing season and the ewes and early lambs were on the mountain. For ten days the weather had been lovely. The thrushes were nesting, and the birches in the dingle were dusted with green. No one had expected any more snow.

'No,' Amos repeated. 'I don't like the look of it.'

He had a chill on his chest, and his legs and back were stiff. Mary fetched his boots and gaiters and noticed, all of a sudden, that he was old. He bent down to tie his laces. Something cricked in his spine, and he sank back into the chair.

'I'll go,' said Benjamin.

'Quickly now!' his father said. 'Before it comes to snow.'

Benjamin whistled for the dog and walked over the fields to Cock-a-loftie. From there he took the steeper path up the escarpment. He reached the rim, and a raven flew off a thornbush, croaking.

Then the cloud came down and the sheep, when he could see them, were like little packs of vapour – and then it began to snow.

The snow fell in thick woolly flakes. The wind got up and blew drifts across the track. He saw something dark close by: it was the dog shaking the snow off his back. Icy trickles ran down his neck, and he realized his cap was gone. His hands were in his pockets but he could not feel them. His feet felt so heavy it was hardly worth bothering to take the next step – and, just then, the snow changed colour.

The snow was not white any more, but a creamy golden rose. It was not cold any more. The tussocks of reed were not sharp, but soft and downy. And all he wanted now was to lie down in this nice, warm comfortable snow, and sleep.

His knees began to weaken, and he heard his brother bellowing in his ear:

103

'You've got to go on. You mustn't stop. I'll die if you go to sleep.'

So he went on, dragging one foot after the other, back to the rocks along the cliff edge. And that really was the place to curl up, out of the wind, with the dog, and sleep.

It was white when he woke, and it took him some time to realize that the whiteness was not snow, but bed-linen. Lewis was by the bedside, and the sharp spring sunlight streamed through the window.

'How do you feel?' he said.

'You left me,' said Benjamin.

XXII

BENJAMIN'S RIGHT HAND was frostbitten. For a while, he seemed likely to lose a finger or two; and until he recovered, Lewis stayed at his side. He was a week away from work. Then, when he did go back to Rhydspence, the bailiff lost his temper, said his farm was not some institution for shirkers, and sacked him.

Ashamed and footsore, Lewis reached home at suppertime, took his place at table, and rested his head in his hands.

'I am sorry, Father,' he said, after coming to the end of his story.

'Hm!' Amos replaced the cover of the cheese-dish.

Twenty minutes went by, silent but for the chink of cutlery and the ticking of the grandfather clock.

'You're not to blame,' he said, and reached for his tobacco-pouch. He rose from the table, put his hand on the boy's shoulder, and then went to sit by the fire.

For the whole of the following week he fretted about the Tribunal, blaming himself, blaming Lewis, and wondering what to do next. Finally, he decided to confide in Mr Arkwright.

The solicitor was very reticent about his origins but was known to have lived in Chester before buying the Rhulen practice in 1912. His manner was unbending towards the 'lower orders', although he blossomed in the presence of a squire. He lived with his ailing wife in a mock-Tudor villa called 'The Cedars' and prided himself on a lawn free of dandelions. There were those who said there was 'something fishy about the fellow'.

A brass plaque, engraved with his name in Roman capitals, gleamed outside his office at Number 14, Broad Street.

The articled clerk showed Amos upstairs into a room of knobbly beige wallpaper, where there were stacks of black tin deed boxes and a bookcase crammed with *Law Society Reports*. The carpet had a pattern of blue flowers, and on the grey slate mantelpiece sat a carriage clock.

Without attempting to stir from his desk, the solicitor leaned back in his leather chair, tugging at his pipe, while Amos, red in the face and flustered, explained how his sons were not two persons, but one.

'Quite so!' Mr Arkwright stroked his chin. After hearing the story of the snowstorm, he started to his feet and slapped his visitor across the back.

'Don't give it another thought!' he said. 'A simple matter! I'll arrange it with my colleagues.

'We're not ogres, you know,' he went on, extending a cold dry hand to Amos, and ushered him on to the street.

It was glorious summery weather on the day of the Tribunal; and four of its five members were in a rip-roaring mood. The morning papers carried news of the Allied 'breakthrough' in France. Major Gattie, the Military Representative, called for a 'dashed good luncheon to celebrate'. Mr Evenjobb, an agricultural merchant, agreed. The vicar agreed; and Mr Arkwright confessed to feeling 'pretty peckish' himself.

So the members treated themselves to a tip-top luncheon at the Red Dragon, downed three bottles of claret, drowsily took their places in the Committee Room of the Town Hall, and waited for their Chairman, Colonel Bickerton.

The room reeked of Jeyes Fluid and was so hot and airless that even the flies stopped droning round the skylight. Mr Evenjobb nodded off. The Reverend Pile felt exhilarated by notions of youth and sacrifice, while the conscripts who hoped for exemption sat outside in a gloomy green corridor on benches, with a police constable guarding them.

The Colonel arrived a little late from his own luncheon party at Lurkenhope. Flushed in the face, and with a rosebud in his buttonhole, he was in no mood to grant any further exemptions, having, at the previous session, exempted two of his hunt servants, and his valet.

'This Tribunal must be fair,' he opened the proceedings. 'The agricultural needs of the community must be taken into account. Yet there is a great and barbarous enemy which must be destroyed. And to destroy it, the Army needs men!'

'Seconded,' said Major Gattie, scrutinizing his fingernails.

The first to be called was Tom Philips, a shepherd lad from Mousecastle, who mumbled about his sick mother and no one to look after the sheep.

'Speak up, my boy,' the Colonel interrupted. 'Can't hear one word of what you're saying.'

But Tom still couldn't make himself understood and the Colonel lost his patience. 'Report to Hereford Barracks within five days.'

'Yessir!' he said.

The panel next heard the case of a pallid youth who loudly affirmed he was a Socialist and a Quaker. Nothing, he said, could force him to reconcile military discipline with his conscience.

'In which case,' said the Colonel, 'I strongly advise you to go to bed early and get up early and your conscience will soon cease to trouble you. Case dismissed. Report to Hereford Barracks within five days.'

The twins had hoped the Colonel would smile: he had known them, after all, since they were three. His face was a blank when they appeared in the doorway.

'One at a time, gentlemen! One at a time! You, on the left, kindly step forward, please. The other gentleman should retire!'

The floorboards creaked as Lewis approached the panel. He had hardly opened his mouth when Mr Arkwright rose and whispered in the Colonel's ear. The Colonel nodded, 'Ah!' and with an air of benediction, said, 'Exemption granted! Next please!'

But when Benjamin edged into the room, Major Gattie eyed him up and down and drawled, 'We need that man!'

Later, Benjamin recalled only the drift of what followed. But he did remember the vicar leaning forward to ask whether, or not, he believed in the sanctity of the Allied Cause. And he remembered hearing his own voice reply, 'Do you believe in God?'

The vicar's head shot up like a startled hen.

'What gross impertinence! Do you realize I'm a clergyman?'

'Then do you believe in the Sixth Commandment?'

'The Sixth Commandment?'

' "Thou shalt not kill!" '

'Damned cheek, what?' Major Gattie lifted an eyebrow.

'Damnable cheek!' echoed Mr Arkwright. And even Mr Evenjobb stirred from his torpor, as the Colonel pronounced the standard formula:

'This Tribunal, having carefully considered your case, finds itself unable to grant exemption from service in His Majesty's Armed Forces. Report to Hereford Barracks within five days!'

Mary was heating beeswax to seal some jars of blackcurrant jam. The smell of boiling fruit filled the kitchen. She heard the clip of hooves in the yard. She gave a start at the sight of Lewis's blotchy face, and knew what had happened to his brother.

'I shall go, Mama,' said Benjamin, calmly. 'The war's as good as over now.'

'I don't believe it,' she said.

The evening was muggy and airless. Clouds of midges spiralled around a couple of heifers. They heard the flop of cowpats and the burbling of geese in the orchard. The sheepdog slunk up the path with his tail between his legs. All the flowers in the garden — the gaillardias, the fuchsias, the roses — were purple or yellow or red. It never occurred to Mary that Benjamin would come back alive.

She believed that Amos had sacrificed their weaker son, her favourite son. She believed Mr Arkwright had offered him a choice. He had chosen Lewis, the twin who would survive on his own.

Amos hung his cap in the porch. He tried to stammer excuses, but she spun round and screamed, 'Don't lie to me, you brute!'

She wanted to hit him, to spit in his face. He stared across the darkening room, dumbfounded by her fury.

She took a taper to light the lamp. The wick flared up: then, as she replaced the green glass shade, a band of light fell across the frame of her wedding photograph. She jerked it off its hook, dashed it to the floor, and disappeared upstairs.

Amos crouched.

The frame had split, the glass shattered, and the mount was bent, but the photo itself was unharmed. He swept up the slivers of glass into a dustpan. Then he picked up the frame and began to fit the pieces together.

Without undressing, Mary spent a sleepless night on Old Sam's palliasse, and the clouds passed over the moon. By breakfast-time, she had shut herself in the dairy — anywhere to avoid another confrontation. Benjamin found her aimlessly cranking the butter-churn.

'Don't be hard on Papa,' he said, touching her sleeve. 'It wasn't his fault. It was my fault, really.'

She went on turning the handle and said, 'You know nothing about it.'

Lewis offered to substitute himself. No one, he said, would ever know the difference.

'No,' said Benjamin. 'I'll go on my own.'

He was very brave and packed up his things, methodically, in a canvas bag. On the morning of his departure, he blinked into the rising sun and said, 'I'll stay till they come and get me.'

Amos made plans to hide both sons, in a secret place, high up in the Radnor Forest; but Mary scoffed and said, 'I suppose you've never heard of bloodhounds.'

On September 2nd, Police Constables Crimp and Bannister drove up to The Vision and made a big show of searching the barn. They hardly hid their disappointment when Benjamin walked from the house, pale, but with the suggestion of a smile, and bared his wrists to the handcuffs.

After a night in the cells, he appeared before the Rhulen magistrate, who 'deemed' him to be a soldier, and fined him £2 for failing to report for duty. A Non-Commissioned Officer then took him by train to Hereford.

At The Vision, they waited for news, and there was none. A month later, certain warning signals told Lewis that the Army had given up trying to train his brother, and was using force.

From the ache in his coccyx, Lewis knew when the N.C.O.s were frog-marching Benjamin round the parade-ground; from the pain in his wrists, when they lashed him to the bed-frame; from a patch of eczema on his chest, when they rubbed his nipples with caustic. One morning, Lewis's nose began to bleed and went on bleeding till sundown: that was the day when they stood Benjamin in a boxing ring and slammed straight-lefts into his face.

Then, one drizzly November morning, the war was over. The Kaiser and his crew had 'gone down like ninepins'. The World was Safe for Democracy.

On the streets of Hereford, Scotsmen played bagpipes, the jam factory sounded its hooter, railway engines whistled, and Welshmen roamed about playing mouth-organs or chanting 'Land of Our Fathers'. A soldier, deaf and dumb since the Dardanelles, saw the Union Jack floating above the newspaper office and recovered his speech, though not his hearing.

In the Cathedral, the Bishop, in a cope of cloth-of-gold, read the First Lesson from the altar: ' "I will sing unto the Lord, for he hath triumphed gloriously: the horse and his rider hath he thrown into the sea..." '

In faraway London, the King came out on to the balcony of Buckingham Palace, accompanied by Queen Mary in a sable coat.

Meanwhile, Benjamin Jones lay gasping for air in the sick-bay of the Hereford Detention Barracks.

He had Spanish influenza.

Outside the gate, Lewis Jones clamoured to be let in. A sentry with a bayonet kept him back.

XXIII

FOR THREE MONTHS after his 'dishonourable discharge' Benjamin refused to leave the farm. He slept late, stayed indoors, and did a few odd jobs around the house. There were sharp lines across his forehead, and dark rings under his eyes. His face was screwed up with a tic. He seemed to have slipped back into childhood, and only wanted to bake cakes for his brother – or to read.

Mary heaved a sigh at the sight of him slumped, unshaven, on the settle: 'Couldn't you go outside and help them today? It's a lovely day, and they're lambing, you know.'

'I know that, Mother.'

'You used to love the lambing.'

'Yes.'

'Please, please, don't sit there doing nothing.'

'Please, Mother, I'm reading,' – but he was only reading the advertisements of the *Hereford Times*.

Mary blamed herself for his moods. She felt guilty for allowing him to be taken, guiltier by far for the day of his return.

The morning had been foggy, and the train from Hereford was late. Icicles hung in a frieze from the canopy, and the melting drops smacked on the flagstones. She had been standing beside the station-master, wrapped in a winter coat, her hands in a fur muff. When the train pulled in, the last two carriages were hidden from view, in the fog. Doors opened and slammed shut. The passengers – grey shapes looming up the platform – handed in their tickets and filed out through the gate. Eager and smiling, she pulled her right hand from the muff, ready to fling it around Benjamin's neck. Then Lewis dashed up to a gaunt, crop-haired man, who was dragging a kitbag by its cord.

She called out, 'That's not Benj——' It was Benjamin. He had heard her. She threw herself towards him: 'Oh, my poor darling!'

He wanted to forget — willed himself to forget — the Detention Barracks: but even the squeak of bed-springs reminded him of the Nissen-hut dormitory; even Amos's hobnails, of the corporal who came to 'get him' at reveille.

To avoid showing his face in public, he stayed behind while the others went to Chapel. Only on Good Friday did Mary persuade him to come: he sat between her and Lewis, neither singing a note nor raising his eyes above the pew in front.

Fortunately, Mr Gomer Davies had gone back to Bala; and the new minister, a Mr Owen Nantlys Williams, was a far nicer person, who came from the Rhymney Valley, and held pacifist views. As soon as the meeting was over, he took Benjamin by the arm and led him round the back of the building.

'From what they tell me,' he said, 'you're a very brave young man. An example to all of us! But you have to forgive them now. They'd no idea what they were doing.'

Spring came. The apples were matted with blossom. Benjamin went for walks, and began to look better. Then, one evening, Mary slipped out to pick a sprig of parsley and found him, spreadeagled by some nettles, banging his head against the wall.

At first, she thought he was having an epileptic fit. She crouched down and saw his eyes and tongue were normal. Crooning softly, she cradled his head in her lap:

'Tell me! Tell me what's the matter! You can tell your mother everything.'

He picked himself up, shook the dirt from his clothes and said, 'It's nothing.'

'Nothing?' she pleaded, but he turned his back and walked away.

For some time she had noticed his look of resentment when his brother came in from the fields. After supper, she made Lewis carry a meat-dish to the back-kitchen, and rounded on him, sharply: 'You're going to tell me what's the matter with Benjamin.'

'I don't know,' he faltered.

So that's it, she thought. A girl!

Amos had rented the grass-keep of two adjoining fields and, after deciding to increase his head of beef cattle, sent Lewis to inspect a Hereford bull, at stud on a farm near Glan Ithon.

On the way home, Lewis took a short cut through Lurkenhope Park. He skirted the lake and then entered the gorge that leads to the mill. The sky was hazy and the beeches were bursting into leaf. Above the path was the grotto, reeking of bats, where – so the story went – a forbear of the Bickertons paid a hermit to gaze at a skull.

Below, the river splashed against the boulders in midstream, and big trout lazily flicked their fins in the deep green pools. Pigeons cooed, and he could hear the *toc-toc* of a woodpecker.

In places, the winter floods had washed away the path: he had to watch his footing. Twigs and dead branches had caught in the bushes along the bank. He climbed a bluff. On the downward slope some lilies-of-the-valley pushed up through a carpet of moss. He sat down and peered past the branches at the river.

Upstream was a thicket of ash-saplings, leafless as yet, and beneath them a carpet of bluebells, wild garlic, and a woodspurge with sharp green flowers.

Suddenly, above the sound of the rushing water he heard a woman's voice, singing. It was a young voice, and the song was slow and sad. A girl in grey was walking downstream through the bluebells. He froze until she started to climb the bluff. Her head had reached the level of his feet when he called out, 'Rosie!'

'Oh Lord, how you scared me!' Breathlessly, she took a seat beside him. He spread out his jacket to cover the damp moss. He was wearing black braces and a striped wool shirt.

'I was walking to work,' she said, her face contracting with sorrow: already he knew of her two tragic years.

Her mother had died of tuberculosis in the winter of '17.

Her brother had died, from fever, in Egypt. Then, as the war was ending, Bobbie Fifield had been taken by the Spanish flu. On hearing that she was homeless, Mrs Bickerton gave her a job as a chambermaid. But the big house scared her: there was a lion on the landing. The other servants made her life a misery, and the butler had tried to corner her in the pantry.

Mrs B. wasn't too bad, she said. She was a lady. But the Colonel was a real rough one...and that Miss Nancy! So awfully upset about losing her husband. Never stopped picking. Pick, pick, pick! And her dogs! Something dreadful! Yap, yap, yap!

She chattered on, her eyes sparkling with all the old malice as the sun went down and the ash-trees hung their shadows over the river.

And Mr Reginald! She couldn't think what to do about Mr Reggie. Couldn't think which way to look! Lost his leg in the war...but that didn't stop him! Not even at breakfast! She'd bring in his breakfast tray and he'd try and drag her down on to the bed——

'Sshh!' Lewis put his finger to his lips. A pair of mallard had landed below them. The drake was mounting the duck in an eddy under a rock. He had a lovely sheeny green head.

'Oo-ooh! He's a beauty!' She clapped her hands, scaring the birds, which took off and flew upriver.

She reminded him of the games they had played here as children.

He grinned: 'Remember the time you caught us by the pool?'

She jerked her head back with a throaty laugh: 'Remember the evening primrose?'

'We could find another one, Rosie!'

She stared for a second into his taut, puzzled face: 'We couldn't.' She squeezed his hand. 'Not yet, we couldn't.'

She stood and flicked a dead leaf from the hem of her skirt. She gave him a rendezvous for Friday. Then she brushed her cheek against his, and left.

After that, they would meet once a week outside the grotto, and go for long walks in the woods.

Benjamin watched his brother's comings and goings, said

nothing, and knew all.

In the middle of July, Lewis and Rosie arranged to meet in Rhulen for the National Peace Celebrations: there was to be a Thanksgiving Service in the parish church, and sports in Lurkenhope Park.

'You don't have to come,' Lewis said, as he adjusted his tie in a mirror.

'I'm coming,' said Benjamin.

XXIV

THE MORNING of the celebrations began in brilliant sunshine. From the early hours, the townspeople had been scrubbing their doorsteps, polishing their doorknockers and festooning their windows with bunting. By nine, Mr Arkwright, the moving spirit behind the festivities, could be seen, bird-necked in a double starched collar, bustling hither and thither to make sure things were going to plan. To every stranger, he touched the brim of his Homburg, and wished him a happy holiday.

Under his 'all-seeing eye', the façade of the Town Hall had been tastefully adorned with trophies and bannerets. Only the week before, he had hit on the idea of planting a patriotic display of salvias, lobelias and little dorrit around the base of the municipal clock; and if the result looked a bit scraggy, his colleague Mr Evenjobb declared it a 'stroke of genius'.

At the far end of Broad Street – on the site set aside for the War Memorial – stood a plain wood cross, its base half hidden under a mound of Flanders poppies. A glazed case contained a parchment scroll, illuminated with the names of the 'gallant thirty-two' who had made the 'Supreme Sacrifice'.

The service had ended before the Jones twins reached the church. A band of ex-servicemen was playing a selection from

'The Maid of the Mountains', and the triumphal procession to Lurkenhope was gradually gathering coherence.

The Bickertons and their entourage had already left by car.

In an 'act of spontaneous generosity' — the words were Mr Arkwright's — they had 'thrown open their gates and hearts to the public', and were providing a sit-down luncheon for the returning heroes, for their wives and sweethearts, and for parishioners over the age of seventy.

All comers, however, were welcome at the soup-kitchen: the Sports and Carnival Pageant were scheduled to start at three.

All morning, farmers and their families had been pouring into town. Demobbed soldiers peacocked about with girls on their arms and medals on their chests. Certain 'females of the flapper species' — again, the words were Mr Arkwright's — were 'garbed in indecorous dress'. The farm wives were in flowery hats, little girls in Kate Greenaway bonnets, and their brothers in sailor-suits and tams.

The grown men were drabber; but here and there, a panama or stripy blazer broke the monotony of black jackets and hard hats.

The twins had put on identical blue serge suits.

Outside the chemist's some urchins were blowing their pea-shooters at a Belgian refugee: 'Mercy Bow Coop, Mon Sewer! Bon Jewer, Mon Sewer!'

'Zey sink zey can laffe.' The man shook his fist. 'Bott soon zey vill be khryeeng!'

Benjamin doubted the wisdom of appearing in public, and tried to slink out of sight — in vain, for Lewis kept elbowing forward, looking high and low for Rosie Fifield. Both brothers tried to hide when P.C. Crimp detached himself from the crowd and bore down on them:

'Ha! Ha! The Jones twins!' he boomed, mopping the sweat from his brow and clamping his hand on Lewis's shoulder: 'Now which one of you two is Benjamin?'

'I am,' said Lewis.

'Don't think you can get away from me, young feller-me-lad!' the policeman chortled on, pressing the boy to his silver buttons. 'Glad to see you looking so fit and hearty! No hard feelings, eh? Bunch o' bloomin' hooligans in Hereford!'

Nearby, Mr Arkwright was deep in conversation with a W.A.A.C. officer, an imposing woman in khaki who was voicing a complaint about the order of the procession: 'No, Mr Arkwright! I'm not trying to do *down* the Red Cross nurses. I'm simply insisting on the unity of the Armed Forces...'

'See those two?' the solicitor interrupted. 'Shirkers! Wonder they dare show their faces! Some people certainly have a bit of gall...!'

'No,' she took no notice. 'Either my girls march *behind* the Army boys or in *front* of them... But they must march together!'

'Quite so!' he nodded dubiously. 'But our patron, Mrs Bickerton, as head of Rhulen Red Cross——'

'Mr Arkwright, you've missed the point. I——'

'Excuse me!' He had caught sight of an old soldier propped up on crutches against the churchyard wall. 'The Survivor of Rorke's Drift!' he murmured. 'Excuse me one moment. One must pay one's respects...'

The Survivor, Sergeant-Major Gosling, V.C., was a favourite local character who always took the air on such occasions, in the scarlet dress uniform of the South Wales Borderers.

Mr Arkwright threaded his way towards the veteran, lowered his moustache to his ear, and mouthed some platitude about 'The Field of Flanders'.

'Eh?'

'I said, "The Field of Flanders".'

'Aye, and fancy giving them a field to fight in!'

'Silly old fool,' he muttered under his breath, and slipped away behind the W.A.A.C. officer.

Meanwhile, Lewis Jones was asking anyone and everyone, 'Have you seen Rosie Fifield?' She was nowhere to be found. Once, he thought he saw her on a sailor's arm, but the girl who turned round was Cissie Pantall the Beeches.

'If you please, Mr Jones,' she said in a shocked tone, while his eye came to rest on the bulldog jowls of her companion.

———

At twenty past twelve, Mr Arkwright blew three blasts on his whistle, the crowd cheered, and the procession set off along the low road to Lurkenhope.

At its head marched the choristers, the scouts and guides, and the inmates of the Working Boys' Home. Next in line were the firemen, the railway workers, Land Girls with hoes over their shoulders, and munitions girls with heads bound up, pirate-fashion, in the Union Jack. A small delegation had been sent by the Society of Oddfellows, while the leader of the Red Cross bore a needlework banner of Nurse Edith Cavell, and her dog. The W.A.A.C.s followed—having assumed, after a vitriolic squabble, their rightful place in the parade. Then came the brass band, and then the Glorious Warriors.

An open charabanc brought up the rear, its seats crammed with pensioners and war-wounded, a dozen of whom, in sky blue suits and scarlet ties, were waving their crutches at the crowd. Some wore patches over their eyes. Some were missing eyebrows or eyelids; others, arms or legs. The spectators surged behind the vehicle as it puttered down Castle Street.

They had come abreast of the Bickerton Memorial when someone shouted in Mr Arkwright's ear, 'Where's the Bombardier?'

'Oh my God, whatever next?' he exploded. 'They've forgotten the Bombardier!'

The words were hardly off his lips when two schoolboys in tasselled caps were seen racing in the direction of the church. Two minutes later, they were racing back, pushing at breakneck speed a wheeled basket-chair containing a hunched-up figure in uniform.

'Make way for the Bombardier!' one of them shouted.

'Make way for the Bombardier!'—and the crowd parted for the Rhulen hero, who had given his gas-mask to an officer at Passchendaele. The Military Medal was pinned to his tunic.

'Hurrah for the Bombardier!'

His lips were purple and his ashen face stretched taut as a drumskin. Some children showered him with confetti and his eyes revolved in terror.

'Hrrh! Hrrh!' A spongy rattle sounded in his throat, as he

tried to slither down the basket-chair.

'Poor ol' boy!' Benjamin heard someone say. 'Still thinks there's a bloody war on.'

Shortly after one, the leaders of the procession sighted the stone lion over the North Lodge of the Castle.

Mrs Bickerton had planned to hold the luncheon in the dining-room. Faced with a revolt from the butler, she had it transferred to the disused indoor dressage-school: as a war-time economy, the Colonel had given up breeding Arabs.

She had also planned to be present, with her family and house-party, but the guest-of-honour, Brigadier Vernon-Murray, had to drive back to Umberslade that evening; and he, for one, wasn't wasting his whole day on the hoi polloi.

All the same, it was a right royal feed.

Two trestle tables, glistening with white damask, ran the entire length of the structure; and at each place setting there was a bouquet of sweet-peas, as well as a saucer of chocolates and Elvas plums for the sweet of tooth. Dimpled tankards were stuck with celery; there were mayonnaises, jars of pickle, bottles of ketchup and, every yard or so, a pyramid of oranges and apples. A third table bent under the weight of the buffet — round which a score of willing helpers were waiting to carve, or serve. A pair of hams wore neat paper frills around their shins. There were rolls of spiced beef, a cold roast turkey, polonies, brawns, pork pies and three Wye salmon, each one resting on its bed of lettuce hearts, with a glissando of cucumber slices running down its side.

A pot of calf's-foot jelly had been set aside for the Bombardier.

Along the back wall hung portraits of Arab stallions — Hassan, Mokhtar, Mahmud and Omar — once the pride of the Lurkenhope Stud. Above them hung a banner reading 'THANK YOU BOYS' in red.

Girls with jugs of ale and cider kept the heroes' glasses topped to the brim; and the sound of laughter carried as far as the lake.

Lewis and Benjamin helped themselves to a bowl of mulligatawny at the soup-kitchen, and sauntered round the shrubbery, stopping, now and then, to talk to picnickers. The weather was turning chilly. Women shivered under their shawls, and eyed the inky clouds heaped up over the Black Hill.

Lewis spotted one of the gardeners and asked if he'd seen Rosie Fifield.

'Rosie?' The man scratched his scalp. 'She'd be serving lunch, I expect.'

Lewis led the way back to the dressage-school, and pushed through the crush of people who were thronging the double doors. The speeches were about to begin. The port decanters were emptying fast.

At his place at the centre of the table, Mr Arkwright had already toasted the Bickerton family *in absentia* and was about to embark on his oration.

'Now that the sword is returned to the scabbard,' he began, 'I wonder how many of us recall those sunny summer days of 1914 when a cloud no bigger than a man's hand appeared on the political sky of Europe —'

At the word 'cloud' a few faces tilted upward to the skylight, through which the sun had been pouring but a minute before.

'A cloud which grew to rain death and destruction upon well nigh the whole continent of Europe, nay, upon the four corners of the globe...'

'I'm going home,' Benjamin nudged his brother.

An N.C.O. — one of his torturers from the Hereford Barracks — sat leering at him loutishly through a cloud of cigar smoke.

Lewis whispered, 'Not yet!' and Mr Arkwright raised his voice to a tremulous baritone:

'An immense military power rose in its might, and forgetting its sworn word to respect the frontiers of weaker nations, tore through the country of Belgium...'

'Where's old Belgey?' a voice called out.

'...burned its cities, towns, villages, martyred its gallant inhabitants...'

'Not him they didn't!' — and someone shoved forward the

Refugee, who stood and gaped blearily from under his beret.

'Good old Belgey!'

'But the Huns never reckoned with the sense of justice and honour which are the attributes of the British people...and the might of British righteousness tipped the scales against them...'

The N. C. O.'s eyes had narrowed to a pair of dangerous slits.

'I'm going,' said Benjamin, edging back towards the door.

The speaker raked his throat and continued: 'This is no place for a mere civilian to trace the course of events. No need to speak of those glorious few, the Expeditionary Force, who pitted themselves against so vile a foe, for whom the meaning of life was the study of death...'

Mr Arkwright looked over his spectacles to assure himself that his listeners had caught the full flavour of his *bon mot*. The rows of blank faces assured him they had not. He looked down again at his notes:

'No need to speak of the clarion call of Lord Kitchener – for men and yet more men...'

A serving-girl, in grey, was standing close to Lewis with a jug of cider in her hand. He asked if she'd seen Rosie Fifield.

'Not all morning,' she whispered back. 'She's probably off with Mr Reggie.'

'Oh!'

'No need to record the disappointments, the months that lengthened into years, and still no chink was found in the enemy's armour...'

'Hear! Hear!' said the N.C.O.

'Everyone in this room will recall how the demon of warfare swallowed up our most promising manhood, and still the monster flourished...'

The last remark obviously tickled the N.C.O.s fancy. He shook with laughter, bared his gums, and went on staring at Benjamin. A clap of thunder shook the building. Raindrops pocked on the skylight, and the picnickers pressed forward through the doors, pushing the twins to within feet of the speaker.

Undeterred by the storm, Mr Arkwright carried on: 'Men

and more men was the cry, and meanwhile submarine piracy threatened with starvation those whose lot it was to remain at home...'

'Not 'im it didn't,' muttered a woman nearby, who must have known, at first hand, of the solicitor's black-market peccadillo.

'Sshh!' – and the woman fell silent; for he appeared to be moving towards the final coda: 'So at last, righteousness and justice prevailed and, with God's help, a treacherous and inhuman foe was laid low.'

The rain slammed on the roof. He raised his hands to acknowledge the clapping; but he had *not* finished: 'In that glorious consummation, all those present have played an honourable part. Or should I say,' he added, removing his glasses and fixing a steely stare on the twins, 'almost all of those present?'

In a flash, Benjamin saw what was afoot and, clawing his brother's wrist, began to squirm towards the door. Mr Arkwright watched them go and then turned to the tricky topic of contributions to the War Memorial Fund.

The twins stood under the cedar of Lebanon, alone, in the rain.

'We didn't ought to have come,' said Benjamin.

They sheltered until the rain blew over. Benjamin still wanted to leave, but Lewis lingered on and, in the end, they stayed for the Carnival Pageant.

For four days, Mr Arkwright and his committee had 'moved heaven and earth' to prepare the ground for the afternoon's events. Hurdles had been erected, white lines drawn on the grass, and, in front of the finishing-post, a canvas awning covered the podium to shield the notabilities from sun or shower. Garden seats had been reserved for the heroes and pensioners: the others had to sit where they could.

The sun shone fitfully through a confused mass of cloud. In the far corner of the field, beside a stand of wellingtonias, the entrants for the Carnival were putting the finishing touches to their floats. Mr Arkwright looked anxiously from his watch to the cloud, and to the gate of the Italian garden.

'I do wish they'd come,' he fretted, wondering what on earth was detaining the Bickertons.

To occupy himself, he darted about, blew his whistle, escorted the pensioners and made a show of pushing the Bombardier's wheel-chair into the place of honour.

At last, the gate swung open and the luncheon party emerged through a gap in the topiary like a parade of prize beasts at a show.

The crowd parted for Mrs Bickerton, who walked ahead of the others in her Red Cross uniform. On seeing the Jones twins, she stopped: 'Do give your mother my love. I wish she'd come and see me.'

Her husband limped along on the arm of Lady Vernon-Murray, an ample woman from whose hat a bird-of-paradise plume curled downwards and tickled the corner of her mouth. A frock of fog-blue voile framed her ankles, and she looked extremely cross. The Brigadier, an immense purple-faced presence, appeared to be trapped in a web of polished brown leather straps. Members of the local gentry followed; and, lastly, in magenta, came the Bickerton war-widow, Mrs Nancy. A young man from London was with her.

She was halfway to the podium when she paused and frowned: 'Re-eggie! Re-eggie!' she called with a stammer. 'N-now whe-ere's he gone? He was here a se-econd ago.'

'Coming!' a voice called back from behind the topiary peacocks, and a youngish man, in a blazer and whites, appeared in the open, on crutches. His left leg was off at the knee.

At his side, conspicuous as a magpie against the evergreens, was a girl in a maid's uniform, with white flounces on her shoulders.

It was Rosie Fifield.

'I told you,' Benjamin said, and Lewis began to tremble.

The twins moved towards the podium where Mr Arkwright, as Master of Ceremonies, had the privilege of escorting the guests-of-honour to their seats.

'I hope we shall be amused,' said Lady Vernon-Murray, as he slid a cane-seated chair beneath her haunches.

'Surely yes, my lady!' he replied. 'We have a pot-pourri of entertainment on the programme.'

'Well, it's dashed cold,' she said, sourly.

Reggie had chosen a chair on the far left of the platform, and Rosie was standing beneath him. He tickled her vertebrae with the toe of his shoe.

'Ladies and gentlemen,' Mr Arkwright succeeded in silencing the crowd. 'Permit me to introduce our illustrious guests – the Hero of Vimy Ridge, and his lady...'

'Gosh, it's perishing,' said her ladyship, as the Brigadier acknowledged the cheers.

He was preparing to open his mouth when two stable-lads rushed forward carrying effigies of the Kaiser and Prince Ruprecht, gagged and bound to a pair of kitchen chairs. On top of the Kaiser's helmet was a stuffed canary, smeared with gold paint.

The Brigadier glared, with mock ferocity, at the foe.

'Ladies and gentlemen,' he began, 'soldiers of the King, and you two misewable specimens of humanity, whom we shall soon have the pleasure of consigning to the bonfire...'

Another round of cheers went up.

'Now sewiously sewiously...' The Brigadier raised a hand as if passing to serious matters. 'This is a memowable day. A day that will go down in the annals of our history...'

'I thought we said we weren't having speeches.' Mrs Bickerton turned coldly to the solicitor.

'Unfortunately, there are people here today who may think they can't wejoice with us because they've lost a dear one. Well, my message to them is this. Wejoice with the west of us now the whole thing's over. And wemember that your husbands or fathers, bwothers or sweethearts have all died in a good cause...'

This time the applause was fainter. Mrs Bickerton bit her lip and stared at the mountain. Her face was white as her nurse's cap.

'I...I...' The Brigadier was warming to his theme. 'I can count myself one of the lucky ones. I was at Vimmy. I was at Wipers. And I was at Passiondale. I witnessed appalling gas-shelling...'

All eyes turned to the five gas victims, who sat lined up on a bench, coughing and wheezing like an exhibition for the horrors of war.

'Our conditions were absolutely filthy. One went for days without a change of clothes, nay, weeks without so much as a bath. Our casualties, especially among the gunners, were quite dweadful...'

'I can't bear it,' murmured Mrs Bickerton, and shielded her face with her hand.

'I often think back to the time I was wounded and in hospital. We'd been thwough an absolute bloodbath near Weemes. But we happened to have a chap in the wegiment...turned out to be something of a poet. Well, he jotted down a few lines, and I'd like to wepeat them to you. At the time, anyway, they were a gweat comfort to me:

> '*If I should die, think only this of me:*
> *That there's some corner of a foweign field*
> *That is fowever England.*'

'Poor Rupert,' Mrs Bickerton leaned across to her husband. 'He'd turn in his grave.'

'Christ, this man's a bore!'

'How can we shut him up?'

'And what of the future for our belovèd country?' The Brigadier had changed tack. 'Or should I say our belovèd county? Our cwying need is not just to feed the people of these islands, but to export bloodstock to our partners overseas. Now I have seen Heweford cattle in evewy part of the globe. Indeed, whewever you will find the white man, there you will find the white-faced bweed. I know you must all feel twemendously pwoud of the Lurkenhope Hewefords...'

'Be damned if they are,' said the Colonel, reddening.

'But it's always been a mystewy to me, why, when one looks wound the countwyside, one sees so many infewior animals...half-bweeds...diseased...deformed...'

The war-wounded, already in agony from the hard benches, began to look frayed and fidgety.

'The only way forward is to eliminate second-wate animals

for good and all. Now in the Argentine and Austwalia...'

Mrs Bickerton glanced about helplessly; and, in the end, it was Mr Arkwright who saved the day. It was time for the Carnival Procession. Another storm, the colour of black grapes, was brewing over the mountain.

Plucking up courage, he whispered in Lady Vernon-Murray's ear. She nodded, tugged her husband by the coat-tails and said, 'Henry! Time's up!'

'What, m'dear?'

'Time's up!'

So he hurriedly bid his audience adieu, hoped to meet them all ' 'ere long on the hunting field', and sat down.

The next item on the agenda was the presentation, by her ladyship, of a silver cigarette-case to 'each and every man returned from these wars'. Loud acclamations greeted her as she descended the steps. She held out the Bombardier's, and a clawlike hand shot out from the basket-chair, and grabbed it.

'Hrrh! Hrrh!' came the same spongy rattle.

'Oh, it's too cruel,' breathed Mrs Bickerton.

'Ladies and gentlemen,' Mr Arkwright called through the megaphone. 'We now come to the principal attraction of the afternoon: the judging of the Carnival floats. I give you Number One...' He consulted his programme. 'The Lur-kenhope Stable Boys, who have chosen as their theme..."The Battle of Om-dur-man"!'

A team of white-fronted shires came into view hauling a hay-waggon, on which was a *tableau-vivant* with Lord Kit-chener surrounded by potted palms and half a dozen lads, some with leopard-skins round their tummies, some in under-pants, and all smeared head to toe with soot, waving spears or assegais, yelling, or beating a tom-tom.

The spectators yelled back, chucked paper darts, and the Survivor of Rorke's Drift shook his crutch: 'Lemme get me mits on 'em Sambos,' he shrieked, as the cart drew off.

Cart Number Two arrived with 'Robin Hood and his Merrie Men'. Next came 'The Dominions' with Miss Bessel of Frogend as Britannia and, fourthly, The Working Boys' Pierrot Troupe.

The boys sang to the accompaniment of a ragtime piano,

and when they rhymed the words 'German sausage' with 'abdominal passage', there was a hushed and horrified silence — except for the cackles of Reggie Bickerton, who laughed and laughed and hardly seemed able to stop. Rosie hid her own sniggers by burying her face in her apron.

Meanwhile, Lewis Jones was edging towards her. He whistled to attract her attention and she stared straight through him, smiling.

The last float but one, showing 'The Death of Prince Llewellyn', roused a clique of Welsh Nationalists to song.

'Enough, gentlemen!' shouted Mr Arkwright. 'Enough is enough. Thank you!' Then a burst of hurrah-ing brought everyone to their feet.

The men whistled. Women craned their necks and offered tender-hearted comments: 'Isn't she lovely?... Lovely!... Oh! And do look at the little angels!... The little darlings!... Aren't they sweet?... Oh, it's Cis... Do look! It's our Cissie... Oh! Oh! Isn't she bee-yewtiful?'

'Miss Cissie Pantall the Beeches,' Mr Arkwright continued in a tone of rapture, 'who has deigned to honour us with her presence — as "Peace". Ladies and gentlemen! I give you..."Peace"!'

Fluid folds of white calico covered the floor and sides of the cart. Laurel swags hung down over the wheel-hubs and on all four corners there were pots of arum lilies.

A choir of angels formed a ring around the throne, and on it sat a big blonde girl in a snowy tunic. She held a wicker cage containing a white fantailed pigeon. Her hair fell like a fleece on to her shoulders, and her teeth were chattering with cold.

The ladies looked up at the chutes of rain already tumbling over the Black Hill, and cast around for the nearest umbrella.

'Let's be going,' said Benjamin.

After a brief conference with Lady Vernon-Murray, Mr Arkwright hastily announced the foregone conclusion: Miss Pantall the Beeches was the winner. Her proud father then led his horse-team round in a circle, so that Cissie could step on to the podium and collect her trophy.

Frightened by the applause and approach of thunder, the Dove of Peace panicked and shredded its wings against the bars of the cage. Feathers flew, fluttered in the wind, and fell near Rosie Fifield's feet. She stooped and picked up two of them. Flushed in the face and smiling, she stood provocatively in front of Lewis Jones.

'Fancy you showing up!' she said. 'I've got a present for you.' And she handed him one of the feathers.

'Thank you very much,' he said, with a puzzled smile. He took the feather before his brother could stop him: he had never even heard of 'white-feathering'.

'Shirkers!' she jeered. And Reggie Bickerton laughed, and the group of soldiers round her also burst out laughing. The N.C.O. was with them. Lewis dropped the feather, and the rain began to fall.

'The Sports will be postponed,' the solicitor called through the megaphone as the crowd broke ranks and ran for the trees.

Lewis and Benjamin crouched under some rhododendrons, and the water ran in trickles down their necks. When the rain let up, they stole away towards the edge of the shrubbery and out onto the carriage drive. Four or five Army louts were blocking their paths. All of them were wet through, and tipsy.

' 'Ad it soft in 'Ereford, didn't ya, mate?' The N.C.O. swung a fist at Lewis, and he ducked.

'Run!' he yelled, and the twins ran back to the bushes. But the path was slippery; Lewis tripped on a root, and fell full-length in the mud. The N.C.O. fell on top of him and twisted his arm.

Another soldier shouted, 'Wipe their bloody snouts in the muck!' And Benjamin booted him behind the knees and toppled him. Then all his world was wheeling, and the next thing he heard was a sneering voice, 'Aw! Leave 'em to stew!'

Then they were alone again, with swollen eyes and the taste of blood on their lips.

That night, climbing the crest of Cefn Hill, they saw a bonfire blazing on Croft Ambrey, another on the Clee and far off, faintly, a dull glow over the Malverns – blazing as they had blazed at the time of the Armada.

The Bombardier did not survive the celebrations. While clearing up the mess in the Park, an estate worker found him in the wheeled basket-chair. No one had remembered him in the rush for shelter. He had ceased to breathe. The man was amazed by the strength of his grip as he prized his fingers from the silver cigarette-case.

XXV

JIM THE ROCK spent the Great Day at a military hospital on Southampton Water.

Serving as a muleteer with the South Wales Borderers, he had survived the First and Second Battles of Ypres, and then the Somme. He came through the war without a scratch until, in the final week, two lumps of shrapnel caught him behind the kneecaps. Septicaemia set in and, for a time, the doctors considered amputation.

When at last he came home after the long months of therapy, he was still very shaky on his pins; his face was pitted with black specks, and he was inclined to snap.

Jim had loved his mules, treated them for ophthalmia and mange, and dragged them from the mud when they fell in up to their fetlocks. He had never shot a wounded mule unless there was no hope of saving him.

The sight of dead mules had distressed him far more than the sight of dead men. 'I see'd 'em,' he'd say in the pub. 'All along the road and stinkin' summut 'orrible. Poor ol' boys what never did no 'arm.'

He had hated it most when the mules got gassed. In one gas attack, he survived when the whole of his mule-train died – and that made him extremely angry. Marching up to his lieutenant, he saluted sullenly and blurted out, 'If I can 'ave me gas mask, why can't me mules?'

This piece of logic so impressed the lieutenant that he sent a report to the general, who, instead of ignoring it, sent back a note of commendation.

By 1918, most British units had equipped their horses and mules with gas-masks, whereas the Germans went on losing supplies; and though no military historian would credit Jim the Rock with the invention of the equine mask, he persisted in the illusion that it was he who had won the war.

So whenever it came to another round — at the Red Dragon in Rhulen, the Bannut Tree in Lurkenhope, or the Shepherd's Rest at Upper Brechfa — he'd stare defiantly at his fellow-drinkers: 'Aw, stand us another pint. I won the war, I did!' And when they jeered back, 'Get ye off, y'old scalliwamp,' he'd fish in his pocket for the general's letter, or the photo of himself and a pair of mules — all three of them in their gas-masks.

Jim's sister Ethel was immeasurably proud of him and his shining medals, and said he needed a 'good long rest'.

She had grown into a strong, big-boned woman who stamped around in an ex-Army greatcoat and stared at the world from under her mossy eyebrows. 'Never you mind,' she'd say, if Jim gave up on a job. 'I'll a-finish it myself.' And when he rode off to the pub, a placid smile would spread across her face. 'That Jim!' she'd say. 'He be wonderful fond of scenery.'

Aggie also doted on Jim and looked on him as one arisen from the grave. But Tom the Coffin — by now a craggy, matt-bearded old man with a luminous stare — had resented the lad for volunteering, and doubly resented his return. At the sight of the war-hero sunning himself, he'd yell in a hoarse and terrible voice: 'I've warned you. I've warned you. This is your last chance. Get yourself to work or I'll clout you. I'll knobble you, you good-for-nothing lump! I'll moil your fat face...'

One evening, he accused Jim of stealing a snaffle-bit and beat his cheeks like a tambourine — whereupon Aggie glowered and said, 'That's it. I've had enough.'

At suppertime, her husband found that the bolts had been drawn against him. He banged and banged, but the door was solid oak, and he went away nursing his knuckles. Around midnight, they heard a terrifying whinny from the beast-house. In the morning he was gone, and Jim's mare lay dead with a nail through her skull.

The next news of the old man, he was living in the Ithon Valley with a farmer's widow, whom he'd gotten with child. People said he'd 'fixed the devil's stare' on her when he went to deliver her husband's coffin.

Without the money from the coffins, Aggie no longer had enough to keep a 'nice house' and, after scouring round for other sources of income, hit on the idea of boarding unwanted children.

The first of her 'rescues' was a baby girl called Sarah, whose mother, the miller's wife at Brynarian, had been seduced by a seasonal shearer. The miller had refused to rear the child under his own roof, but offered £2 a week for her upkeep.

This arrangement brought in Aggie a clear profit of £1 and, on the strength of it, she took in two more illegitimates — Brenda and Lizzie — and, in this way, maintained her standards. The tea-caddy was full. They ate pickled lamb once a week. She bought a new white linen table-cloth, and a tin of pineapple chunks sat proudly on the Sunday tea-table.

As for Jim, he lorded it over his female brood, shirked work, and would sit on the hillside playing his penny-whistle to the whinchats and wheatears.

He hated to see any creature in pain; and if he found a rabbit in a snare, or a gull with a broken wing, he'd carry it home and bind the wound with a bandage, or the wing with a splint of twigs. Sometimes, there'd be several birds and animals festering in boxes by the fire; and when one of them died, he'd say, 'Poor ol' boy! An' I dug a hole an' put 'im in the ground.'

For years he went on harping about the war, and had the habit of slipping down to The Vision to hector the Jones twins.

They were scything one sunset in their shirtsleeves, when Jim limped up and launched into his usual harangue: 'An' them tanks I'm a-tellin' yer! Baroom!...Baroom!' The twins went on scything, stooping occasionally to whet their blades and, when a fly blew into Benjamin's mouth, he spat it out: 'Aagh! Them pithering flies!'

Of Jim they took no notice and he ended up losing his temper: 'An' you? You'd a-lasted a fraction of a second in that war. An' you'd a farm to fight for! An' I...I'd only me own skin to save!'

Since the day of the peace celebrations, the twins' world had contracted to a few square miles, bounded on one side by Maesyfelin Chapel and on the other by the Black Hill: both Rhulen and Lurkenhope now lay on enemy soil.

Deliberately, as if reaching back to the innocence of early childhood, they turned away from the modern age; and though the neighbours invested in new farm machinery, they persuaded their father not to waste his money.

They shovelled muck on to the fields. They broadcast seed from a basketwork 'lip'. They used the old binder, the old single-furrow plough, and even did their threshing with a flail. Yet, as Amos was forced to admit, the hedges had never been neater, the grass greener, the animals healthier. The farm even made money. He had only to set foot in the bank for the manager to slip round the counter, and shake his hand.

Lewis's only extravagance was a subscription to the *News of the World*, and after lunch on Sundays, he would riffle through its pages in case there was an air-crash to paste in his scrapbook.

'Really,' Mary pretended to protest. 'What a morbid imagination you have!' Already, though they were only twenty-two, her sons were behaving like crabby old bachelors. But her daughter gave her greater concern.

For years, Rebecca had basked in her father's infatuation: nowadays they seldom spoke. She would steal off to Rhulen and come back with cigarette smoke on her breath and rouge rubbed off around her lips. She raided Amos's cash-box. He called her a 'harlot' and Mary despaired of reconciling them.

To get her out of the house, she found the girl a job as a sales assistant at the old Albion Drapery, which, in a flush of post-war francophilia, had changed its name to 'Paris House'. Rebecca lodged in an attic above the shop and came home at weekends. One Saturday afternoon, as the twins were washing out the milk-churns, they heard the shouts and screams of a dreadful row in the kitchen.

Rebecca had confessed to being pregnant – and worse: the man was an Irish navvy, a Catholic, who worked on the railway. She left the house with a bleeding lip and fifteen gold sovereigns in her purse, astonishing everyone with her sly smile and the coolness of her behaviour.

'And that's all she'll ever have from me,' Amos thundered.

They never heard from her again. From an address in Cardiff she sent her old employer a postcard with news of a baby girl. Mary took a train-journey to see her grandchild, but the landlady said the couple had emigrated to America, and slammed the door in her face.

And Amos never recovered from her disappearance. He kept crying out 'Rebecca!' in his sleep. An attack of shingles maddened him to the point of frenzy. Then, to add to his troubles, the rent went up.

The Bickertons were in financial trouble.

Their Trustees had lost a fortune in Russian bonds. Their stud-farming experiments had failed to repay the investment. The sale of Old Masters was a disappointment and, when the Colonel's lawyers broached the subject of avoiding death-duties, he flared up: 'Don't speak to me about death-duties! I'm not dead yet!'

A circular letter from his new agent warned all tenants to expect substantial rises in the coming year – an awkward time for Amos, who was hoping to buy some land.

Even at his angriest, Amos assumed that both the twins would marry, and continue to farm; and since The Vision could never support two families, they needed extra land.

For years he had had his eye on The Tump – a smallholding of thirty-three acres, set in a circle of beeches, on high ground half a mile from the Rhulen lane. The owner was an old recluse – a defrocked priest, so they said – who lived alone in scholarly squalor until one snowy morning Ethel the Rock saw no smoke from his chimney and found him spreadeagled in his garden, with a Christmas rose in his hand.

On making enquiries, Amos was told the place would be

sold at auction. Then, one Thursday evening, he took Lewis aside and said sourly:

'Your old friend, Rosie Fifield, moved herself into The Tump.'

XXVI

WHILE WORKING at Lurkenhope, one of Rosie's duties had been to carry the bathwater upstairs to Reggie Bickerton's bedroom.

This place, to which few people were ever admitted, was situated in the West Tower, and was a perfect bachelor's den. The walls were hung with deep-blue paper. The tapestry curtains and bed-hangings were worked in green with a design of heraldic beasts. There were chintz-covered chairs and ottomans; the carpet was Persian and in front of the fireplace lay a polar-bearskin rug. On the mantelpiece was an ormolu clock, flanked with figures of Castor and Pollux. Most of the paintings were of oriental subjects, bazaars, mosques, camel caravans and women in latticed rooms. His Eton photographs showed groups of young athletes with imperturbable smiles; and the evening sun, filtering through roundels of stained glass, shed flecks of blood-red light over the frames.

Rosie would spread out the bath-mat, drape a towel over a chair, and lay out the soap and sponge. Then, after plunging a thermometer into the water — to be sure of not scalding the young master's stump — she tried to slip away without his calling her back.

Most evenings, he'd be lying on the ottoman loosely wrapped in a yellow silk dressing-gown, sometimes pretending to read or jotting down notes with his serviceable hand. He watched her every movement from the corner of his eye.

133

'Thank you Rosie,' he'd say, as she turned the door-handle.
'Er...Er...Rosie!'

'Yes, sir!' She would stand, almost to attention, with the door half-open.

'No! Forget it! It's of no importance!' – and, as the door closed behind her, he would reach for his crutch.

One evening, stripped to the waist, he asked her to help him into the water.

'I can't,' she gasped, and rushed for the safety of the passage.

In 1914, Reggie had gone to war with a head full of chivalric notions of duty to caste and country. He had come home a cripple, with a receding hairline, three fingers missing from his right hand, and the watery eyes of a secret drinker. At first, he made light of his injuries with upper-class stoicism. By 1919, the first wave of sympathy had worn off, and he had become 'a case'.

His fiancée had married his best friend. Other friends found the Welsh Border too far from London for frequent visits. His favourite sister, Isobel, had married and gone to India. And he was left in this huge gloomy house, alone with his squabbling parents and the sad, stuttering Nancy, who showered him with unwanted affection.

He tried his hand at writing a novel about his wartime experiences. The strain of composition tired him: after twenty minutes of left-handed scribbling, he would be staring out of the window – at the lawn, the rain and the hill. He longed to live in a tropical country and he longed for a tumbler of whisky.

One May weekend, the house was full of guests and Rosie was mouthing her supper in the Servant's Hall, when the bell of Bedroom Three began to ring: she had already seen to his bathwater.

She knocked.

'Come in.'

He was on the ottoman, half-dressed for dinner, trying with his wounded hand to press a gold stud through his shirtfront:

'Here, Rosie? I wonder if you could do these for me?'

Her thumb felt for the back of the stud, but just as it went 'pop' through the starched-up hole, he caught her off balance and pulled her on top of him.

She struggled, shook him off and backed away. A rush of crimson coloured her neck, and she stammered, 'I didn't mean to.'

'But I did, Rosie,' and he protested his love.

He had teased her before. She said it was mean of him to make fun of her.

'But I'm not making fun of you,' he said, in real despair.

She saw he was serious and went out slamming the door.

All through Sunday, she pretended to be sick. On the Monday, when the house-party was over, he apologized with the full force of his charm.

He made her laugh by describing the private lives of all the guests. He spoke of travelling to the Mediterranean, and the Isles of Greece. He gave her novels, which she read by candlelight. She admired the clock above the mantelpiece: 'They're the Heavenly Twins,' he said. 'Take it. It's a present. Anything here can be yours.'

She held him at bay another week. He suspected a rival. Maddened by her resistance, he proposed to her.

'Oh!'

Calmly and slowly, she walked towards the leaded window and looked out over the topiary, and the woods behind. A peacock squawked. In her imagination, she saw the butler bringing in her breakfast-tray; and in the deepening evening, she slipped between the sheets.

Thereafter, they established a regular pattern of deception. She felt humiliated by having to leave him at five, before the house began to wake. When the whispering started they had to be even more careful. One night, she had to hide in the wardrobe while Nancy lectured him to lay off:

'Re-eally, Re-eggie!' she protested. 'It's the s-s-candal of the village!'

Rosie pressed him to tell his parents. He promised to do so once the peace celebrations were over. Another month went by. He came to his senses when she missed her first period.

'I shall tell them,' he said. 'Tomorrow, after breakfast.'

Three days later, his mother had left for the South of France, and he said, 'Please, please, please, please will you give me a

135

little more time?'

The leaves were yellowing in the park, and sportsmen came from London to stay in the house. On the second Saturday of pheasant shooting, the butler ordered her to take a picnic to the Colonel's party over by Tanhouse Wood. A groom was driving her and the hampers back across the park. She saw a blue motor speeding towards the West Lodge.

Reggie had packed his bags and was off, abroad.

She did not cry. She did not break down. She was not even greatly surprised. By creeping off like a coward, he had confirmed her opinion of men. On her bed, she found a letter and tore it to contemptuous shreds. A second letter advised her to visit a Mr Arkwright, Solicitor, in Rhulen.

She went. The offer was for five hundred pounds.

'Make it six,' she said, returning to Mr Arkwright an even icier stare.

'Six,' he agreed. 'And not a penny more!' She walked away with the cheque.

That winter, she took lodgings at a dairy farm and paid her way by making cheeses. When her boy was born, she left him with a wet-nurse and went out to work.

She had always suffered from bronchial troubles, and loved the clean air of the mountains. One summer evening with the swifts whooshing low over her head, she was rambling back along the ridge from the Eagle Stone, and stopped to talk to an old man resting by a hump of reddish rock.

He told her the names of the surrounding bluffs: she asked him the name of the rocks they were sitting on.

'Bickerton's Knob,' he said, perplexed by the hoots of derisive laughter with which she greeted his reply.

The old recluse was lame and stiff. He pointed to his cottage, far below in its ring of beech trees. She escorted him down the slope, then sat with him till dark while he recited his poems. She took to fetching his groceries. He died two winters later, and she was able to buy his property.

She bought a small flock of sheep, and a pony, and taking her son, she shut herself off from the world. She burned the poet's rubbish, but saved his papers and his books. Her only protection was a squeaky door, and a dog.

One day, Lewis Jones went chasing after a runaway ram. He came to a stream in a copse of hazels, where the water combed over a rock, and there were piles of bleached bones brought down by the winter flood. Peering through the leaves, he saw Rosie Fifield, in a blue dress, sitting on the far side of the gully. Her washing was laid out to dry on the gorsebushes, and she was buried in a book. A little boy ran up to her, and held a buttercup under her chin.

'Please, Billy!' she stroked his hair. 'No more now!' – and the child settled down to make a daisy-chain.

Lewis watched them for ten minutes, frozen as you would watch a vixen playing with her cubs. Then he went back to the house.

XXVII

O N BOXING DAY of 1924, the hounds met at Fiddler's Elbow and began drawing the coverts of Cefn Wood. Around eleven-thirty, Colonel Bickerton was thrown from his hunter and kicked in the spine by an oncoming horse. The schoolchildren were given a holiday for the funeral. In the pub, the drinkers toasted the old squire's memory, and said, 'It's the way he'd have wanted to go.'

His widow came for three days, and went back to Grasse.

Having quarrelled with the rest of her family, she had chosen to live in France, painting and gardening in a small Provençal house. Mrs Nancy lived on at Lurkenhope, 'holding the fort' for Reggie, who was away, on his coffee-plantation, in Kenya. Most of the servants were given their notice. In July, Amos Jones heard a rumour that the hill-farms would be sold to pay the death-duties.

This was the moment for which he had waited all his life.

He called on the land-agent, who confirmed, in confidence, that all tenants of ten or more years' standing would be offered their farms at a 'fair valuation'.

'And what would a fair valuation be?'

'For The Vision? Hard to say exactly! Somewhere between two and three thousand, I expect.'

Amos next called in on the bank-manager, who foresaw no difficulty in securing a loan.

The prospect of owning his own farm made him feel young again. He seemed to forget his daughter. He looked over the land with the new eyes of love, dreamed of buying modern machinery, and delivered moralistic sermons on the decline of the gentry.

The Hand of God, he said, had delivered the land unto him and his seed; and when he spoke of 'seed', the twins both blushed and looked at the floor. One day, during the grouse season, he hid among the larches and watched Mrs Nancy striding up the pasture with a party of guns and beaters.

'And next year,' he shouted down the supper-table, 'next year, if they so much as show their fat faces in my field, I'll see them off...I'll set the dogs on them...'

'Good heavens!' said Mary, as she set down a dish of shepherd's pie. 'What did they ever do to you?'

Autumn slipped by. Then, towards the end of October, two valuers came from Hereford and asked to be shown the fields and the buildings.

'And what do you two gentlemen think the place might be worth?' Amos asked, deferentially opening the door of their saloon.

The older man rubbed his chin: 'Around three thousand on the open market. But I'd keep that figure dark if I were you.'

'Open market? But it's not to be sold on the open market.'

'I dare say you're right,' the valuer shrugged, and pulled the self-starter.

Amos suspected that something was wrong. But never, in his wilder moments of anxiety, was he prepared for the announcement in the *Hereford Times*: that the farms were to be sold, at public auction, on a date six weeks hence, at the Red Dragon in Rhulen. Apprehensive of the new Labour Government, and alert to new legislation that might go against the landlord, the Lurkenhope Trustees had opted to go for the last farthing, and were forcing their tenants to compete with outside buyers.

Haines of Red Daren called a meeting in the hall at Maesyfelin where, one after the other, the tenants protested against 'this monstrously underhand behaviour', and promised to disrupt the sale.

The sale went ahead as planned.

It was sleeting on the big day. Mary put on a warm grey woollen dress, her winter coat, and the hat she wore for funerals. As she took her umbrella, she turned to the twins and said, 'Please, do come! Your father needs you. Today, he needs you more than ever.'

They shook their heads and said, 'No, Mother! We'd not go to town.'

The Banqueting Hall of the Red Dragon had been cleared of tables, and the manager, alarmed for his parquet floor, was hovering in the entrance on the look-out for hobnail boots. The auctioneer's clerk was setting slips of paper on the chairs reserved for bidders. Nodding to friends and acquaintances, Mary sat down in the third row, while Amos went to join the other tenants, who — Welshmen to a man — stood in a ring with waterproofs over their arms, speaking in low murmurs as they tried to agree on a strategy.

The ringleader was Haines of Red Daren, now a gaunt, stringy man in his fifties with a squashed-up nose, a mop of greyish curls and crooked teeth. He had recently lost his wife.

'Right!' he said. 'If anyone bids against a tenant, I shall kick him from this room with my own boot.'

The room was filling up, with both bidders and spectators. Then a youngish, frowsy-looking woman came in wearing a rain-drenched hat of green feathers. On her arm was old Tom Watkins the Coffin.

Amos broke from the circle to greet his former enemy, but Watkins turned his back and glared at a hunting print.

At twenty past two, Mr Arkwright, the vendors' solicitor, appeared as if dressed for a shooting-party, in chequered tweed plus-fours. He, too, had recently lost his wife; but when David Powell-Davies went up to commiserate 'on behalf of all members of the Farmers' Union', the solicitor returned a withering smile:

'A sad business to be sure! But a mercy! Believe me, Mr Powell-Davies! A great mercy!'

Mrs Arkwright had spent her last year in and out of the Mid Wales Insane Asylum. The widower walked away to engage the auctioneer in conversation.

The auctioneer was a Mr Whitaker, a tall, bland, sandy-haired man with a high complexion and oyster-coloured eyes. He was dressed in the uniform of the professional classes – a black jacket and striped trousers – and his Adam's apple jerked up and down in the V of his winged collar.

At half-past two precisely, he mounted the rostrum and announced, 'By Order of the Trustees of Lurkenhope Estates, the sale of fifteen farms, five parcels of accommodation land, and two hundred acres of mature forest.'

'Shall I not die in the farm I were born in?' A deep voice, resonant with irony, sounded from the rear of the room.

'Of course you shall,' said Mr Whitaker, pleasantly. 'By making the appropriate bid! I do assure you, sir, the reserves are low. Are we ready to begin then? Lot One...Lower Pen-Lan Court...'

'No, sir!' It was Haines of Red Daren. 'We are not ready to begin. We are ready to put an end to this nonsense. Is it right to put up property of this kind without giving the tenants a chance to buy?'

Mr Whitaker turned from the muttering crowd to Mr Arkwright: they had been warned in advance to expect a disturbance. He laid down his ivory gavel and addressed the chandelier:

'All this, gentlemen, is a little late in the day. But I will say the following: as farmers you advocate open markets for selling your stock. Yet you come here expecting a closed market against your landlord.'

'Is there government control of the price of land?' It was Haines again, his sing-song voice rising in anger. 'There is government control of the price of stock.'

'Hear! Hear!' – and the Welshmen started clapping, slowly.
'Sir!' Mr Whitaker's mouth quivered and turned down at
the corners. 'This is a sale by public auction. It is not a political
meeting.'
'It'll turn political soon enough.' Haines waved a fist in the
air. 'You Englishmen! You think you've had troubles enough
in Ireland. I can tell you, there's a room full of Welshmen to
make trouble enough right here.'
'Sir!' The gavel sounded, *rat-tat-tat!* 'This is not the time or
place to discuss imperial questions. There is one question
before us, gentlemen! Do we, or do we not, wish this sale to
proceed?'
From all sides came cries of 'No!'…'Yes!'…'Chuck the
bugger out!'…'Bloody Bolshevik!'…'God Save the King!'
– while the core of Welshmen joined hands and sang in
chorus, *Hen Wlad Fu Nhadau*, 'O Land of My Fathers'.
Rat-tat-tat-tat-tat-tat-tat!
'Unfortunately, I cannot compliment you on your singing,
gentlemen!' The auctioneer paled. 'I shall say one thing more.
If this disturbance continues, the lots will be withdrawn and
offered for sale by private treaty in a single block.'
'Bluffer!…Chuck him out!…' But the shouts carried little
conviction and soon petered off into silence.
Mr Whitaker folded his arms and gloated over the effective-
ness of his threat. In the shadows, David Powell-Davies was
remonstrating with Haines of Red Daren.
'All right! All right!' Haines raked his fingernails down his
pitted cheeks. 'But if I catch any man, woman or dog bidding
against a tenant, I'll boot him——'
'Very well, then.' The auctioneer surveyed the lines of
tense, self-centred faces. 'The gentleman has given us permission to proceed. Lot One, then…Lower Pen-Lan Court…Five
hundred pounds, am I bid?' – and within twenty-five minutes
he had sold off the land, woodland, and fourteen farms, every
one of them to their tenants.
Dai Morgan gave £2,500 for The Bailey. Gillifaenog went
to Evan Bevan for £2,000 only, but the land was poor. The
Griffithses had to pay £3,050 for Cwm Cringlyn; and Haines
bought Red Daren for a full £400 below the estimate.

That certainly perked him up. He circulated round his cronies, pumping their hands and promising a round of drinks at opening time.

'Lot Fifteen...'

'This is it,' breathed Mary. Amos was trembling, and she slipped her grey-gloved hand over his.

'Lot Fifteen, The Vision Farm. House and outbuildings, with a hundred and twenty acres and grazing rights on the Black Hill...What am I bid? Five hundred pounds?...Five hundred it is! Your bid, sir!...At five hundred...!'

Amos pushed his bids against the reserve: it was like pushing a cart uphill. He clenched his fists. His breath came in sharp bursts.

At £2,750, he glanced up and saw the gavel poised to fall.

'Your bid, sir!' said Mr Whitaker; and Amos felt that he had reached a sunny summit and the clouds had all dispersed. Mary's hand lay over his relaxing knuckles, and his mind flashed back to that first evening, together in the overgrown farmyard.

'Very well, then,' Mr Whitaker was winding up the sale. 'Sold to the tenant for two thousand, seven hun——'

'Three thousand!'

The voice fell like a pole-axe on the base of Amos's skull.

Chairs squeaked as the spectators turned to stare at the unexpected bidder. Amos knew the bidder, but would not turn round.

'At three thousand,' Mr Whitaker beamed with pleasure. 'The bid is at the back of the room at three thousand.'

'Three thousand one hundred,' Amos choked.

'And five hundred!'

The bidder was Watkins the Coffin.

'And six at the front!'

And where was Red Daren now, Amos wondered. Where was his boot now? He felt, with each bid, that he was going to burst. He felt he was fighting for air, that each hundred was his final breath, but the cold voice behind him continued.

Now he opened his eyes and saw the complacent, coaxing smile on the auctioneer's face.

'Yours at the back,' the voice was saying. 'Sold to the

bidder at the back for five thousand two hundred pounds. Have you all done? Against you, sir!'

Mr Whitaker was enjoying himself. You could tell he was enjoying himself by the way he moistened his lower lip with the tip of his tongue.

'Five thousand three hundred!' said Amos, his eyes agape in a trance-like stare.

The auctioneer caught the bids in his mouth, like flowers flying.

'Near me, at five thousand three hundred!'

'Stop!' Mary's fingers clawed at her husband's shirt-cuff. 'He's mad,' she hissed. 'You've got to stop!'

'Thank you, sir! Five thousand four hundred at the back!'

'And five,' Amos barked.

'Near me again, at five thousand five hundred!'

Again, Mr Whitaker stretched his gaze beyond the chandelier — and blinked. A look of perplexity passed over his face. The second bidder had bolted for the door. People were leaving their seats and putting on their coats.

'Very well, then!' He raised his voice above the crinkle of oilskins. 'Sold to the tenant for five thousand five hundred pounds!' — and the gavel descended with an onanistic thud.

XXVIII

IT WAS SLEETING again next afternoon as Mary drove the dog-cart on her way to the solicitor. The fields were full of sodden sheep, and there were sheets of muddy water in the lane. Amos had taken to his bed.

The clerk showed her into the office, where a coal fire was blazing.

'Thank you, I'd prefer to stand here a moment,' she said, warming her hands while she collected her thoughts.

Mr Arkwright came in and rearranged some papers on his

desk: 'Dear lady, how good of you to call in so soon!' he said, and went on to discuss the deposit and exchange of contracts: 'We'll soon have the matter sewn up.'

'I haven't come to speak of the contract,' she said, 'but the unfair price at the sale.'

'Unfair, madam?' The monocle popped out of his eye-socket and swung to and fro on its black silk ribbon. 'In what way unfair? It was a public auction.'

'It was a private vendetta.'

The steam spiralled up from her skirt as she explained the feud between her husband and Watkins the Coffin.

The solicitor toyed with his paper-knife, adjusted his cravat-pin, leafed through a journal; then he rang for his secretary and asked, very pointedly, for 'one cup of tea'.

'Yes, Mrs Jones, I am listening,' he said, as Mary came to the end of her tale. 'Is there anything more you wish to tell me?'

'I was hoping...I was wondering...if the Trustees would agree to reduce the price...'

'Reduce the price? What a suggestion!'

'Is there no way——?'

'None!'

'No hope of——?'

'Hope, madam? I call it sheer effrontery!'

She stiffened her backbone and curled her lip: 'You won't get that price from anyone else, you know!'

'I beg your pardon, madam. On the contrary! Mr Watkins came to see me this very morning. Only too willing to place his deposit if the purchaser defaults!'

'I don't believe you,' she said.

'Don't,' he said, and pointed to the door. 'You have twenty-eight days in which to decide.'

A pity, he thought, as he listened to her footsteps on the linoleum. She must have been a handsome woman once: and she had caught him lying! But then she had—had she not? —betrayed her class. He was twitching nervously when the secretary fetched in the tea.

The evening clouds were darker than the hill. Great flocks of starlings flew low over Cefn Wood, expanding and condensing in arcs and ellipses, then sweeping in a whirlwind and settling on the branches. On ahead, Mary saw the lights of her home, but hardly dared advance towards it.

The twins came out, unharnessed the pony and wheeled the cart into its shed.

'How's Father?' she said, shivering.

'Acting strange.'

All day, he had called on God to smite him for the sin of pride.

'And what can I tell him now?' she said, crouching on a footstool by the grate. Benjamin fetched her a mug of cocoa. She closed her eyes to the blaze and seemed to see the lines of red corpuscles streaming over her eyelids.

'What can we, any of us, do?' she addressed the flames; and the flames, to her amazement, answered back.

She stood up. She went to the piano and opened the marquetry box in which she kept her correspondence. Within seconds, she had fished out Mrs Bickerton's Christmas card from last year. Under the signature was an address, near Grasse.

The twins ate their supper and went off to bed. A gale blew over the roof and, in the bedroom, she could hear Amos groaning. The flames crackled, the nib scratched. She wrote letter after letter, crumpling them up until she achieved the right effect. Then she stamped the envelope and left it for the postman.

She waited a week, two weeks, twenty days. The twenty-first day was a bright chilly morning, and she told herself not to run out to the postman, but to wait for the postman's knock.

The letter had come.

As she slit it open, something yellow, the colour of a baby chick, bounced out on to the hearthrug. She held her breath as her eyes raced over Mrs Bickerton's confident scrawl:

'Poor you! What an ordeal! I do so agree...some people are absolutely mad! Thank heavens, I still have *some* clout with the Trustees! And I should think so too!...Wonderful invention,

145

the telephone...Got through to London in ten minutes flat!...Sir Vivian most understanding...Couldn't remember offhand what the reserve on The Vision was...Under three thousand, he thought...But whatever it was, you can certainly have it for that!'

Mary raised her eyes to Amos and a tear dropped on to the notepaper. She went on reading aloud:

'... Garden lovely! ... Mimosa time ... and almond blossom...Heaven! Love you to come down if you can get away...Ask that awful Arkwright to get you the ticket...'

Suddenly, she was terribly embarrassed. She looked again at Amos.

'Big of them!' he snarled. 'Very very big of them!' – and he stamped out on to the porch.

She picked up the thing that had fallen from the letter. It was a flowerhead of mimosa, squashed but still fluffy. She held it to her nostril and inhaled the smell of the South.

One year, in the late Eighties, she and her mother had met the missionary's ship when it docked in Naples. Together they had travelled through a Mediterranean spring.

She remembered the sea, the olives blown white in the wind, and the scents of thyme and cistus after rain. She remembered lupins and poppies in the fields above Posilippo. She remembered warmth and ease in her body, under the sun. And what would she give now, for a new life, in the sun? To shrivel and die in the sun? Yet this letter, the letter she had prayed for, was it not also a sentence to stay, trapped for ever and ever, for the rest of her existence, in this gloomy house below the hill?

And Amos? If he could have smiled, or been grateful, or even understanding! Instead of which, he banged and stamped and broke crockery, and cursed the bloody English, and the Bickertons in particular. He even threatened to burn the place down.

And finally, when the Trustees' letter came – offering The Vision for £2,700 – all the years of brewed-up resentment burst into the open:

It had been *her* connections that got them the lease. *Her* money that stocked the farm. *Her* furniture furnished the house. Because of *her*, his daughter had run off with the Irishman. It was *her* fault that his sons were idiots. And now, when everything'd gone to whinders, it was *her* class and her clever clever letter that had saved all that he, Amos Jones — man, farmer, Welshman — had worked for, saved for, ruined his health for — and now did not want!

Did she hear that? DID — NOT — WANT! No! Not at that price! Nor at any price! And what did he want? He knew what he wanted! His daughter! Rebecca! He wanted her. Back. Back home! And the husband! Bloody Irishman! Couldn't be worse than them two halfwits! And he'd find them! And bring her back! Bring 'em both back! Back! Back! Back!——

'I know...I know...' Mary stood behind him, cradling his head in her hands. He had collapsed onto the rocking-chair, and was shaking with sobs.

'We'll find her,' she said. 'Somehow we'll find her. Even if we have to go to America, we'll somehow get her back.'

'Why did I put her out?' he whimpered.

He clung to Mary as a frightened child clings to a doll, but to his question she could find no answer.

XXIX

SPRING HAD DUSTED the larches. The cream was coming thick and yellowy in the cream-separator when a call from Benjamin made Mary drop the handle and rush for the kitchen. Amos lay stretched out on the hearthrug, mouth open and fish-eyes gaping at the rafters.

He had had a stroke. He had just passed his fifty-fifth birthday, and had been bending to tie a bootlace. On the table there was a mug of primroses.

Dr Galbraith, the jovial young Irishman who had taken over the practice, congratulated his patient on having the 'strength of an ox' and said he'd have him on his feet in no time. Then, taking Mary aside, he warned her to expect a second attack.

Yet despite one paralysed arm, Amos recovered sufficiently to hobble round the yard, wave his stick, curse the twins and get in the way of the horses. He was very hard to handle when his thoughts harked back to Rebecca.

'Well, 'ave you found her?' he'd snap each time the postman brought a letter.

'Not yet,' Mary'd say, 'but we'll keep on trying.'

She knew the Irishman's name was Moynihan, and wrote letters to the police, to the Home Office, and to his old employers on the railway. She advertised in the Dublin newspapers. She even wrote without success to the immigration authorities in America.

The couple had vanished.

That autumn, she announced with an air of finality, 'There's nothing more we can do.'

From then on, since neither twin went out, and even Benjamin had lost the habit of handling money, it was she who ruled The Vision; she who kept the accounts; she who decided what to plant. She was a shrewd judge of business and a shrewd judge of men, knowing when to buy and when to sell; when to placate the stock-dealers and when to send them packing.

'Phew!' a man was heard to complain after she'd struck some ferocious bargain. 'That Mother Jones is the stingiest woman on the hill.'

The remark was passed back to her, and it gave her great pleasure.

To avoid any question of paying death-duties, she put the deeds of The Vision in the twins' joint name. Her triumphant stare was enough to send Mr Arkwright scuttling down the street. She hooted with laughter at the news of the solicitor's arrest – for murder.

'Murder, Mother?'

'Murder!'

At first, Mrs Arkwright was thought to have died from nephritis and the effects of insanity. Then a rival solicitor, Mr Vavasour Hughes, asked the widower certain embarrassing questions about a client's will. At a tea-party designed to dispel his doubts, Mr Arkwright pressed him to eat a bloater paste sandwich, from which he nearly died in the night. A fortnight later Mr Hughes received a box of chocolates 'from an admirer'; and again he nearly died. He reported his suspicions to the police, who found that each chocolate had been syringed with arsenic. They put two and two together, and ordered the dead woman to be exhumed from Rhulen churchyard.

Dr Galbraith professed himself shocked by the result of the forensic tests: 'I knew she was martyr to indigestion,' he said, 'but I never expected this.'

To avail himself of her capital, Mr Arkwright had laced his wife's Benger's Food with arsenic purchased for the persecution of dandelions. He was convicted in Hereford and hanged in Gloucester.

'They've hanged old Arkwright,' Lewis waved the *News of the World* in his father's face.

'Eh?' Amos was now very deaf.

'I said, they've hanged old Arkwright,' he bellowed.

'An' 'e should a-been hanged at birth,' he said, decisively, bubbles of saliva dribbling down his chin.

Mary watched for signs of the second stroke; but it was not a stroke that killed him.

Olwen and Daisy were The Vision's two heavy brood-mares, and they foaled alternate years.

Lewis loved them dearly, saw whole worlds in their gleaming flanks, and liked to scrub them, comb them, polish their brasses, and fluff the white 'feathering' out around their hoofs.

A mare came on heat around the end of May, and waited for the visit of the stallion – a magnificent animal called Spanker who made a tour of the hill-farms with his master, Merlin Evans.

This Merlin was a wiry, tow-haired fellow with a pitted triangular face and a set of brown broken teeth. Around his neck he wore a number of ladies' chiffon scarves – until they rotted off—and a single gold hoop through his earlobe. He astonished the twins with his tales of conquest. They had only to mention some saintly, Chapel-going woman and he would grin: ''Ad her in the dingle over by Pantglas,' or ''Ad her standing up in the beast-house.'

Some nights he slept behind a haystack, others between linen sheets. People said he had sired a good few more offspring than Spanker: in fact there were farmers who, with an eye to fresh blood in the family, made a point of leaving their wives alone in the house.

Every year, before Christmas, he took a week's holiday in the capital; and once, when Lewis paid him twenty-five shillings for the stallion's services, Merlin spread the coins in his palm: 'Them'll get me one woman in London,' he said, 'and five in Abergavenny!'

In the spring of '26 a girl delayed him in Rosgoch, and he arrived at The Vision a week late.

Shreds of cloud hung motionless in the sky. The hills were silvery in the sunlight, the hedges white with hawthorn, and the buttercups spread a film of gold over the fields. The paddock was thick with bleating sheep. A cuckoo called. Sparrows chattered, and house-martins sliced the air. The two mares stood in their stalls, their muzzles in their oat-bags, kicking because of the flies.

Lewis and Benjamin were expecting the shearers at any moment.

All morning, they had been lashing the pens, boiling the tar-pot, oiling rusty shears, and taking the greasy oak shearing-benches down from the hayloft.

Indoors, Mary made lemon barley water for the men's refreshment. Amos was taking a nap, when a sharp voice sounded by the gate: 'Giddy-up then! Here comes the old lecher!'

The clatter of horseshoes woke the invalid. He went out to see what was going on.

The sun was very bright, and it dazzled him. He didn't seem to see the mares.

Nor did the twins see him as he limped into the strip of shadow between the stalls and the stallion. Nor did he hear

Merlin Evans bawling, 'Watch it, yer old fool!'
It was too late.

Olwen had kicked. The hoof caught him under the chin, and the sparrows went on chattering.

XXX

FROM THE MOMENT he set foot on the staircase, Mr Vines the undertaker registered an expression of doubt. The doubts increased as he cast a professional eye on the gap between the newel-post and the passage wall. He took a tape-measure to the corpse, and descended to the kitchen.

'He's a big man,' he said. 'We'll have to coffin him down here, I suppose.'

'I suppose so,' said Mary. A black crêpe handkerchief was tucked into her sleeve, in readiness for the tears that would not come.

In the afternoon, she scrubbed the kitchen floor and, sprinkling some bed-sheets with lavender-water, tacked them to the picture rail, so that they hung in folds over the frames. She fetched a branch or two of laurel from the garden, and made a frieze from the shining leaves.

The weather continued hot and muggy: the twins went on with the shearing. Five of the neighbours had come to help, clipping all day in competition for the prize of a costrel of cider.

'I'll put my money on Benjamin,' said old Dai Morgan, as Benjamin dragged another ewe from the pen. He was five beasts ahead of Lewis. He had strong, agile hands, and was a wonderful shearer.

The sheep lay quietly under the shears, and endured the torture. Then, creamy white again—though some with bloody cuts about their udders—they bounded out into the

151

paddock, jumping in the air, as if over an imaginary fence, or simply to be free. None of the shearers spoke of the dead man.

Two boys – Reuben Jones's grandsons – rolled up the fleeces, teased the neck-wool into cords, and tied them. Now and again, Mary appeared in the doorway, in a long green dress, with a jug of the lemon barley water.

'You must be terribly thirsty,' she smiled, cutting short their efforts to commiserate.

When Mr Vines drove up at four, the twins downed tools and carried the coffin in through the porch. Their hands were greasy and their overalls shiny black from the lanolin. They wrapped their father in a sheet and fetched him down the staircase. They laid him on the kitchen table, and left the undertaker to his business.

Mary went for a walk, alone, over the fields to Cock-a-loftie. She watched a kestrel quivering under a curdled sky. Around sunset, like crows at the lambing season, women in black came to pay their last respects, and kiss the corpse.

The coffin lay open on the table. Candles stood on either side, and their light flickered up through the bacon-rack and made a grid of shadow with the rafters. Mary, also, had changed into black. Some of the women were crying:

'He was a fine man.'

'He was a good man.'

'The Lord have mercy!'

'God be with him!'

'God have mercy on his soul!'

The coffin was lined with wadding and domett. To conceal the contusions on his chin, a white scarf had been wrapped around the lower half of his face, but the mourners saw the wisps of reddish hair poking out of his nostrils. The room smelled of lavender and lilac. Mary was unable to cry.

'Yes,' she replied. 'He was a good man.'

She showed her guests into the parlour and served each one a glass of mulled ale with lemon peel. This, she recalled, was custom in the valleys.

'Yes,' she nodded. 'There are no friends like old friends.'

The twins stood silently against the kitchen wall, eyeing

the people who were eyeing their father.

Mary went into Rhulen and bought for the funeral a black velvet skirt, a black straw hat, and a black blouse with a collarette of accordion-pleated chiffon. She was still in the bedroom, dressing, as the hearse drew up to the gate. The kitchen was full of people. The pall-bearers shouldered the coffin; but she continued to gaze at her reflection in the pier-glass, slowly swivelling her head and surveying her profile. Her cheeks were like crumpled rose-petals beneath the chenille-spot veil.

She held up through the service and the committal. She walked from the grave without a final look — and within a week she gave way to despair.

First, she blamed herself for Amos's stroke. Then she assumed those aspects of his character which had once annoyed her most. She lost her appetite for the least of luxuries. She bought no clothes. She lost her sense of humour, no longer laughing at the little absurdities that had lightened her existence; and she even remembered his mother, old Hannah, with affection.

She carried her devotion to the point of eccentricity.

She patched his jacket and darned his socks, laid a fourth place for supper and would heap his plate with food. His pipe, his tobacco-pouch, his spectacles, his Bible — all were set out in their familiar places; also his box of chisels in case he wanted to carve.

They held conversations three times a week — not through table-turning or the techniques of spiritism, but from the simpler belief that the dead were alive and would answer if called.

She would take no decision without his assent.

One November night, when a field belonging to Lower Brechfa was coming up for sale, she parted the curtains and whispered into the darkness. Then, turning to face her sons, she said, 'Lord knows where we'll find the money, but Father says we should buy.'

On the other hand, when Lewis wanted a new McCormick binder – he no longer held to his hatred of machinery – she tightened her lips, and said, 'Definitely not!'

Then, havering, she said, 'Yes!'

Then she said, 'Father says, "No!"'

Then she said, 'Yes!' again; but by that time, Lewis was so confused he let the matter drop, and they didn't buy a binder till after the Second World War.

Nothing – not even a teacup – was replaced; and the house began to look like a museum.

The twins never ventured out, rather from force of habit now than fear of the outside world. Then, during the summer of '27, there was a very disagreeable incident.

XXXI

TWO YEARS AFTER Jim the Rock came home from the war, his sister Ethel gave birth to a boy. His name was Alfie, and he grew up simple. Who the father was, Ethel wasn't saying; but because the lad had Jim's carroty hair and cauliflower ears, unkind people used to say, 'Brother and sister! What can you expect? Small wonder the kid's a halfwit!' – which was quite unfair, because Jim and Ethel were not blood-relations.

Alfie was a troublesome child. He was always stripping off his clothes and playing naked in the beast-house, and sometimes he went missing for days. Ethel shrugged at these absences, and said, 'He be bound to show up sooner or later.' One summer evening, Benjamin Jones found him frolicking on the hill and, having a childish streak himself, the two of them went on playing till sundown.

But the boy had only one true friend and that was a clock.

The clock – its glass always filthy from peatsmoke – had a white enamel dial and Roman numerals, and lived in a wooden case on the wall above the fireplace.

As soon as he was tall enough, Alfie would climb a chair, stand on tiptoe, open the tiny trap-door and peer at the pendulum swinging to and fro, *tick-tock...tick-tock...*Then he would crouch by the grate, as if his icy eyes could quench the embers, clicking his tongue, *tick-tock...tick-tock...*and nodding his head in time.

He thought the clock was alive. He would come home with presents for the clock — a pretty pebble perhaps, a piece of moss, a bird's egg or a dead fieldmouse. He longed to make the clock say something other than *tick-tock...*He fiddled with the hands and the pendulum. He tried to wind it up and, in the end, he broke it.

Leaving the case behind on the wall, Jim took the mechanism to Rhulen. The clock-repairer examined it — it was a fine eighteenth-century model — and offered him £5. Jim left the shop whistling happily on his way to the pub, but little Alfie was heartbroken.

He missed his friend, screamed, searched the barn and buildings, and butted his blazing head against the whitewashed wall. Then, convinced the clock was dead, he vanished.

Ethel made no special effort to find him and, even three days later, merely grumbled that Alfie'd 'gone the devil knows where'.

Below Craig-y-Fedw there was a boggy pool, hidden among hazels, where Benjamin went picking watercress for tea. Some bluebottles were buzzing around a clump of kingcups. He saw a pair of legs poking out of the mud, and ran back home to fetch Lewis.

By the time the police came on the scene, Ethel the Rock had thrown a fit of hysterics, and was moaning and wailing that Benjamin was the murderer.

'I knew it,' she bawled. 'I knew he was that kind!' — and poured forth a rigmarole of how Benjamin took the boy on lonely walks.

Benjamin was dumbstruck: the presence of policemen carried him back to the terrible days of 1918. Escorted to The Vision for questioning, he hung his head and was unable to return a single coherent answer.

As usual, it was Mary who saved the day: 'Officer, don't you see it's a complete fabrication. Poor Miss Watkins! She's a little bit out of her mind.'

The interview ended with the policemen doffing their helmets and offering apologies. At the inquest, the coroner returned a verdict of 'death by misadventure'; but relations between The Vision and The Rock were sour again.

XXXII

As AMOS's WIDOW, Mary wanted at least one daughter-in-law and a brood of grandchildren. As the mother of twins, she wanted to keep both sons for herself, and in her daydreams made a mental picture of the scene at her death.

She would be lying, a withered husk with wisps of silver hair on the pillow, and her hands stretched out over a patchwork quilt. The room would be filled with sunshine and birdsong; a breeze would stir the curtains, and the twins be standing, symmetrically, on either side of the bed. A beautiful picture – and one she knew to be a sin!

There were times when she chided Benjamin, 'What is all this nonsense about not going out? Why can't you find a nice young lady?' But Benjamin's mouth would tighten, his lower lids quiver, and she knew he would never get married. At other times, wilfully displaying the perverse side of her character, she took Lewis by the elbow and made him promise never, never to marry unless Benjamin married too.

'I promise,' he said, slumping his head like a man receiving a prison sentence; for he wanted a woman badly.

All through one winter, he became very jumpy and argumentative, would snap at his brother and refuse to eat. Mary feared a repetition of Amos's black moods and, in May, she made a momentous decision: both the boys were going to the Rhulen Fair.

'No.' She shot a piercing look at Benjamin. 'I won't hear any excuses.'

'Yes, Mama,' he said, lifelessly.

She packed them a picnic lunch and waved goodbye from the porch.

'Mind you pick the pretty ones!' she called out. 'And don't come back till dark!'

She strolled into the orchard and gazed across the valley at the two ponies, one cantering round in circles, the other ambling at a trot, until they vanished over the skyline.

'Well, at least we've got them out of the house.' She scratched Lewis's sheepdog behind his ear, and the dog wagged his tail and nuzzled his head against her skirt. Then she went indoors to read a book.

She had lately discovered the novels of Thomas Hardy, and she wanted to read them all. How well she knew the life he described — the smell of Tess's milking-parlour; Tess's torments, in bed and in the beetfield. She, too, could whittle hurdles, plant pine saplings, or thatch a hayrick — and if the old unmechanized ways were gone from Wessex, time had stood still, here, on the Radnor Hills.

'Think of The Rock,' she told herself. 'Nothing's changed there since the Dark Ages.'

She was reading *The Mayor of Casterbridge*. She liked it less than *The Woodlanders*, which she had read the week before, and Hardy's 'coincidences' had begun to grate on her nerves. She read three more chapters; then, letting the book fall into her lap, she allowed herself to slide into a reverie of certain nights and mornings — in the bedroom with Amos. And suddenly, he came to her — with his flaming hair and the light streaming out round his shoulders. And she knew she must have slept because the sun had come round to the west and sunbeams were pouring past the geraniums, in between her legs.

'At my age!' she smiled, shaking herself awake — and heard the sound of horses in the yard.

The twins were standing by the gate, Benjamin puffed into

a state of exalted indignation, while Lewis looked over his shoulder as if searching for somewhere to hide.

'Whatever's the matter?' she burst out laughing. 'Were there no young ladies at the fair?'

'It was terrible,' said Benjamin.

'Terrible?'

'Terrible!'

Skirts, since the twins were last in Rhulen, had risen not above the ankle, but above the knee.

At eleven that morning, they had stopped on the hilltop and looked down over the town. Already the fair was in full swing. They heard the hum of the crowd, the whine of Wurlitzer organs, and the odd snarl or bellow from the beasts in the menagerie. In Broad Street alone, Lewis counted eleven merry-go-rounds. There was a Ferris-wheel in the market-place, and a little Tower of Babel, which was a helter-skelter.

For the last time, Benjamin begged his brother to turn back.

'Mother'd never know,' he said.

'I'd tell her,' said Lewis, and kicked his pony.

Twenty minutes later, he was wandering round the fairground like a man possessed.

Farm lads strolled the streets in gangs of seven or eight, puffing at cigarettes, ogling the girls, or daring one another to spar with 'The Champ' — a Negro boxer in red satin shorts. Gipsy fortune-tellers offered lilies-of-the-valley, or your fortune. *Ping...ping* sounded from the shooting galleries. An exhibition of freaks showed the 'smallest mare and foal in the world', and one of its larger women.

By noon, Lewis had ridden an elephant, flown in a 'Chairoplane', drunk the milk of a coconut, licked a lollipop, and was looking for other amusements.

As for Benjamin, all he saw were legs — bare legs, legs in silk stockings, legs in fish-net stockings — kicking, dancing, prancing, and reminding him of his one and only visit to an abattoir and the kicks of the sheep in their death throes.

Around one o'clock, Lewis paused outside the 'Theatre de Paris' where four can-can girls, encased in raspberry velvet, were doing a come-on act, while, behind painted draperies, a Mamzelle Delilah performed the 'Dance of the Seven Veils' to an audience of heavy-breathing farmers.

Lewis felt for the sixpence in his pocket, and a hand clamped around his wrist. He turned to meet his brother's flinty stare:

'You'll not go in there!'

'Just you try and stop me!'

'Won't I just?' Benjamin sidestepped across his brother's path, and the sixpence slid back down into his pocket.

Half an hour later, Lewis's gaiety had left him. He moped around the booths looking desolate. Benjamin dogged him, a few paces behind.

A beatific vision had been offered — offered for the price of a drink — and Lewis had turned aside. But why? Why? Why? He asked the question a hundred times, until it dawned on him that he was not just afraid of hurting Benjamin: he was afraid of him.

At a hoop-la stand, he almost accosted a girl in flamingo straining every fibre of her torso to land her hoop over a five pound note. He saw his brother glaring through a stack of tea-sets and goldfish bowls; and his courage failed.

'Let's go home,' said Benjamin.

'To hell with you,' Lewis said, and was on the point of relenting when two girls accosted him.

'Want a cigarette?' asked the elder one, poking her stubby fingers in her handbag.

'Thank you very much,' said Lewis.

The girls were sisters. One wore a green frock, the other a tunic of mauve jersey with an orange sash around her bottom. Their cheeks were rouged, their hair shingled, and their nostrils were cavernous. They winked at one another with insolent pale blue eyes, and even Lewis saw that skimpy hemlines looked absurd on their short, heavy-breasted bodies.

He tried to shake them off: they clung on.

Benjamin watched from a distance as his brother treated

them to lemonade and brandy-snaps. Then, realizing they were no competition, he joined the group. The girls burst into fits at the thought of walking out with twins.

'What a lark!' said the mauve one.

'Let's go on the Wall of Death!' said the green one.

A huge cylindrical drum stood beside its steam-engine at the top end of Castle street. Lewis paid the grimy youth at the ticket kiosk; and all four stepped inside.

Several other passengers were waiting for the start. The youth shouted, 'Stand against the wall!' The door slammed and the drum began to spin faster and faster on its axis. The floor rose, pushing the passengers upward till their heads were almost level with the rim. When the floor fell again, they were stranded, pinned by centrifugal force, in attitudes of the Crucifixion.

Benjamin felt his eyeballs being squashed back into his skull. For three endless minutes, the agony continued. Then, as the drum slowed up, the girls slithered down and their frocks concertina-ed above their hips, so that gaps of bare flesh showed between their stockings and suspender-belts.

Benjamin staggered on to the street and vomited into the gutter.

'I've had enough,' he spluttered, and mopped his chin. 'I'm off.'

'Spoil-sport!' squealed the girl in green. 'He's only putting it on.' The sisters linked their arms around Lewis's and tried to march him up the street. He did shake them off, and turned on his heels and followed the tweed cap through the crowd in the direction of the ponies.

That night, on the staircase, Mary brushed her cheek against Benjamin's and, with a sly smile, thanked him for bringing his brother home.

XXXIII

S HE BOUGHT THEM Hercules bicycles for their thirty-first
birthday, and encouraged them to take an interest in local
antiquities. At first, they went for short rides on Sundays.
Then, moved by the spirit of adventure, they extended their
range to take in the castles of the Border Barons.

At Snodhill they ripped the ivy off a wall, and uncovered
an arrow-slit. At Urishay they mistook a rusty pannikin for
'something mediaeval'. At Clifford they pictured the Fair
Rosamond, lovelorn in a wimple; and when they went to
Painscastle, Benjamin thrust his hand down a rabbit-hole and
pulled out a fragment of iridescent glass.

'A goblet?' suggested Lewis.

'A bottle,' Benjamin corrected.

He borrowed books from the Rhulen Lending Library and
read aloud, in condensed versions, the chronicles of Froissart,
Giraldus Cambrensis and Adam of Usk. Suddenly, the world
of the Crusading Knights became more real than their own.
Benjamin vowed himself to chastity; Lewis to the memory of
a fair damsel.

They laughed — and laying their bikes behind a hedge,
went off to laze beside a stream.

They imagined battering-rams, portcullises, crucibles of
boiling pitch and bloated bodies floating in a moat. Hearing
of the Welsh archers at Crécy, Lewis stripped a yew branch,
hardened it with fire, strung it with gut and fletched some
arrows with goose feathers.

The second arrow whizzed across the orchard and pierced
a chicken through the neck.

'A mistake,' he said.

'Too dangerous,' said Benjamin, who, meanwhile, had
unearthed a most interesting document.

A monk of Abbey Cwmhir relates that the bones of
Bishop Cadwallader lie in a golden coffin beside St Cynog's
Well at Glascoed.

'And where be that?' Lewis asked. He had read about the
Tomb of Tutankhamun in the *News of the World*.

'There!' said Benjamin, placing his thumbnail under some Gothic lettering on the Ordnance Survey Map. The place was eight miles from Rhulen, off the road to Llandrindod.

After Chapel next Sunday, Mr Nantlys Williams saw the twins' bicycles propped against the palings, and a spade lashed to Lewis's crossbar. He chided them gently for labouring on the Lord's Day, and Lewis blushed as he bent down to fix his cycle-clip.

At Glascoed, they found the Holy Water gurgling from a mossy cleft, then dribbling away among some burdocks. It was a shady spot. There were cowpats in the mud, and horseflies buzzing round them. A boy in braces saw the two strange men and took to his heels.

'Where do we dig?' Lewis asked.

'Yonder!' said Benjamin, pointing to a hummock of earth half-hidden by nettles.

The soil was black and glutinous and wriggling with earthworms. Lewis dug for half an hour and then handed his brother a piece of porous bone.

'Cow!' said Benjamin.

'Bull!' said Lewis, only to be interrupted by a strident voice shouting across the fields: 'I tell you to get from here!'

The boy in braces had come back with his father, a farmer who was fuming on the far side of the bushes. The twins saw a shotgun. Remembering Watkins the Coffin, they crept out, sheepishly, into the sunshine.

'And I'll be keeping the spade,' the farmer added.

'Yes, sir!' said Lewis, and dropped it. 'Thank you, sir!' — and they mounted their bikes, and rode off.

Forswearing gold as the root of all evil, they turned their attention to the early Celtic saints.

Benjamin read, in a learned paper by the Rector of Cascob, that these 'spiritual athletes' had retreated into the mountains to be at one with Nature and the Lord. St David himself had settled in the Honddhu Valley, in 'a mean shelter covered with moss and leaves' — and there were several other sites within cycling distance.

At Moccas, they found the place where St Dubricius saw a white sow suckling her litter. And when they went to Llanfrynach, Benjamin teased his brother about the woman who tried to tempt the saint with 'wolfsbane and other lustful ingredients'.

'I'll thank you for keeping your mouth shut,' Lewis said.

In Llanveynoe Church, carved on a Saxon stone, they saw a sturdy youth suspended from the Tree: the church's patron, St Beuno, had once cursed a man for refusing to cook a fox.

'Fox wouldn't pass my mouth neither,' said Lewis, pulling a face.

They considered taking up the life of anchorites – an ivy bower, a babbling brook, a diet of berries and wild leek and, for music, the chatter of blackbirds. Or perhaps they'd be Holy Martyrs, clinging to the Host while hordes of marauding Danes looted, burned and raped? It was the year of the Slump. Perhaps there was going to be a revolution?

One August afternoon, pedalling as fast as they could go beside the Wye, they were 'buzzed' by an airplane.

Lewis braked and stopped in the middle of the road.

The crash of the R 101 had given a tremendous boost to his scrapbook, although his true loves, now, were the lady aviators. Lady Heath...Lady Bailey...Amy Johnson...The Duchess of Bedford: he could string off their names as if saying his prayers. His favourite, of course, was Amelia Earheart.

The plane was a Tiger Moth, with a silver fuselage. It circled a second time and the pilot dipped, and waved.

Lewis waved back, passionately, in case it was one of his ladies; and when the plane zoomed low on its third circuit, the figure in the cockpit flicked back her goggles, and showed her tanned and smiling face. The plane was so close that Lewis swore he saw her lipstick. Then she soared her machine, back into the eye of the sun.

Over supper, Lewis said that he, too, would like to fly.

'Hm!' Benjamin grunted.

He was far more concerned about their next-door neighbour than the likelihood of Lewis flying.

XXXIV

THE FARMHOUSE at Lower Brechfa lay in a very windy position and the pine-trees around it slanted sideways. Its owner, Gladys Musker, was a strong meaty woman, with glossy cheeks and tobacco-coloured eyes. A widow of ten years' standing, she somehow managed to keep a tidy house and support her daughter, Lily Annie, and her mother, Mrs Yapp.

Mrs Yapp was an irritable old scrounger, more or less crippled with rheumatism.

One day, soon after the Joneses bought her field, Lewis was pleaching a hedge between the two properties when Mrs Musker came out and watched him hammering in the stakes. Her defiant gaze unnerved him. She heaved a sigh and said, 'Life's all moil and toil, isn't it?' and asked if he'd come and rehang a gate. At tea, he polished off six mince-pies, and she put him on her list of possible husbands.

At suppertime, he happened to mention that Mrs Musker was an excellent pastrycook, and Benjamin shot an anxious glance at his mother.

Lewis warmed to Mrs Musker, and she was certainly very friendly to him. He stacked her straw, slaughtered her porker, and one day she came running over the fields, out of breath:

'For the love of God, Lewis Jones. Come and help me with the cow! She gone down like the Devil kicked her!'

The cow had colic, but he succeeded in coaxing her to her feet.

Sometimes, Mrs Musker tried to show him upstairs into the bedroom; but he never went that far, preferring to sit in

164

her nice fuggy kitchen and listen to her stories.

Lily Annie had a pet fox cub that answered to the name of Ben and lived in a wire-netting cage. Ben ate kitchen scraps and was so tame she could handle him like a dolly. Once, when he escaped, she ran down the dingle, calling, 'Bennie! Bennie!' – and he bounded out of the brambles and curled in a ball at her feet.

Ben became quite a local celebrity, and even Mrs Nancy the Castle came to see him.

'But he's very choosy, you know,' crowed Mrs Yapp. 'He don't take to every Tom, Dick or Harry! Mrs Nancy brought the Bishop of Hereford a while back, and Our Bennie jumped up on the mantelpiece and done his business. It was an awful foxy smell, I can tell you.'

'Unlike her mother, Mrs Musker was an uncomplicated soul, who enjoyed having a man about the place; and if a man did her a favour, she'd give a favour in return. Among her callers were Haines of Red Daren and Jim the Rock – Haines because he gave her tiddling lambs, and Jim because he gave her a good long laugh.

Lewis hated the idea of her seeing these two and she was plainly disappointed in him. Some days, she was all smiles: at other times, she'd say, 'Oh, it's you again! Why don't you sit and have a chat with mother?' But Lewis was bored by Mrs Yapp, who only wished to talk about money.

One morning, having strolled over to Lower Brechfa, he saw the fox's skin nailed to some barnsiding and Haines's grey cob tethered to the gate. He left, and did not see Mrs Musker again till February, when he met her in the lane. Draped around her neck there was a red fox-fur.

'Yes,' she said, clicking her tongue. 'It's poor old Ben. He bit into Lily Annie's hand, and Mr Haines says that's the way to get lock-jaw, so we had him shot. I cured him myself with saltpetre. And fancy! I only fetched him from the furrier's Thursday.'

She added, smiling silkily, that she was alone in the house.

He waited two days and then trudged through the snow-drifts to Lower Brechfa. The pines were black against a crystalline sky, and the rays of the setting sun seemed to rise, not fall, as if toward the apex of a pyramid. He blew through his hands to warm them. He had made up his mind to have her.

The cottage was windowless on the north side. Icicles hung from the gutter, and a drop of cold water trickled down his neck. Coming round the end of the house, he saw the grey horse and heard the groans of love in the bedroom. The dog barked, and he ran. He was halfway across the field when Haines's voice came bawling after him.

Four months later, the postman confided in Benjamin that Mrs Musker was expecting Haines's baby.

She was ashamed to show herself in Chapel, so she stayed at home, cursing the lot of women and waiting for Mr Haines to do the proper thing.

This he did not. He said his two sons, Harry and Jack, had set their teeth against the marriage, and offered to pay her.

Indignantly, she refused. But the neighbours, instead of despising her, overwhelmed her with sympathy and kindness. Old Ruth Morgan offered to act as midwife. Miss Parkinson, the harmonium player, brought a lovely gloxinia, and Mr Nantlys Williams himself said a prayer at the bedside.

'Don't fret, my child,' he consoled her. 'It is the woman's part to be fruitful.'

She held her head high the day she drove to Rhulen to register the birth of her daughter.

'Margaret Beatrice Musker,' she printed the capitals when the clerk handed her the form, and when Haines came knocking on the door to see his daughter, she shooed him away. A week later she relented and allowed him to hold her for half an hour. After that, he behaved like a man possessed.

He wanted to have her baptized Doris Mary, after his mother, but Mrs Musker said, 'Her name is Margaret Beatrice.' He offered wads of pound notes: she threw them in his face. She cuffed him when he tried to make love to her. He begged her, pleaded on his knees for her to marry him.

'Too late!' she said, and locked him out for good.

He would mooch round the yard, uttering threats and curses. He threatened to kidnap the baby, and she threatened him with the police. He had a terrible temper. Years earlier, he and his brother had slogged at one another with bare fists, for three whole days, until the brother slunk away and disappeared. Somewhere in his family there was said to be a 'touch of the tarbrush'.

Mrs Musker was frightened to leave the house. On a page of almanac, she scribbled a note to Lewis Jones and gave it to the postman to deliver.

Lewis went; but when he came to the gate, Haines was lurking by the beast-house with a lurcher straining on a leash.

Haines yelled, 'Get yer dirty interfering nose from here!' The dog slavered, and Lewis headed for home. All afternoon he wondered whether to call the police but, in the end, thought better of it.

A gale blew in the night. The old pine creaked; windows rattled, and twigs flew against their bedroom window. Around twelve Benjamin heard someone on the door. He thought it was Haines and woke his brother.

The hammering went on and above the shrieking wind, they heard a woman's voice calling, 'Murder! There's been a murder!'

'God in Heaven!' Lewis jumped out of bed. 'It's Mrs Yapp.'

They led her into the kitchen. The embers were still whispering in the grate. For a while she sat babbling, 'Murder!...Murder!' Then she pulled herself together and said, grimly, 'He done hi'self as well.'

Lewis lit a hurricane lamp and loaded his shotgun.

'Please,' said Mary – she was on the staircase in a dressing-gown – 'please, I beg of you, be careful!' The twins followed Mrs Yapp into the darkness.

At Lower Brechfa, the kitchen window had been broken. Dimly, in the lamplight, they saw the body of Mrs Musker, her brown homespun dress spread round her, hunched over the rocking-cradle, in the centre of a blackish pool. Lily Annie crouched in the far corner cradling a dark object, which was the baby – alive.

At nine o'clock, Mrs Yapp had gone, as she usually went, to answer Haines's knock; but instead of waiting on the doorstep, he had slipped round the house, smashed his gunstock through the window, and fired both barrels, point-blank, at his lover.

She, in her final flash of instinct, threw herself over the cradle, and so saved the child. The shot sprayed Lily Annie's hands; and she hid with her grandmother in a cupboard under the stair. Half an hour later, they heard two further shots, and after that there was silence. Mrs Yapp had waited two hours more before she went for help.

'Swine!' Lewis said, and went outside with the lamp.

He found Haines's body in the blood-spattered Brussels sprouts. The gun was at his side, and his head was off. He had tied a length of twine around the triggers, passed it round the stock, put the barrel in his mouth, and pulled.

'Swine!' he kicked the corpse, once, twice, but checked himself before blaspheming the dead three times.

The inquest was held in the hall at Maesyfelin. Almost everyone was sobbing. Everyone was in black except for Mrs Yapp, who arrived dry-eyed in a hat of crimson plush with a pink chiffon sea-anemone that waved its tentacles when she nodded.

The Coroner addressed her in a sad, sepulchral voice: 'Did the Chapel folk forsake your daughter in the hour of her distress?'

'No,' said Mrs Yapp. 'Some of them come up to the house and was very nice to her.'

'Then all honour to this little Bethel which did not forsake her!'

He had intended to pass a verdict of 'wilful murder followed by suicide', but when Jack Haines read his father's final note, he changed his mind to 'manslaughter in a sudden transport of passion'.

The inquest adjourned and the mourners trooped out for the funeral. There was a sharp wind. After the service, Lily Annie followed her mother's coffin to the grave. Her wounded hands were wrapped in a flapping black shawl, and she carried a wreath of daffodils to lay on the mound of red soil.

Mr Nantlys Williams bade all present stay for the second committal, which took place in the far corner of the churchyard. On Haines's coffin there was a single wreath – of laurel leaves with a card affixed: 'To dearest Papa, from H & J.'

Mrs Yapp ransacked the house for anything of value and went with Lily Annie to live at her sister's in Leominster. She refused to spend 'one single penny' on her daughter's memory: so it was left to Lewis Jones to buy the funerary monument. He chose a rustic stone cross carved with a single snowdrop and a legend reading, 'Peace! Perfect Peace!'

Every month or so, he forked the gravel free of weeds. He planted a clump of daffodils to flower each year in the month of her death; and though he never, ever pardoned himself, he was able to enjoy some consolation.

XXXV

BEFORE LEAVING the district, Mrs Yapp let it be known she had no intention of harbouring the 'child of such a union'; and without telling his mother or twin, Lewis offered to raise her at The Vision.

'I'll think about it,' the old woman said.

He heard nothing further until the postman told him that Little Meg had been parked at The Rock. He ran over to Lower Brechfa, where Mrs Yapp and Lily Annie were piling their possessions on a cart. The Rock, he protested, was no place to bring up a baby.

'It's where she belongs,' the old woman retorted tartly: letting it be known that, to her way of thinking, Jim, not Haines, had been the father.

'I see.' Lewis hung his head, and sadly walked home to tea.

He was right: The Rock was no fit place for any baby. Old

Aggie, her face a web of grimy wrinkles, was too frail for housework except to jab a poker at the fire. Jim was too idle to sweep the chimney and, on windy days, the smoke blew back into the room, and they could hardly see across it. The three adopted girls — Sarah, Brennie and Lizzie — padded about with smarting eyes and snivelling colds. Everyone itched with lice. Ethel was the only one who worked.

To feed her hungry mouths, she would slip out after dark and snaffle what she could from other farms — a duckling, perhaps, or a tame rabbit. Her thefts from The Vision were unnoticed until the morning Benjamin opened the door of the meal-shed, and a dog shot past his legs and raced up the fields to Craig-y-Fedw. The dog was Ethel's. She had raided the corn-bin: he wanted to call the police.

'No,' Mary restrained him. 'We shall do nothing about it.'

Because of his reverence for animal life, Jim never sent a single beast for slaughter and his flock became more and more decrepit. The oldest animal, a wall-eyed ewe called Dolly, was over twenty years old. Others were barren, or missing their back teeth, and in winter they died from lack of feed. After the snowmelt, Jim would collect the carcasses and dig a communal grave — with the result that, over the years, the farmyard became one big cemetery.

Once when Ethel was at the end of her tether, she ordered him to sell five ewes in Rhulen; but on the outskirts of town, he heard the bleats of other sheep, lost the will to continue and drove his 'girlies' home.

At the end of an auction, he would hang round the sales clerks, and if there was some clapped-out nag that nobody wanted — not even the knacker — he'd step forward and stroke her muzzle: 'Aye, I'll give her a home. All she needs is a bit o' feedin' up.'

Dressed like a scarecrow, he would drive his cart through the neighbouring valleys, picking up bits of scrap metal and cast-off machinery, but instead of trying to turn a profit, he turned The Rock into a fortress.

At the outbreak of Hitler's war the house and outbuildings were encircled with a stockade of rusty hayrakes and plough-shares; mangles, bedsteads and cartwheels, and harrows with their teeth pointing outward.

His other mania was to collect stuffed birds and animals and, eventually, the attic was crammed so full of moth-eaten taxidermy that the girls had no place to sleep.

One morning as Mary Jones was listening to the nine-o'clock news, she looked up and saw Lizzie Watkins pressing her nose against the kitchen window. The girl's hair was lank and greasy. A skimpy floral dress hung from her wasted body, and her teeth were chattering with cold.

'It's Little Meg,' she blurted out, wiping her nose with her forefinger. 'She's dying.'

Mary put on her winter coat and walked out into the wind. For the past week she had not been feeling well. It was the time of the equinoctial gales, and the heather was purple on the hill. As they approached Craig-y-Fedw, Jim came out and cursed the yelping sheep-dogs: 'Atcha! Yer buggers!' She ducked her head to clear the lintel, and entered the murky room.

Aggie was feebly fanning the fire. Ethel sat on the box-bed with her legs apart; and Little Meg, half-covered with Jim's jacket, gaped at the rafters with brilliant blue-green eyes. Her cheeks were inflamed. A tinny cough rattled in her throat. She had a fever and was gasping for breath.

'She's got bronchitis,' said Mary, adding in an expert tone: 'You'll have to get her out of this smoke, or it'll turn to pneumonia.'

'You take her,' Jim said.

She looked him square in the eyes. They were the same as the eyes of the child. She saw he was pleading and knew that he really was the father.

'Of course I will,' she smiled. 'Let Lizzie come with me and we'll soon make her better.'

She prepared a eucalyptus inhaler and, even after the first few gulps, Meg began to breathe more freely. She spooned some cream of wheat between her lips, and camomile as a sedative. She showed Lizzie how to sponge her with water, and so keep the fever down. All night they kept vigil, holding her warm and upright by the fire. Now and then, Mary sewed a few black stars on to her patchwork quilt. By morning, the crisis had passed.

Long afterwards, when Lewis cast his mind over his mother's last years, one particular image remained in his memory: the sight of her sewing the patchwork quilt.

She had begun the work on threshing day. He remembered coming indoors for a drink and shaking the chaff-dust from his clothes and hair. Her best black skirt lay like a shroud on the kitchen table. He remembered her look of alarm in case the dust disfigured the velvet.

'I shall only go to one funeral now,' she had said. 'And that will be my own.'

Her scissors sliced the skirt into strips. Next, she cut into the dresses of gaily-coloured calico – all reeking of camphor after forty years in a trunk. Then she stitched together the two halves of her life – the early days in India, and her days on the Black Hill.

She had said, 'It will be something to remember me by.'

The quilt was ready by Christmas. Some time before that, though, Lewis had stood behind her chair and noticed, for the first time, her shortness of breath and the solid blue veins on her hands. She had seemed far younger than seventy-two, partly on account of her unlined face, partly because of her hair which grew, if anything, browner with the years. He had realized then that the triangle – of son, mother and son – would shortly cease to be.

'Yes,' she had said, wearily. 'I have a heart.'

For some time, the household had been troubled and divided.

Lewis suspected both his mother and brother of conspiring against him: the fact that he was womanless was all a part of their plan. He resented the way they kept him in ignorance of the farm's finances. Surely he too should have his say? He insisted on checking the accounts; but as he puzzled over the columns of credits and debits, Mary would brush his cheek with her sleeve and murmur softly, 'You've no head for figures, that's all. It's nothing to be ashamed of. So why not leave it to Benjamin?'

He resented, too, their stinginess, which seemed to him unjust. If ever he asked for a new piece of machinery, she would wring her hands and say, 'I'd love to give it to you. We're broke, I'm afraid. It'll have to wait till next year now.' Yet *they* always had enough money when it came to buying land.

She and Benjamin bought land with a passion, as if with each new acre they could push back the frontier of the hostile world. But extra land meant extra work; and when Lewis suggested replacing the horses with a tractor, they gasped.

'A tractor?' said Benjamin. 'You must be cracked.'

He was terribly angry when both came back from the lawyer's in Rhulen and announced that they had bought Lower Brechfa.

'Bought what?'

'Lower Brechfa.'

Three years had passed since Mrs Musker's death and her smallholding had gone to ruin. Docks and thistles had invaded the pasture. The yard was a sea of nettles. Slates were missing from the roof and, in the bedroom, there was a barn-owl nesting.

'Farm it yourself,' Lewis snapped. 'It's a sin to take a dead woman's land. I'll not set foot on the place.'

In the end he relented — as he always relented — though not before he had sinned on his own. He drank in pubs and went out of his way to befriend some new people who had settled in the neighbourhood.

At Rhulen market, he had found himself standing within a few feet of a strange, long-legged woman, with scarlet lips and nails, and sunglasses set in wedges of white bakelite. On her arm was a large wicker basket. A younger man was with her and, when he let fall a couple of eggs, she pushed the sunglasses up on to her forehead and drawled in a gravelly voice, 'Darling, don't be so hopeless...'

XXXVI

JOY AND NIGEL LAMBERT were an artist's wife and an artist, who had rented a cottage at Gillifaenog.

The artist had once had a successful exhibition in London and was soon to be seen, with paintbox and easel, sketching the effects of cloud and sunshine on the hill. His wreath of fair curls must once have been 'angelic', and already he was running to fat.

The Lamberts shared a conspiracy of gin, but not a bed. They had kicked around the Mediterranean for five years, and had come back to England in the belief that there was going to be a war. Both lived in terror of being considered middle class.

Because of their fondness for peasants — the 'Earlies' as they called them — they drank three nights a week at the Shepherd's Rest, where Nigel impressed the locals with his stories of the Spanish Civil War. On wet nights, he would sweep into the bar wearing a thick wool cape with a brown smear down the front. This, he said, was the blood of a Republican soldier, who had died in his arms. But Joy was bored by his stories, having heard them all before: 'Did you really, duckie?' she'd chip in. 'God! It must have been ghastly!'

As long as she was decorating her house, Joy was too busy to pay much attention to her neighbours: if she did take in the Jones twins, they were 'two boys living with their mum'.

She had always been famous for her taste, and her ability to 'make do' on a shoestring. She would add a touch of blue to the whitewash of one wall, and a dash of ochre to the other. Instead of a dining-table, she used an old paper-hanger's trestle. The curtains were made of wadding, the sofa covered in horse-blankets, and the cushions in saddler's plaid. She loathed 'amusing' objects on principle. She owned one work of art, a Picasso etching, and she banished Nigel's paintings to the studio-barn.

One day, looking round the room, she said, 'What this

room needs is one...good...chair!' And she must have cast
her eye over hundreds of rush-seated cottage chairs before
finding the *one*, beautifully battered example at The Rock.

Nigel had been sketching there all day, and she went up to
fetch him: her foot was hardly through the door before she
whispered, 'God! There's my chair! Ask the old girl how
much she wants for it!'

On another occasion, calling in at The Vision to buy some
of Mary's farm-butter, she spotted an old brawn jar poking
out of the rubbish dump: 'Gosh! What a pot!' she cried,
fingering the crackled grey glaze.

'Well, you can have it if you can use it,' said Lewis,
doubtfully.

'I need it for flowers.' She grinned. 'Wild flowers! Hate
garden flowers,' she added, sweeping her arm contemp-
tuously over Benjamin's pansies and wallflowers.

A month later, Lewis passed her in the lane with a foxglove in either hand, one of them freakishly pale:

'Now, Mr Jones, I need your advice. Which one would
you choose?'

'Thank you very much,' said Lewis, completely non-
plussed.

'No! Which one d'you like best?'

'That one.'

'Quite right,' she said, chucking the darker one over the
hedge. 'The other was awful.'

She asked him to call in, and he went, astonished to find
her, in pink sailor pants and a red headscarf, hacking down a
lilac bush and dragging the branches onto a bonfire.

'Don't you absolutely loathe lilac?' she said, the smoke
billowing round her legs.

'I can't say I've given much thought to it myself.'

'I have,' she said. 'Smell's made me sick as a dog all week.'

Later in the afternoon, when Nigel came in for his mug of
tea, she said, 'Know something? I've rather taken a shine to
Lewis Jones.'

'Oh?' he said. 'Which one's that?'

'Really, darling! You *are* unobservant!'

She next met Lewis, on the day of the sheep drive, in the bar of the Shepherd's Rest.

From seven in the morning, farmers on horseback had been clearing the hill, and the bleating white mass was now safe in Evan Bevan's paddock, waiting to be sorted after lunch.

The day was hot, the hills hazy, and the thornbushes looked like little bits of fluff.

Nigel, in a boisterous mood, insisted on buying drinks all round. Lewis was leaning on his elbows with his back to the sill. The net curtains ballooned around his shoulders. His hair was glossy black, parted in the centre, with a fleck or two of grey. He blinked through his steel-rimmed glasses, smiling occasionally as he tried to follow Nigel's story.

Joy glanced up from her gin. She liked his strong white teeth. She liked the way his belt bunched up his corduroys. She liked his big hand around the dimples of the tankard. She had caught him looking at the lipstick on the rim of her glass.

'O.K. You prude!' she thought. She stubbed out a cigarette and came to two conclusions: (a) that Lewis Jones was a virgin; (b) that this was going to be a long operation.

Halfway through the shearing, Nigel walked up to The Vision and asked if he could make some drawings of the men at work.

'I'd not be the one to stop you,' said Benjamin, pleasantly.

It was cool and dark in the shearing shed. Flies were spinning round the dusty sunbeams that fell through the chinks in the roof. All afternoon, the artist sat crouched against a hay-bale with the sketch-pad on his knees. At sunset, when the cider keg came out, he followed Benjamin to the fowl-house and said he had something to discuss.

He wanted to make a set of twelve etchings to illustrate 'The Sheep Farmer's Year'. He had a poet friend in London who, he was sure, would write a sonnet for every month. Would he, Mr Jones, consent to pose as the model?

Benjamin frowned. Instinctively, he mistrusted anyone

'from off'. He knew what a sonnet was, but wasn't so sure about an etching.

He shook his head: 'We're busy just now. I couldn't see my way to sparing the time.'

'It wouldn't take *time!*' Nigel cut him short. 'You'd go on with your work, and I'd just follow and make drawings.'

'Well,' Benjamin stroked his chin apprehensively. 'That's all right then, isn't it?'

During the summer and autumn of '38, Nigel sketched Benjamin Jones — with his dogs, with his crook, with his castrating knife, on the hill, in the valley, or with a sheep slung over his shoulder like an Ancient Greek statue.

On the damp days, he wore his Spanish cape and carried a brandy flask in his pocket. He always bragged a bit when he drank; and it was a relief to have, as an audience, someone who knew nothing of Spain and couldn't check the details of his stories.

And there were things in the stories that reminded Benjamin of his weeks in the Detention Barracks — things the guards made him do; dirty, shameful things; things he had never told Lewis, which now he could get off his chest.

'Yes, they often do that,' Nigel said, eyeing him up and down, and then looking at the ground.

Both the Lamberts grated on Mary's nerves. She knew they were dangerous and tried to warn her sons that these strangers were only playing games. She despised Nigel for lacing his plummy voice with working-class slang. To Benjamin she said, 'He's such a wet': to Lewis, 'I can't think why you like that woman. All that make-up! She looks like a parrot!'

Every week or so, Mrs Lambert hired Lewis to take her riding. And one misty evening, when they were out on the hill, Nigel appeared at The Vision with news that he'd be leaving next day for London.

'How long'll you be gone?' asked Benjamin.

'Can't say,' the artist answered. 'It all depends on Joy; but we're bound to be back for the lambing.'

'Better be!' Benjamin grumbled, and went on cranking the beet-pulper.

At two that afternoon, Joy had gulped down a quick snack, swallowed three cups of strong black coffee, and was pacing up and down outside her cottage, waiting for Lewis Jones.

'He's late! Damn and blast him!' She whisked her riding-crop at a dead thistle.

The valley was lost in the fog. Spider's webs, wavering white with dew, were stretched over the dead grass; and all she could see, down the line of the hedge, were the grey receding shapes of oak trees. Nigel was in his studio, playing Berlioz on the gramophone.

'Hate Berlioz!' she cried out loud when the record came to an end. 'Berlioz, my dear one, is a bore!'

She examined her reflection in the kitchen window – a pair of long, clean-cut legs in beige breeches. She flexed her knees so that they fitted more snugly into the fork. She undid the button of her russet riding-coat. Underneath she wore a pale grey jersey. She felt comfortable and energetic in these clothes. Her face was framed in a white headscarf and, pinned to it, there was a man's pork-pie.

She smoothed her lipstick with her little finger. 'God! I'm too old for this kind of caper,' she murmured, and heard the ponies thudding over the turf.

'Late!' she grinned.

'Very sorry, mam!' said Lewis, smiling shyly from under his hat-brim. 'I had a spot of bother with my brother. Him was none too keen on it. Says as we might get lost in the fog, like.'

'Well, you're not afraid of getting lost?'

'No, mam!'

'So there! Besides, it'll be sunny on the tops. Just you wait!'

He handed her the reins of the grey. She cocked her leg and swung into the saddle. She led and he followed. They trotted along the track to Upper Brechfa.

The hawthorns made a tunnel over their heads; the branches ripped against her hat, and showered her with crystal drops.

'Hope to God the pins stay in,' she said and kicked the horse into a canter.

They passed the Shepherd's Rest and stopped at the gate that leads on to the mountain. She opened the latch with her riding-crop. When she closed it behind him, he said, 'Thank you very much.'

The path was muddy and the gorse brushed their boots. She leaned forwards, rubbing herself against the pommel. The damp mountain air filled her lungs. They saw a buzzard. On ahead it was already looking lighter.

Coming to a clump of larches, she cried, 'Look! What did I tell you? The sun!' The golden hair of the larches shone out against a milky blue sky.

Then they cantered on into the sunlight with the clouds spread out below, on and on, for miles it seemed, until she reined in her pony at the edge of a gully. In a hollow, out of the wind, there were three Scots pines.

She dismounted and walked towards them, dribbling a pine-cone over the close-cropped turf.

'I love Scots pines,' she said. 'And when I'm very very old I'd like to look like one. Know what I mean?'

He was breathing beside her, hot under his mackintosh. She clawed at the bark, a flake of which came away in her hand. An earwig scuttled for safety. Judging that the moment had come, she transferred her lacquered fingers from the tree-trunk to his face.

It was dark when she pushed through the door of the cottage, and Nigel was drowsing by the fire. She banged her riding-crop on the table. There were moss-stains on her breeches: 'You lost the bet, duckie. You owe me a bottle of Gordon's.'

'You had him?'

'Under an ancient pine! Very romantic! Rather damp!'

From the moment Lewis crossed the threshold, Mary knew exactly what had happened.

He was walking differently. His eyes roamed the room like a stranger's. He stared at her, as if she too were a stranger. With trembling hands, she served a giblet pie. The silver spoon glinted. A wisp of steam curled up. He went on staring as though he'd never sat at supper in his life.

She toyed with her food, but could not bring herself to eat it. She sat waiting for Benjamin to explode.

He pretended to notice nothing. He cut a sliver of bread and began mopping the juices off his plate. Then his voice rasped out: 'What's that you got on your cheek?'

'Nothing,' Lewis faltered, fumbling for a napkin to wipe away the lipstick, but Benjamin had nipped round the table and rammed his face up close.

Lewis panicked. His right fist smashed into his brother's teeth, and he ran from the house.

XXXVII

H E WENT AWAY, to work on a pig farm near Weobley in Herefordshire. Two months later, drawn irresistibly in the direction of home, he got a job in Rhulen, as a porter for an agricultural merchant. He bunked on the premises and spoke to no one. The farmers who came into the offices were astonished by the blankness of his stare.

Because he sent no word to his mother, she arranged, one afternoon, for a neighbour to give her a lift into town.

A sharp wind was whistling down Castle Street. Her eyes watered; and the shops, the housefronts and pedestrians dissolved into a greyish blur. Holding her hat, she pushed her steps along the pavement and then turned left, out of the wind, into Horseshoe Yard. Outside the merchant's a cart was being loaded with meal-sacks.

Another sack came out through the double doors.

She gave a start at the sight of the bony, sunken-eyed man

in dirty dungarees. His hair had gone grey. Around one wrist there was a vicious purple scar.

'What's that?' she asked when they were alone.

'If thy right hand offend thee...' he murmured.

She gasped, covered her mouth – and breathed out, 'Thank heaven for that!'

She slipped her arm into his, and they walked towards the river and out along the bridge. The Wye was in spate. A heron stood in the shallows and, on the far bank, a fisherman was casting for salmon. Snow lay on the tops of the Radnor Hills. With their backs to the wind they watched floodwater sluicing past the piles.

'No.' She was quivering all over. 'You can't come home yet. It's terrible to see your brother in such a state.'

Benjamin's love for Lewis was murderous.

Spring came. The celandines made stars in the hedgerows. It still seemed that Benjamin's anger would never die down. To take her mind off her misery, Mary wore herself out with housework; she darned every moth-hole she could find in the blankets; she knitted socks for both her sons; she stocked the store-cupboard and cleaned the dirt from hidden crevices – as though these were preparations before leaving on a journey. Then, when she could work no more, she would collapse into the rocking chair and listen to the beating of her heart.

Images of India kept passing before her eyes. She saw a shimmering flood-plain, and a white dome afloat in the haze. Men in turbans were bearing a cloth-bound bundle to the shore. There were fires smouldering, and kitehawks spiralling above. A boat glided by downstream.

'The river! The river!' she whispered, and shook herself out of her reverie.

One day in the first week of September, she woke with flatulence and indigestion. She fried a few rashers of bacon for Benjamin's breakfast but lacked the strength to fork them from the skillet. A pain gripped her chest. He had carried her to the bedroom before the attack.

He jumped on his bike, rode to the call-box at Maesyfelin, and phoned for the doctor.

At six that evening, Lewis came in from delivering a load

of cow-cake. In the office the clerk was glued to the wireless, listening to the latest news from Poland. He glanced up and told him to call the surgery.

'Your mother's had a coronary,' Dr Galbraith told him. 'Looks like a bad one to me. I've given her morphine and she's hanging on. But I'd get up there quick as you can.'

Benjamin was kneeling on the far side of the bed. The evening sunlight raked in through the larches, and touched the black frame of the Holman Hunt engraving. She was sweating. Her skin was yellowish, and her gaze fixed intently on the doorknob. The name of Lewis rustled on her lips. Her hands lay motionless on the black velvet stars.

A motor sounded in the lane.

'He's come,' said Benjamin. From the dormer window, he watched his brother paying off the taxi.

'He's come,' she repeated. And when her head dropped sideways on the pillow, Benjamin was holding her right hand, and Lewis her left.

In the morning they hung black crêpe over the beehives to tell the bees that she had gone.

The night after the funeral was the night of their weekly bath.

Benjamin boiled the copper in the back-kitchen, and spread a cloth over the hearthrug. They took turns to soap each other's backs, and scrub them with a loofah. Their favourite sheepdog crouched beside the tub, his head on his forepaws, and the flamelight fluttering in his eyes. Lewis rubbed himself dry and saw, laid out on the table, two of their father's unbleached white calico nightshirts.

They put them on.

Benjamin had lit the lamp in their parents' room. He said, 'Give us a hand with the sheets.'

From the chest of drawers they unfolded a pair of fresh linen sheets. Grains of lavender fell at Lewis's feet. They made the bed and smoothed down the patchwork quilt. Benjamin plumped up the pillows; and a feather, that had worked its way through the ticking, floated upwards in the lamplight.

They climbed into bed.

'Goodnight now!'

'Goodnight!'

United at last by the memory of their mother, they forgot that all of Europe was in flames.

XXXVIII

THE WAR WASHED over them without disturbing their solitude.

Now and then, the drone of an enemy bomber, or some niggling wartime restriction, reminded them of the fighting beyond the Malvern Hills. But the Battle of Britain was too big for Lewis's scrapbook. An invasion scare – of German parachutists on the Brecon Beacons – was a false alarm. And when, one November night, Benjamin saw a red glow on the horizon and the sky lit up with incendiary flares – it was the Coventry Raid – he said, 'And a good job t'isn't we!' – and went back to bed.

Lewis thought of joining the Home Guard but Benjamin dissuaded him from doing so.

In Chapel, the twins sat side by side in their parents' pew. Before each meeting they spent an hour or so, lost in silent meditation by the grave. Some Sundays, especially if there was a Bible-class beforehand, Little Meg the Rock came with one of her foster-sisters; and the sight of her, an angular waif in a moth-eaten beret, revived in Lewis memories of lost love, and sadness.

One blustery morning, she came in, blue with cold, clutching at a bunch of snowdrops. The preacher had the habit of reciting the first verse of a hymn, and then making one of the children repeat it line by line. After announcing

Hymn Number Three—William Cowper's 'Praise for the Fountain Opened'—his finger fell on Meg:

There is a fountain fill'd with blood
Drawn from Emmanuel's veins
And sinners plunged beneath that flood
Lose all their guilty stains.

Tightening her grip on the snowdrops, Meg struggled through the first line, but the effort of 'Emmanuel's veins' choked her to silence. The crushed flowers fell at her feet, and she started sucking her thumb.

The schoolteacher said there was 'nothing to be done with the child'. Yet, though Meg neither read nor wrote nor did the simplest sums, she could mimic the voice of any animal or bird; and she embroidered white lawn handkerchiefs with garlands of flowers and leaves.

'Yes,' the teacher confided in Lewis, 'Meg's a handy little needlewoman. I believe it was Miss Fifield as taught her the art'—adding, for the sake of gossip, that young Billy Fifield was a pilot in the R.A.F., and that Rosie was alone at The Tump, laid up with bronchitis.

After lunch, Lewis packed a basket of provisions and filled a can of milk from the dairy. A pewter sun hung low over the Black Hill. The milk sloshed against the lid as he walked. The beeches were grey behind the cottage, and rooks flew off, their wingtips glinting like flakes of ice. There were Christmas roses flowering in the garden.

It was twenty-four years since they had met.

Rosie shuffled to the door in a man's overcoat. Her eyes were blue as ever, but her cheeks were hollow and her hair was grey. Her jaw dropped when she saw the tall greying stranger on the doorstep.

'I heard you was poorly,' he said. 'So I brought you some things.'

'So it's Lewis Jones,' she wheezed. 'Come on in and warm yourself.'

The room was cramped and dingy, and the whitewash flaking from the wall. On a ledge over the fireplace were tea-canisters and her clock of the Heavenly Twins. A chromolithograph hung on the back wall — of a blonde girl picking a posy along a woodland path. Slung over an armchair was a needlework sampler, half completed. A tortoiseshell butterfly, awoken by the sunlight, flapped against the window, although its wings were trapped in a dusty cobweb. The floor was strewn with books. On the table were some jars of pickled onions — which were all she had to eat.

She unpacked the basket, greedily examining the honey and biscuits, the brawn and bacon, spreading them out without a word of thanks.

'Sit down and I'll make you a cup of tea,' she said, and went to the scullery to rinse the teacups.

He looked at the picture and remembered their walks along the river.

She took a bellows to sharpen up the fire, and as the flames licked the sooty underside of the kettle, her coat fell open revealing a pink flannelette nightie slipping off her shoulder. He asked about Little Meg.

Her face lit up: 'She's a good girl. Honest as the day! Not like them others and all their thieving! Ooh! It makes my blood boil the way they treat her. Her as never harmed a living thing. I've seen her in the garden here, and the finches feeding out of her hand.'

The tea was scalding hot. He sipped it, uneasily, in silence.

'He's dead, isn't he?' Her voice was sharp and accusing.

He paused before taking another sip, and said, 'I'm very sorry to hear it.'

'What's it to you?'

'In an aeroplane, was it?'

'Not him!' she snapped. 'I don't mean my Billy. I mean the father!'

'Bickerton?'

'Aye, Bickerton!'

'Well, him's dead for sure,' he answered. 'In Africky, as I did hear it. It was the drink as killed him.'

'And a good job!' she said.

Before leaving, he foddered her sheep, which had gone a whole week without hay. He took the milk-can and promised to come back on Thursday.

She clutched his hand and breathed, 'Till Thursday then?'
She watched him from the bedroom window walking
away along the line of hawthorns, with the sunlight passing
through his legs. Five times, she wiped the condensation
from the pane until the black speck vanished from view.

'It's no good,' she said out loud. 'I hate men – all of them!'

On the Thursday, her bronchitis was better and though
she was able to talk more freely, only one topic held her
attention: Lurkenhope Castle, which had just been requisi-
tioned for American troops.

The place had lain empty for five years.

Reggie Bickerton had died, of D.T.s in Kenya, in the year
that his coffee plantation failed. The Estate had passed to a
distant cousin, who had had to pay a second round of
death-duties. Isobel, too, had died, in India; and Nancy had
moved into a flat above the stables – which, so her father said,
were better built than the house. And there she lived, alone
with her pugs, fretting about her mother who was interned in
the South of France.

She gave a dinner-party for some black G.I.s and people
said the strangest things.

Apart from the Negro boxer at the Rhulen Fair, the twins
had never set eyes on a black man. Now, hardly a day passed
without their meeting these tall dark strangers, sauntering
round the lanes in twos and threes.

Benjamin pretended to be shocked by the stories coming
out of the Castle. Could it be true they ripped up the
floorboards and burned them in the grate?

'Ooh!' he rubbed his hands. 'It be hot where them do come
from.'

One frosty evening, walking home from Maesyfelin, he
was hailed by a nattily turned-out giant:

'Hi, feller! I'm Chuck!'

'I'm not so bad myself,' said Benjamin, shyly.

The man's expression was grave. He stopped to talk, and
spoke of the war and the horrors of Nazism. But when
Benjamin asked what it was like to live 'in Africky', he

creased with laughter, and clung to his stomach as if he were never going to stop. Then he disappeared into the darkness, flashing a broad white grin over the turned-up collar of his greatcoat.

Another memorable occasion was the day when troops from the Dominions staged a mock-assault on Bickerton's Knob.

The twins came back from drenching some calves at Lower Brechfa to find the farmyard swarming with 'darkies', some in lop-sided hats, some with their heads 'wrapped in towels' — they were Gurkhas and Sikhs — all 'chittering away like monkeys and scaring off the fowls'.

But the big event of the war was the crashed plane.

The pilot of an Avro Anson, flying home from a reconnaissance, misjudged the height of the Black Hill and pancaked into the bluff above Craig-y-Fedw. A survivor limped down the escarpment and roused Jim the Rock, who went up with the search-party and found the pilot dead.

'I see'd 'im,' Jim said afterwards. 'Froze to death, like, an' 'is face split open an' all 'angin' down.'

The Home Guard sealed off the area, and removed seven cartloads of wreckage from the site.

Lewis was very disappointed that Jim had seen the crash and he had not. All he found, strewn over the heather, were some shreds of canvas and a strip of aluminium with a bolt through it. He stuffed these into his pockets, and kept them as souvenirs.

Meanwhile, Benjamin had taken advantage of a depressed market to add a farm of sixty acres to the list of their possessions.

The Pant lay half a mile down the valley, and had two big arable fields on either side of the brook. Ploughed and planted, these yielded an excellent crop of potatoes; and to help with the harvest, the man from the Ministry assigned the twins a German prisoner-of-war.

His name was Manfred Kluge. He was a beefy, pink-cheeked fellow from a country district of Baden-Württemburg, whose father, the village woodman, had flogged him sadistically, and whose mother was dead.

Drafted into the Army, he had served in the Afrika Korps: his capture at El Alamein was one of the few strokes of fortune he had known.

The twins never tired of listening to his stories:

'I have seen the Führer with my eyes, *Ja!* I am in Siegmaringen. *Ja!*...And many peoples! Verrymanypeoples! *Ja! "Heil Hitler!"*..."*Heil Hitler!" Ja?*...*Ja?* And I say "Fool!" LOUD!! And this man next me in crowd...Verrybigman. RED-FACE-BIG-MAN...*Ja?* He say me, "You say, Fool!" And I say him, "*Ja*, very fool!" And he hit! *Ja?* And other peoples all hit! *Ja?* And I run away...! Ha! Ha! Ha!'

Manfred was a hard worker. At the end of the day, there were sweat-rings under the armpits of his uniform; and with the indulgence of doting parents, the twins gave him other clothes to wear about the house. A third cap in the porch, a third pair of boots, a third place at table — all helped remind them that life had not entirely passed them by.

He wolfed his food and was always ready with a show of affection as long as there was a square meal in sight. He was neat in his personal habits, and slept in the attic in Old Sam's room. Every Thursday, he had to report to barracks. The twins dreaded Thursdays in case he was transferred elsewhere.

Because he had a special talent for poultry, they allowed Manfred to breed his own flock of geese and keep the proceeds as pocket money. He loved his geese, and they could be heard burbling to each other in the orchard: '*Komm, mein Lieseli! Komm...schon! Komm zu Vati!*'

Then, one lovely spring morning, the war came to an end with a bold headline in the *Radnorshire Gazette*:

51½lb SALMON 'GRASSED'
AT COLEMAN'S POOL

*Brigadier tells of 3-hour
struggle with titanic fish*

For readers who wished to keep abreast of international events, there was a shorter column on the far side of the page: 'Allies enter Berlin — Hitler dead in Bunker — Mussolini killed by Partisans.'

As for Manfred, he was equally indifferent to the Fall of Germany, though he brightened up, a few months later, on seeing in the *News of the World* a photo of the mushroom cloud above Nagasaki:

'Is good, *Ja?*'

'No.' Benjamin shook his head. 'It's terrible.'

'*Nein, nein!* Is good! Japan finish! War finish!'

That night, the twins had an identical nightmare: that their bed-curtains had caught fire, their hair was on fire, and their heads burned down to smouldering stumps.

Manfred showed no signs of wanting to go home when the first batches of prisoners were repatriated. He spoke of settling in the district, with a wife and a poultry-farm; and the twins encouraged him to stay.

Unfortunately, he had a very weak head for liquor. Once the wartime restrictions were lifted, he struck up a drinking friendship with Jim the Rock. He would stagger home at all hours, and the twins would find him, next morning, dead drunk in the straw. Benjamin suspected him of messing with one of the Watkins girls, and wondered whether they ought to get rid of him.

One summer afternoon, they heard the gander honking and hissing and Manfred gabbling away in German.

Coming out through the porch, they saw in the farmyard a middle-aged woman in brown corduroy trousers and a blue aertex shirt. She held a map in her hand. Her face lit up as she turned to face them:

'So!' she exclaimed. 'Tvinss!'

XXXIX

A TALL STATUESQUE WOMAN, with slanting grey eyes and golden braids like hawsers, Lotte Zons had left Vienna not a month too soon. Her father, a surgeon, had been too ill to travel, her sister blind to the danger. She had arrived at Victoria Station with a domestic science diploma in her handbag; in the spring of 1939, to come as a servant was the only sure way of getting into England.

Her love of England, deriving as it did from English literature, had mixed in her memory with hikes in the Voraarlberg, gentians, the scent of pines, and the pages of Jane Austen blinding her in the alpine sunlight.

She moved with the ample grace of ladies in the age before Sarajevo. Her life in wartime London had been grimmer than anything she had known.

First, she was interned. Then, because of her training as a psychotherapist, she got a job treating air-raid victims at a clinic in Swiss Cottage. Her salary scarcely paid the rent of a cheerless room. Her strength ebbed away on a diet of corned beef and packet potato. A solitary gas-ring was her only means of cooking.

Sometimes, she met other Jewish refugees in a Hampstead café; but the nusstorte was uneatable, the backbiting made her even more miserable, and she would grope her way home through the foggy, blacked-out streets.

As long as the war went on, she allowed herself the luxury of hope. Now, with victory, hope had gone. No word came from Vienna. After seeing the pictures of Belsen, she broke down completely.

The head of the clinic suggested she take a holiday.

'I could do,' she said, doubtfully, 'but where will I find some mountains?'

She took a train to Hereford, and the bus to Rhulen. For days she lost herself along leafy lanes unchanged since the time of Queen Elizabeth. A pint of draught cider went to her head. She read Shakespeare in ivy-covered church-yards.

On her last day, feeling so much stronger, she climbed the summit of the Black Hill.

'Aah!' she sighed in English. 'Here at last von can breeze...!'

She happened to walk back through The Vision yard and

overheard Manfred talking, in German, to his geese.

Lewis shook hands with the visitor and said, 'Please to come on in.' After tea, she jotted down Benjamin's recipe for Welsh cakes, and he offered to show her the house.

He opened the door of the bedroom without a trace of embarrassment. Her eyebrow arched at the sight of their lace-trimmed pillow-cases: 'So you loved your mother very much?'

Benjamin lowered his head.

Before leaving, she asked if they would welcome her again.

'If you would come,' he said; for something in her manner had reminded him of Mary.

In the following year, she came at the end of September at the wheel of a small grey coupé. She asked for 'my young friend Manfred' and Benjamin frowned: 'We had to put him over the door, like.'

Manfred had got Lizzie the Rock into trouble. He had, however, done the 'gentlemanly thing' and married her, thus securing his right to remain in Britain. The couple had gone to Kington to work on a poultry farm.

Lotte took the twins on motoring expeditions round the countryside.

They visited megalithic tombs, crumbling abbeys, and a church with a Holy Thorn. They walked along a stretch of Offa's Dike and climbed Caer Cradoc, where Caractacus made his stand against the Romans.

Their interest in antiquities revived. Against the chill autumn winds, she wore a plum cord jacket with big patch pockets and padded shoulders. She recorded their comments in a buckram-bound notebook.

She seemed to have absorbed the entire contents of the lending library. There was something terrifying about her grasp of local history; and at times she could be quite tigerish.

On a trip to Painscastle, they met an elderly man in plus-fours, an amateur antiquary who was measuring the moat. He mentioned in passing that Owen Glendower had defended the castle in 1400.

'Qvite hrongg!' she contradicted. The battle was at Pilleth, not Painscastle—in 1401, not 1400. The man looked flustered, excused himself, and fled.

Lewis laughed: 'Oooh! She do have her head screwed on!'—and Benjamin agreed.

She had taken a room in a bed-and-breakfast place in Rhulen, and showed no sign of wanting to return to London. Little by little, she broke through their shyness. She earned her place as the third person in their lives and ended up extracting their most intimate secrets.

Not that she made a secret of her interest in them! She told them that, before the war in Vienna, she had made a study of twins who had never separated. Now, she would like to continue it.

Twins, she said, play a role in most mythologies. The Greek pair, Castor and Pollux, were the sons of Zeus and a swan, and had both popped out of the same egg:

'Like you two!'

'Fancy!' They sat up.

She went on to explain the difference between one-egg and two-egg twins; why some are identical and others not. It was a very windy night and gusts of smoke blew back down the chimney. They clutched their heads as they tried to make sense of her dizzying display of polysyllables, but her words seemed to drift towards the borderland of nonsense: '...psychoanalysis...questionnaires...problems of heredity and environment...' What did it all mean? At one point, Benjamin got up and asked her to write the word 'monozygotic' on a scrap of paper. This he folded and slipped in his waistcoat pocket.

She wound up by saying that many identical twins were inseparable—even in death.

'Ah!' sighed Benjamin in a dreamy voice. 'That's as I always felt.'

She clasped her hands, leaned forward in the lamplight, and asked if they would answer a full range of questions.

'I'd not be the one to stop you,' he said.

Lewis sat upright on the settle and stared into the fire. He did not want to answer questions. He seemed to hear his mother saying, 'Beware of this foreign woman!' But in the end, to please Benjamin, he relented.

Lotte followed the twins on their daily round. Neither was accustomed to making confessions; but her warm understanding and harsh guttural accent struck a proper balance of proximity and distance. She had soon compiled a sizeable dossier.

At first, Benjamin gave her the impression of being a biblical fundamentalist.

She asked, 'Then how do you imagine Hell-fire?'

'Something like London, I expect.' He screwed up his nose and sniggered. Only when she probed a little further did she discover that his concept of the life-to-come — whether in Heaven or in Hell — was a blank and hopeless void. How could you believe in an immortal soul, when your own soul, if you had one, was the image of your brother across the breakfast table?

'Then why do you go to Chapel?'

'Because of Mother!'

Both twins said they hated being mistaken for one another. Both recalled mistaking their own reflection for their other half: 'And once,' Lewis added, 'I mistook my own echo.' But when she steered her enquiry in the direction of the bedroom, she drew an identical, innocent blank.

She noticed it was Benjamin who poured the tea, while Lewis cut the loaf; Lewis who fed the dogs, and Benjamin the fowls. She asked how they divided their labour, and each replied, 'I reckon we done it atween we.'

Lewis remembered how, at school, he had given all his money to Benjamin and ever since, the idea of owning sixpence — let alone a chequebook — was unthinkable.

One afternoon, Lotte found him in the cowshed, in a long brown work-coat, pitching the straw on to a cart. He was red in the face, and bothered. Skilfully timing her question, she asked if he was angry with Benjamin.

'Bloomin' mad!' he said: Benjamin had gone into Rhulen and was buying another field.

There wasn't any sense in it, he said. Not without a man to

193

work it! And Benjamin was far too tight to pay a man a wage! They should buy a tractor! That's what they should do!

'Catch him buying a tractor!' he muttered angrily. 'Sometimes I think I'd be better off on my own.'

Her melancholic gaze met his. He rested his pitchfork, and the anger died in him:

How he'd loved Benjamin! Loved him more than anything in the world. No one could deny that! But he'd always felt left out... 'Pushed out, you might say...'

He paused: 'I was the strong one and him was a poor mimmockin' thing. But him was always the smarter. Had more grounding, see? And Mother loved him for it!'

'Go on!' she said. He was close to tears.

'Aye, and that's the worry! Sometimes, I lie awake and wonder what'd happen if him weren't there. If him'd gone off...was dead even. Then I'd have had my own life, like? Had kids?'

'I know, I know,' she said, quietly. 'But our lives are not so simple.'

On her last Sunday Lotte drove the twins to Bacton to see the memorial to Dame Blanche Parry, a maid of Queen Elizabeth's bed-chamber.

The churchyard was choked with willow-herb. Fallen yew-berries made little red scabs along the path to the porch. The memorial had columns and a Roman arch and stood at the far end of the chancel. On the right sat a white marble effigy of the Queen herself—a jewel-encrusted manikin weighted under a chain of Tudor roses. Dame Blanche knelt beside her, in profile. Her face was drawn but beautiful, and in her hand she held a prayer book. She wore a ruff, and below it there hung a pectoral cross on a ribbon.

The church was chilly: Benjamin was bored. He sat outside in the car, while Lotte copied the inscription in her notebook:

> ...*So that my tyme I thus did passe awaye*
> *A maede in courte and never no man's wyffe*
> *Sworne of Quene Ellsbeths bedd chamber*

Alwaye with the maedn Quene
A maede did ende my lyffe.

She completed the line. The pencil fell from her hand and bounced from the altar-carpet on to the flagstone floor. For suddenly all the loneliness of her life came back to stifle her — the narrow spinster's bed, the guilt of leaving Austria, and the bitterness of the squabbles in the clinic.

Lewis stooped to recover the pencil; and he too recalled the misery of his first loves, and the fiasco of the third. He squeezed her hand and pressed it to his lips.

She withdrew it gently.

'No,' she said. 'It would not be correct.'

After high-tea, she took Benjamin aside and told him, in no uncertain terms, that he was going to buy Lewis a tractor.

XL

AGGIE WATKINS DIED during the terrible winter of '47. She was over ninety years of age. The snow had drifted over the roof, and she died in darkness.

Jim had run out of hay. The cows kept everyone awake with their bellowing. The dogs whimpered, and the cats nipped in and out with hunger-swollen eyes. Seven of his ponies were missing on the hill.

He shoved his mother into a sack, and laid her, frozen stiff on the woodpile, out of reach of the dogs, but not the cats or rats. Three weeks later, when the thaw set in, he and Ethel lashed her to a makeshift sled and hauled her down to Lurkenhope for burial. The sexton was staggered at the state of the corpse.

Jim found his ponies a few days later, all seven together, in a cleft among some rocks. They had died on their feet, in a circle, their muzzles pointing inwards like the spokes of a wheel. He wanted to dig a grave for them, but Ethel made him stay and help with the house.

A big bulge had appeared in the gable-end, and the whole wall seemed likely to collapse. Some rafters had given way under the weight of snow. The icy water had seeped through Jim's stuffed animals, and poured from the attic into the kitchen. And though he kept on saying, 'I'll get me a few tile an' fix 'em up like new,' all he ever did was spread a leaky tarpaulin over the roof.

When the spring came, he tried to buttress the wall with stones and railway-sleepers, but so undermined the foundations that it caved in completely. Next winter, no one lived in the east end of the house, and no one had to; for all the Watkins girls, except Little Meg, had left.

Lizzie, married to Manfred, pretended The Rock did not exist. Brennie had gone off with 'some kind o' darkie', a G.I., of whom nothing was heard until a postcard arrived from California. Then, at the May Fair in Rhulen, Sarah met a haulage contractor, who took her to live with him on his smallholding behind the Begwyns.

Sarah was a big-boned, blowzy young woman, with a tangle of black hair and a very unpredictable temper. Her one great fear was of lapsing into poverty; and this sometimes made her seem callous and grasping. Unlike Lizzie, however, she kept her eye on The Rock and made it her business to see they never starved.

In 1952, after another storm had made the kitchen uninhabitable, Ethel abandoned it to the hens and ducks and piled all the furniture into the one remaining room.

This place now looked like a junk-dealer's shed. Behind the curving settle was an oak chest, on top of which stood a tall-boy and a stack of cardboard boxes. Strewn over the tables were an assortment of pots, pans, mugs, jamjars, dirty plates, and usually a bucket of fowl-mash. All three occupants slept in the box-bed. The perishable food was stored in baskets that dangled from the roofbeams. Heaped up on the mantelpiece was every kind of object – from shaving bowls to sheep-shears – rusty, worm-eaten, smeared with candle-grease and speckled with the excrement of flies.

A file of headless lead soldiers marched along the window-sill.

As the wall-plaster crumbled, Jim tacked up sheets of newspaper and roofing felt.

'Aye,' he'd say optimistically, 'I be makin' it wind-proof, like.'

The smoke from the chimney covered everything with a film of brown resin. In time, the walls were so sticky that if a picture took his fancy – a postcard from California, the label off a tin of Hawaiian pineapple, or the legs of Rita Hayworth – all he had to do was slap it up – and there it stuck!

If a stranger came near, he would reach for his ancient muzzle-loader – without the shot or powder to charge it – and when the Tax Inspector came asking for a 'Mr James Watkins', Jim poked his head over the stockade and shook his head: ' 'Aven't see'd 'im in a good while. 'Im be gone to France! Fightin' the Germins, as I did 'ear it.'

Despite her attacks of emphysema, Ethel would walk into town on market day, striding briskly down the middle of the lane, always in the same dirty orange tweed coat, and a pair of shopping-bags slung at either end of a horse girth round her neck.

One day, on the crest of Cefn Hill, Lewis Jones drove up behind on his new tractor, whereupon she waved him to a halt, and nipped up on to the footplate.

From then on, she timed her departure to coincide with his. She never said a word of thanks for the lift, and would jump down at the War Memorial. The morning she spent scavenging round the stalls. Around noon, she called in at Prothero's Grocery.

Knowing her to be light-fingered, Mr Prothero winked at his assistant, as if to say, 'Keep an eye on the old girl, will you?' A kindly, shiny-faced man, bald as a Dutch cheese, he would always let her lift a can of sardines or cocoa. But if she overstepped the mark and took, say, a large tin of ham, he would slip round the counter, and block the door:

'Come along, Miss Watkins! What have we got in the bag

this morning? That one shouldn't be there, should it now?'
—and Ethel would stare stiffly out of the window.

This went on year after year until Mr Prothero retired and
sold his business. He told the new owners they should
pardon her peccadilloes; yet the first time Ethel stole a can
of Ideal Milk, they worked themselves into a fever of right-
eous indignation and called the police.

The next time it was a £5 fine: after that, six weeks in
Hereford jail.

She was never the same again. People saw her moving
through the market like a sleepwalker, stooping now and
then to pick up an empty cigarette packet and stuff it in her
bag.

One drizzly November night, the passengers waiting for
the last bus saw a figure slumped in the corner of the shelter.
The bus drew up and a man called, 'Wake up! Wake up!
You'll miss the bus.' He shook her, and she was dead.

Meg was nineteen at the time, a nice compact little person
with dimpled cheeks and eyes that seemed to outglare the
sun.

She woke at dawn and worked all day, never leaving The
Rock unless to gather whimberries on the hill. Sometimes, a
hiker saw her tiny figure rattling a bucket on the edge of the
pond, and a file of white ducks waddling towards her. She
would bolt for the house if anyone came near.

She never took off her clothes or her hat.

The hat, a grey felt cloche, had with age and greasy fingers
come to resemble a cowpat. Her two pairs of breeches—a
brown pair over a beige—had ripped around the knees,
leaving the lace-up parts as leggings, while the rest flapped,
in panels, from her waist. She wore five or six green jerseys
at a time, all so riddled with holes that patches of her skin
showed through. And when one jersey rotted away, she
would keep the wool and use it to mend the others with
hundreds of tiny green bows.

The sight of Meg in these clothes made Sarah feel very
vexed. She brought her blouses and cardigans and wind-

cheaters: but Meg only wore green jumpers and only if they were falling off her back.

On one of Sarah's visits, she found Jim squelching up to his ankles in the ooze:

'An' 'ow's you?' he grunted. 'An' what d'yer want anyway? Why can't yer leave us alone?'

'I come to see Meg, not you!' she snapped, and he limped off, cursing her under his breath. A week earlier, Meg had been complaining of pains in her abdomen.

Pushing past the hens, Sarah found Meg squatting by the fireside, listlessly fanning the embers in the grate. Her face was twisted with pain, and there were sores up her arms.

'You're coming with me,' Sarah said. 'I'm taking you to the doctor.'

Meg shuddered, swayed back and forth, and began to drone a repetitive dirge:

'No, Sarah, I'd not go from here. Very kind of you, Sarah, but I'd never go from here. Jim and me, we been together, like. We done the work together, like. Aye, and the foddering and the feeding and lived our lives together. And the poor ducks'd starve if I'd be gone. Aye, and the chicks'd starve. An' that poor ol' pullet in the box there! Her was all a-dying and I took her back to life. But her'd die if I'd be gone. And the birdies in the dingle, them'd die if I dinna feed them. And the cat? You canna say what'd happen to the cat if I'd be gone...'

Sarah tried to argue. The doctor, she said, was only three miles away, in Rhulen: 'Don't be daft! You can see his house from the hill. I'll take you down to surgery and bring you straight back.'

But Meg had slipped her fingers under her hat-brim and, covering her face with both palms, said, 'No, Sarah, I'd never go from here.'

A week later, she was in Hereford Hospital.

At dawn on the Friday Sarah was woken with a reverse-charge call from the phone-box at Maesyfelin. It was Jim the Rock, from whose incoherent sputterings she gathered that Meg was sick, if not actually dying.

The fields around Craig-y-Fedw were frozen hard: so she

was able to drive her van to the gate. The house and buildings were blanketed with fog. The dogs howled and tried to burst from their shelters. Jim was in the doorway, hopping up and down like a wounded bird.

'How is she?' Sarah asked.

'Bad,' he said.

In the front room the hens were still drowsing on their perches. Meg lay on the floor, eyes closed, amid the droppings. She was moaning quietly. They rolled her on to a plank and carried her to the van.

Halfway down the hill, the thought of taking Meg to the doctor in such a state made Sarah feel dreadfully ashamed. So instead of driving directly to Rhulen, she took the patient home, where, with soap, hot water and a decent coat, she made her look a little more presentable. By the time they reached the surgery, Meg was delirious.

A young doctor came out and climbed into the back of the van. 'Peritonitis.' He spat the word through his teeth and shouted to his secretary to call for an ambulance. He was very offensive to Sarah for not having brought her in sooner.

Later, Meg had only the haziest recollection of her weeks in hospital. The metal beds, the medicines, the bandages, the bright lights, lifts, trolleys and trays of shining implements were things so removed from her experience that she dismissed them as the fragments of a nightmare. Nor did the doctors tell her they had taken out her womb. All she did remember was what she was told: 'Run down! That's as 'em says I was and that's as I was. Run down! But them didna say the harf of it what buggered me.'

XLI

THE FIRST TRACTOR to arrive at The Vision was a Fordson Major. Its body was blue, its wheels were orange, and it had the name 'Fordson' written in raised orange letters down the sides of the radiator.

Lewis loved his tractor, thought of her as a woman, and wanted to give her a woman's name. He toyed with 'Maudie', then 'Maggie', then 'Annie'; but none of these names suited her personality, and she ended up with no name at all.

To begin with, she was extremely difficult to handle. She gave him a bad fright by slewing sideways into a ditch; and when he mistook her clutch for the brake-pedal, she landed him in the hedge. Yet once he had her under control, he thought of entering a ploughing competition.

He liked nothing better than to hear her firing on all eight cylinders, purring in neutral, or growling uphill with the plough behind.

Her engine, too, was perplexing as a woman's anatomy! He was forever checking her plugs, fiddling with her carburettor, poking his grease gun into her nipples, and fretting about her general state of health.

At the slightest splutter, he would reach for the maintenance manual and read aloud from the list of possible ailments: 'Wrongly set choke-valve...mixture too rich... defective leads...dirt in the float chamber' – while his brother pulled a face as though he were listening to obscenities.

Again and again, Benjamin groused over the cost of running the tractor and kept saying darkly, 'We'll have to go back to horses.' Having paid for a plough, a seed-drill and a link-box, there seemed no end to the number and cost of her accessories. Why did Lewis need a potato-spinner? What was the point of buying a baler? Or a muck-spreader? Where would it ever end?

Lewis shrugged off his brother's outbursts and left it to the accountant to explain that, far from being ruined, they were rich.

In 1953, they had a nasty brush with the Inland Revenue.

They hadn't paid one penny of taxes since Mary's death. And though the inspector treated them leniently, he insisted they take professional advice.

The young man who came to audit their books had the pimply and undernourished complexion of someone living in digs: yet even he was astonished by their frugality. They had clothes to last their lifetime; and since the grocery bill, the vet, and the agricultural merchant were all paid by cheque, they hardly ever handled cash.

'And what shall we put down to incidentals?' asked the accountant.

'Like money in our pockets?' said Benjamin.

'Pocket money, if you like!'

'About twenty pound?'

'A week?'

'Oh no, no...Twenty'd see us through the year.'

When the young man tried to explain the desirability of running at a loss, Benjamin puckered his forehead and said, 'That can't be right.'

By 1957, a large taxable profit had piled up in The Vision's farm account; and the accountant, too, had 'filled out'. A beer-stomach bulged over the belt of his cavalry twills. A hacking-jacket, yellow socks and chukka boots completed his outfit; and he kept foul-mouthing a Mr Nasser.

He thumped his fist on the table: 'Either you spend £5,000 on farm machinery, or you give it as a present to the Government!'

'I suppose we'd better buy another tractor,' said Benjamin.

Lewis pored over prospectuses and decided on an International Harvester. He cleared a stable in which to house her and chose a fine dry afternoon to drive her up from Rhulen.

She was not the kind of tractor one used. He would scrub her tyres, flick her with a duster, and drive her along the lane for an occasional airing; but for years he kept her, idly enshrined in the stable, under padlock and key. From time to time, he would peep through a chink in the door, feasting his eyes over her scarlet paintwork like a little boy peeping into a brothel.

The Fifties were years of spectacular air-crashes: two Comets tumbling from the sky, thirty spectators killed at the Farnborough Air Display. Benjamin had a hernia, The Vision was hitched up to mains electricity, and one by one the older generation fell ill and died. Hardly a month went by without a funeral service in Chapel and when old Mrs Bickerton died in the South of France — at the age of ninety-two she had drowned herself in her swimming-pool — there was a lovely memorial service in the parish church and Mrs Nancy the Castle gave a sit-down lunch for all the old tenants and estate workers.

The Castle itself lay crumbling into ruins until, one August evening, a schoolboy sneaked in to shoot rats with a bow-and-arrow, dropped a lighted cigarette butt, and the place went up in flames. Then in April of 1959, Lewis had his cycling accident.

He had been riding to Maesyfelin with a bunch of wall-flowers to lay on the graves. The afternoon was bitterly cold. The buckle of his overcoat worked loose; the belt caught in the front spokes — and over the handlebars he went! A plastic surgeon rebuilt his nose in Hereford Hospital and, for ever after, he was always a little deaf in one ear.

The day of their sixtieth birthday was almost a day of mourning.

Each time they tore a page from the calendar, they had forebodings of a miserable old age. They would turn to the wall of family photos — row on row of smiling faces, all of them dead or gone. How was it possible, they wondered, that they had come to be alone?

Their wrangles were over. They were inseparable now as they had been before Benjamin's childhood illness. But surely, somewhere, there was a cousin they could trust? What was the point of owning land, or tractors, if the one thing you lacked was an heir?

They looked at the picture of the Red Indian and thought of Uncle Eddie. Perhaps he had grandsons? But they would be in Canada and would never come back. They even considered their old friend Manfred's son, a pale-eyed lad who sometimes came to visit.

Manfred had started up his own poultry farm, in some Nissen huts put up for Polish refugees, and despite his thick guttural accent, he was now 'more English than the English'. He had changed his name by deed poll from Kluge to Clegg. He wore green tweed suits, rarely missed a point-to-point, and was Chairman of the local Conservative Association.

Proudly, he drove the twins to see his establishment; but the wire cages, the smell of chicken-shit and fish-meal, and the birds' raw, featherless necks so nauseated Benjamin that he preferred not to go there again.

In December 1965, the calendar showed a picture of the Norfolk Broads under ice. Then on the 11th—a date the twins would never forget—a rusty Ford van drove into the yard, and a woman in gumboots got out and introduced herself as a Mrs Redpath.

XLII

SHE HAD auburn hair going grey, and hazel eyes, and delicate rose-pink cheeks unusual in a woman of her age. For at least a minute she stood beside the garden gate, nervously fumbling with the latch. Then she said she had something of importance to discuss.

'Come on in now!' Lewis beckoned. 'And you'll have a cup of tea.'

She apologized for the mud on her boots.

'No harm in a bit of mud,' he said pleasantly.

She said, 'No bread-and-butter, thank you!' but accepted a slice of fruitcake, cutting it into neat little strips and placing each one, daintily, on the tip of her tongue. Now and then, she glanced round the room, and wondered out loud how the twins found time to dust 'all those curios'. She spoke of her husband, who worked for the Water Board. She spoke of the clement weather and the cost of Christmas shopping. 'Yes,' she replied to Benjamin, 'I could manage another cup.' She took a further four lumps of sugar and began to tell her story:

All her life, she had believed that her mother was the widow of a carpenter, who had to take in lodgers and had made her childhood a misery. Then last June, as the old woman lay dying, she had learned she was illegitimate, a foundling. Her real mother, a girl from a farm on the Black Hill, had left her to board in 1924 and gone overseas with an Irishman.

'Rebecca's baby,' murmured Lewis, and his teaspoon tinkled on the saucer.

'Aye,' breathed Mrs Redpath, summoning an emotional sigh. 'My mother was Rebecca Jones.'

She had checked her birth-certificate, checked the parish register — and here she was, their long-lost niece!

Lewis blinked at the handsome workaday woman before him, and saw, in her every gesture, a resemblance to his mother. Benjamin kept quiet. In the harsh shadow cast by the naked light bulb, he had noticed her unamiable mouth.

'Just you wait till you see my little Kevin!' She reached for a knife and cut herself another slice of cake. 'He's the spitting image of you both.'

She wanted to bring Kevin to The Vision the very next day, but Benjamin was none too keen: 'No. No. We'll come up and see him some time.'

All through the following week the twins were once again at loggerheads.

Lewis believed that Kevin Redpath had been sent as a gift from Providence. Benjamin suspected — even if the story were true, even if he was their great-nephew — that Mrs Redpath was bent on their money, and no good would come of it.

On the 17th, a Christmas card — of Santa Claus and a reindeer-sleigh — came 'With Seasons Greetings from Mr and Mrs Redpath, and Kevin!!' Tea was again on the table when she reappeared and asked if she could drive them, that very evening, to the nativity play at Llanfechan, where her son was playing Father Joseph himself.

'Aye, I'd come with you,' said Lewis, on impulse. And taking a kettle off the hob, he nodded to his brother and went upstairs to shave and dress. Left alone in the kitchen, Benjamin felt himself covered with embarrassment. Then he, too, followed upstairs to the bedroom.

It was dark when they came to leave. The sky was clear and the stars revolved like little wheels of fire. A hoar-frost blanketed the hedgerows and floury shapes rose up in the glare of the headlights. The van skidded on a bend, but Mrs Redpath was a careful driver. Benjamin sat slumped in the back, on a sack stuffed with straw, gritting his teeth until she drew up outside the Chapel Hall. She hurried off to make sure Kevin was dressed.

Inside, it was freezing. A pair of paraffin stoves did nothing to heat the benches at the back. A draught whined in under the door, and the floorboards reeked of disinfectant. The audience sat muffled in scarves and overcoats. The preacher, a missionary returned from Africa, shook hands with each member of his flock.

Drawn across the stage was a curtain consisting of three grey ex-Army blankets, peppered with moth-holes.

Mrs Redpath rejoined her uncles. The lights were switched off, except for the light onstage. From behind the curtain they heard the whispering of children.

The schoolteacher slipped through the curtain and sat down at the piano-stool. Her knitted hat was the same puce pink as the azalea on the piano; and as her fingers hammered the keyboard, the hat bobbed up and down, and the petals of the azalea quivered.

'Carol Number One,' she announced. ' "O Little Town of Bethlehem" – which will be sung by the children only.'

After the opening bars, the sound of faltering trebles drifted over the curtain; and through the moth-holes, the twins saw flashes of sparkling silver, which were the tinsel haloes of the angels.

The carol ended, and a blonde girl came out front, shivering in a white nightie. In her diadem there was a silver-paper star.

'I am the star of Bethlehem...' Her teeth chattered. ' 'Tis ten thousand years since God put a great star in the sky. I am that star...'

She finished the prologue. Then the curtain jerked back with the noise of squeaky pulleys to reveal the Virgin Mary, in blue, on a red rubber kneeler, scrubbing the floor of her house in Nazareth. The Angel Gabriel stood beside her.

'I am the Angel Gabriel,' he said in a suffocated voice. 'And I have come to tell you that you are going to have a baby.'

'Oh!' said the Virgin Mary, blushing crimson. 'Thank you very much, sir!' But the Angel fluffed the next line, and Mary fluffed the one after, and they both stood helplessly in the middle of the stage.

The teacher tried to prompt them. Then, seeing that no amount of prompting could rescue the scene, she called out, 'Curtain!' and asked all present to sing 'Once in Royal David's City'.

Everyone knew the words without having to open their hymnals. And when the curtain drew back again, everyone guffawed at the two-piece donkey that kicked and bucked and neighed and nodded his papier-mâché head. Two scene-shifters carried in a bale of straw, and a manger for feeding calves.

'That's my Kevin!' whispered Mrs Redpath, nudging Benjamin in the ribs.

A little boy had come onstage in a green tartan dressing-gown. Wound round his head was an orange towel. He had a black beard gummed to his chin.

The twins sat up and craned their necks; but instead of facing the audience, Father Joseph shied away and spoke his lines to the backdrop: 'Can't you find us a room, sir! My wife's going to have a baby at any minute.'

'I ain't got a room in the place,' replied Reuben the innkeeper. 'The whole town's chock-a-block with folks as come to pay their taxes. Blame the Roman Government, not me!

'I got this stable, though,' he went on, pointing to the manger. 'You can sleep in there if you want to.'

'Oh, thanks very much, sir!' said the Virgin, brightly. 'It'll do very nicely for humble folks like us.'

She started rearranging the straw. Joseph still stood facing the backdrop. He raised his right arm stiffly to the sky.

'Mary!' he shouted, suddenly plucking up courage. 'I can see something up there! Looks like a cross to me!'

'A cross? Ugh! Don't mention that word. It reminds me of Caesar Augustus!'

Through the double thickness of their corduroys, Lewis could feel his brother's kneecap, shaking: for Father Joseph had spun round, and was smiling in their direction.

'Yes,' said the Virgin Mary towards the end of the final scene. 'I think it's the loveliest baby I ever set eyes on.'

As for the Jones twins, they, too, were in Bethlehem. But it was not the plastic doll that they saw. Nor the innkeeper, nor the shepherds. Nor the papier-mâché donkey, nor the living sheep that nibbled at the straw. Nor Melchior with his box of chocolates. Nor Kaspar with his bottle of shampoo. Nor Black Balthazar with his crown of red cellophane and a ginger jar. Nor the Cherubim and Seraphim, nor Gabriel, nor the Virgin Mary herself. All they saw was an oval face with grave eyes and a fringe of black hair beneath a wash-towel turban. And when the choir of angels started singing, 'We will rock you, rock you, ro-ock you...' they rocked their heads in time and tears dripped on to their watch-chains.

After the performance, the minister took some snapshots with a flash. The twins waited outside the Chapel where the mothers were changing their children.

'Kevin!...Kevin!' came a shrill voice. 'If you don't come here, I'll slap your bottom...!'

XLIII

HE WAS A NICE BOY, lively and affectionate, who liked his Uncle Benjamin's fruitcake and loved to ride with Uncle Lewis on the tractor.

In the school holidays, his mother sent him to stay for

weeks on end: they came to dread, as much as he did, the first day of term.

Perched on the tractor mudguard, he would watch the plough-share bite into the stubble, and the herring-gulls shrieking and swooping over the fresh-turned furrow. He saw lambs being born, potatoes harvested, a cow calving and, one morning, there was a foal in the field.

The twins said all this, one day, would be his.

They fussed over him like a little prince, waited on him at table, learned never to serve cheese or beetroot and, in the attic, found a humming-top that whined like a contented bee. Wilfully retracing the steps of their own childhood, they even thought of taking him to the seaside.

Some nights, his eyelids heavy with sleep, he'd rest his head in his hands and yawn, 'Please, please will you carry me?' So they carried him upstairs to their old bedroom, and undressed him; and put on his pyjamas, and tiptoed out with the night-light burning.

In a patch of garden, he planted lettuces, radishes and carrots, and a row of sweet-peas. He liked listening to the zinging sound of seeds in their packets, but saw no point in sowing biennials.

'Two years,' he'd moan. 'That's far too long to wait!'

With a bucket slung over his arm, he went off scouring the hedges for anything that took his fancy — toads, snails, furry caterpillars — and once he came home with a shrew. When his tadpoles grew into baby frogs, he built a frog-castle, on a rock in the middle of an old stone trough.

About this time, the farmer below Cwm Cringlyn started a pony-trekking centre; and in the summer months, up to fifty boys and girls might trot through The Vision on their way to the hill. Often, they forgot to shut the gates; churned the pasture into a mud-pie; and Kevin wrote a sign reading 'Trespassers will be Prosecuted'.

One afternoon, Lewis was scything nettles by the pig-sties and saw him racing across the field.

'Uncle! Uncle!' he shouted, breathlessly. 'I seen a very funny person.'

He dragged Lewis by the hand, and together they walked to

the edge of the dingle.

'Sshh!' Kevin raised a finger to his lips. Then, parting the leaves, he pointed at something through the undergrowth. 'Look!' he whispered.

Lewis looked and saw nothing.

The sun filtered through the hazels, spattering the stream-bank with varied light. The stream tinkled. Croziers of young bracken curled up through the cow-parsley. Woodpigeons cooed. A jay chattered nearby, and lots of smaller birds were chirping and twittering around a mossy tree-stump.

The jay glided off its perch and hopped onto the stump. The small birds scattered. The stump moved.

It was Meg the Rock.

'Sshh!' Kevin pointed again. She had brushed off the jay and the other birds were coming back to feed from her hand.

Her skin was plastered with reddish mud. Her breeches were the colour of mud. Her hat *was* a rotting stump. And the tattered green jerseys, tacked one to the other, were the mosses, and creepers, and ferns.

They watched her for a little while, and then they walked away.

'Isn't she lovely?' said Kevin, knee-deep in the ox-eye daisies.

'Yes,' his uncle said.

At the start of the Christmas holidays, Kevin said he wanted to give the 'Bird Lady' a present. He bought an iced chocolate cake with his own pocket-money; and because Thursday was Jim's day at market, he and Lewis chose a Thursday to take it to The Rock.

Slaty clouds were tumbling over the hill as they picked their way through the defences. The wind was whipping the surface of the pond. Meg was indoors, up to her elbows in a bucket of dog-feed. She cringed at the arrival of visitors.

'I brought you a cake,' Kevin stammered, and screwed up his nose at the stench.

Lowering her eyes, she said, 'Aye, and thank you very much!' and then slipped outside with the bucket.

They heard her yelling, 'Quiet, y'old buggers!' And when she came back in, she said, 'Them dogs is wild as hawks.'

She transferred her gaze from the cake to the boy, and her face lit up: 'And will I boil you people a kettle for tea?'

'Yes.'

She split some sticks with a hacker, and set them alight. No one had come to tea for years. Dimly, she remembered the day Miss Fifield showed her how to lay the table. She flitted round the room with the agility of a dancer and, taking a cracked cup here, a chipped plate there, laid three places each with a knife and fork. She put a pinch of tea in the pot, and pierced a can of condensed milk. She wiped the breadknife on her breeches, cut three hefty slices of cake, and threw the crumbs to a pair of bantams.

'Poor ol' boys!' she said. 'Them was buggered by the cold, but I be feedin' 'em up in the house.'

The shyness had left her. She said that Sarah had taken Jim to Hereford to sell some ducks: 'That's as 'em says!' She rested her hands on her hips. 'But them won't get no moneys 'cos them gulls is old. Let 'em live, that's what I say! Let 'em live! Let 'em rabbits live! And 'em hares live! Let 'em stoats go on a-playin'! Aye, and 'em foxes, I won't harm 'em. Let all God's creatures live...!'

She clasped both hands around her cup, and her head swayed to and fro. Her cheeks crinkled with merriment when Lewis mentioned the pony-trekkers:

'Aye, I see'd 'em,' she said. 'Drunk as zowls, and howlin' and hollerin' and fallin' dead drunk off their horses.'

Kevin, horrified by the squalor, was itching to go.

'And I'll cut you another slice?' she asked.

'No, thanks,' he said.

She cut a second, larger slice for herself, and swallowed it. She did not throw the crumbs to the bantams, but mopped them up with her fingers and put them in her mouth. Then she licked her finger tips, one by one, and burped, and slapped her stomach.

'We'll be off now,' said Lewis.

Her eyelids drooped. In a dispirited voice she said, 'And what'll I owe you for the cake?'

'It's a present,' said Kevin.

'But you'll take it along with you?' She put the remains of the cake back in its box and, sadly, shut the lid: 'I wouldn't want Jim to catch me with a cake.'

Outside in the yard, Lewis helped her heave a tarpaulin off some hay-bales. The trapped rainwater sluiced over and splashed down Kevin's wellingtons. On the roof of the barn, a loose tin sheet was rattling in the wind. All of a sudden, a gust lifted it in the air, and it flew, like a monstrous bird, in their direction, and landed with a clatter on the scrap-heap.

Kevin threw himself flat on the mud.

'Bloomin' gale,' said Meg. 'Blaowin' 'em zincs about!'

The boy clung to his uncle's arm as they walked away across the hummocky field. He was filthy and whimpering with fright. The clouds were breaking and patches of blue flew low over their heads. One by one, the dogs stopped barking. They looked back and saw Meg, by the willows, calling in her ducklings. Her voice was carried in the wind: 'Wid! Wid! Come on then! Wid! Wid!...'

'Do you think he'll beat her?' the boy asked.

'I don't know,' said Lewis.

'He must be a very nasty man.'

'Jim's not so bad.'

'I don't ever want to go there again.'

XLIV

KEVIN GREW UP far faster than either of his uncles thought possible. One summer, he was singing with the trebles. The next – or so it seemed – he was the long-haired daredevil riding a bronco at the Lurkenhope Show.

When he was twelve, the twins made out their will in his favour. Owen Lloyd the lawyer pointed out the advantage of giving Vision Farms to Kevin in their lifetime. Far be it from him, he said, to influence them in any way: but providing they lived another five years, their estate would escape paying death-duties.

'Nothing to pay?' Benjamin perked up, thrusting his face across the lawyer's desk.

'Nothing but the Stamp Duty,' said Mr Lloyd.

To Benjamin, at least, the idea of doing down the Government was irresistible. And besides, in his eyes, Kevin could do no wrong. His faults, if he had them, were Lewis's faults – and that made them all the more lovable!

Naturally, Mr Lloyd continued, Kevin would be legally bound to provide for their old age, especially, he added in an undertone, 'if either of you two gentlemen fell ill...'

Benjamin glanced round at Lewis, who nodded.

'That settles it, then,' Benjamin said, and instructed the lawyer to draw up the deed of gift. Kevin would inherit the property at the age of twenty-one – by which time the twins would be eighty.

No sooner were the documents signed than his mother, Mrs Redpath, began to plague them. As long as the inheritance had been in doubt, she had kept her distance and minded her manners. Suddenly, overnight, she changed her tactics. She acted as though the farm was her birthright – almost as though the twins had swindled her out of it. She importuned them for money, rummaged in their drawers, and made jibes about them sharing a bed.

She said, 'Fancy trying to cook on that old range! Small wonder the food tastes of soot! There are such things as electric stoves, you know!...And those stone floors, I ask you? In this day and age! So unhygienic! What that floor needs is a damp course and some nice vinyl tiling.'

One Sunday, simply for the sake of disrupting lunch, she announced that her mother was alive and well, a wealthy widow in California.

Benjamin dropped his fork, then shook his head.

'I doubt it,' he said. 'She'd have wrote if she was living' – whereupon Mrs Redpath burst into a flood of crocodile tears. No one had ever loved her. No one had wanted her. She had always been pushed out, passed over.

In an effort to console her, Lewis unfolded the green baize of the silver box, and gave her Rebecca's christening spoon. Her eyes narrowed. She demanded harshly, 'What else you got of Mother's?'

Leading her to the attic, the twins unlocked a trunk and spread out all that remained of the little girl's belongings. A sunbeam, falling through the skylight, played over the tartan coat, the pairs of white silk stockings, the buttoned boots, a tam with a pompom, and some lace-trimmed blouses.

Moved to silence, the twins stared at these sad, crumpled relics and recalled those other Sundays, long ago, when they all drove to Matins in the dog-cart. Then, without so much as a by-your-leave, Mrs Redpath wrapped the lot in a bundle, and left.

Kevin, too, had begun to disappoint them.

He was charming: he even charmed a motor-bike out of Benjamin. But he was incurably lazy, and attempted to hide his laziness under a patter of technical jargon. He pooh-poohed the twins' farming methods, and worried them silly with his talk of silage and foetus-implantation.

He was supposed to put in two days' work at The Vision and three at a local polytechnic. In practice, he did neither. He would turn up from time to time, in sunglasses and a denim jacket decorated with studs and a death's head mask. A transistor radio dangled from his wrist. He had a snake tattooed on his arm, and he had bad friends.

In the spring of '73, a young American couple called Johnny and Leila bought the old farmhouse at Gillyfaenog in which to set up a 'community'. They had private means. Already their health-food shop in Castle Street was the talk of the town; and when Lewis Jones inspected it, he said it looked 'a bit like a meal-shed'.

Some members of the commune wore loose orange robes, and shaved their heads. Others wore pigtails and Victorian costume. They kept a herd of white goats; played the guitar and flute; and were sometimes to be seen in their orchard, cross-legged in a circle, saying and doing nothing, with their eyes half-closed. It was Mrs Owen Morgan who put around the rumour that the Hippies slept together 'like pigs'.

That August, Johnny built a strange scarlet tower in the vegetable garden, from which hung ribbon-like banners, printed with pink flowers and intertwined with black lettering. These, according to Mrs Morgan, were the symbols of the cult. Indian, she thought it was.

'Something to do with the Pope, then?' said Lewis. He hadn't heard her above the noise of the tractor.

They were standing outside the Chapel at Maesyfelin.

'No,' she shouted. 'That's Italian.'

'Oh!' he nodded.

A week later he gave a lift to a red-bearded giant, dressed in a homespun jerkin, with his feet bound up in sackcloth: his beliefs, he said, forbade him the use of leather.

Lewis dropped him at the gate, and asked about the letters on the flag. The young man bowed, raised his hands in prayer, and chanted very slowly: 'OM MANI PADME HUM' — which he translated equally slowly, 'Hail, Jewel in the Lotus! Hum!'

'Thank you very much,' said Lewis, touching his hat-brim and engaging the gear-shift.

After this encounter the twins revised their opinion of the Hippies, and Benjamin suggested they were 'taking some kind of rest'. All the same, he wished young Kevin wouldn't mess around with them. Halfway through a greenish sunset, the boy had tottered up the garden path, reeled into the kitchen with a glazed and faraway look and dumped his yellow crash-helmet on the rocking chair.

'Been drinking?' said Benjamin.

'No, Uncle,' he grinned. 'I been eating mushrooms.'

XLV

I N THEIR SEVENTIES, the twins found a new, unexpected friend in Nancy, the last of the Bickertons, who now lived at the old Rectory in Lurkenhope.

Arthritic, myopic and with scant control of the foot-pedals, she had somehow persuaded the licensing officer that she was fit to drive her 'rattletrap Sunbeam', and was for ever going off on trips. She had known about The Vision all her life, and now expressed a wish to see it. She came once, and then again and again, always unheralded, at teatime, with an offering of rock cakes, and her five spluttering pugs.

The gentry bored her. Besides, she shared with the Jones twins certain memories of the happier days before the First World War. She said The Vision was the prettiest farmhouse she'd ever set eyes on, and that if Mrs Redpath gave 'one iota of trouble', they should show her the door.

She pressed them to come to the Rectory, which they hadn't seen since the death of the Reverend Tuke: it took them weeks of hesitation before they consented to go.

They found her halfway down the herbaceous border, in a pink smock and raffia hat, yanking at some convolvulus that threatened to smother the phlox.

Lewis coughed.

'Oh, there you are!' She turned to face them: she had long ago lost her stammer.

The two old gentlemen were standing, side by side on the lawn, nervously fingering their hats.

'Oh, I *am* glad you came!' she said, and took them on a tour of the garden.

A thick layer of make-up covered the blotches on her face; and a pair of ivory bangles flew up and down her wasted arm and clacked as they hit her hand.

'That!' she gestured to a cloud of white blossom. 'That's *crambe cordifolium!*'

She kept apologizing for the chaos: 'One can no more find a gardener than the Holy Grail!'

The pillars of the pergola had fallen; the rock garden was a mound of weeds; the rhododendrons were leggy or dying, and the rest of the clergyman's shrubbery had 'gone back to jungle'. On the door of the potting-shed, the twins found a horse-shoe they had nailed up there for luck.

A breeze blew clouds of thistledown across the lily pond. They stood on the margin and watched the goldfish moving under the lily-fronds, lost in a reverie of Miss Nancy being rowed across the lake by her brother. Then the housekeeper called them in for tea.

They passed through the French windows into a sea of memorabilia.

By temperament, Nancy was incapable of throwing anything away, and had crammed into her eight rooms of vicarage the relics from fifty-two rooms of castle.

On one wall of the drawing-room hung a moth-eaten tapestry, of Tobit; on another, a vast canvas of Noah's Ark and Mount Ararat, its treacly surface bubbling with welts of bitumen. There were 'gothick' cupboards, a bust of Napoleon, half a suit of armour, an elephant's foot, and any number of other big-game trophies. Potted pelargoniums shed their yellowing leaves over the piles of pamphlets and *Country Lifes*. A budgie clawed at the bars of its cage; demijohns of home-made wine were busy fermenting under the console, while, dotted here and there over the carpet, were the urine stains of generations of incontinent pugs.

The tea things came rattling in on a trolley.

'China or Indian?'

'Mother lived in India,' said Benjamin, abstractedly.

'Then you must meet my niece, Philippa! Was born in India! Adores it! Goes there all the time! I mean the tea!'

'Thank you,' he said. So to be on the safe side, she poured them two cups of Indian with milk.

At six, they moved out on to the terrace. She served them elderberry wine, and they sat reminiscing of the old times. The twins reminded her of Mr Earnshaw's peaches.

'Now he', she said, 'really *was* a gardener! Wouldn't like it nowadays, would he?'

The wine loosened Lewis's tongue. Flushed in the face, he confessed how, as boys, they had hidden behind a tree-trunk and watched her ride past.

'Really,' she sighed, 'if only I'd known...'

'Aye,' Benjamin chuckled. 'And you should have heard what this one told Mother!'

'Tell me!' She gave Lewis a square look.

'No. No,' he said, smiling sheepishly. 'No. I couldn't.'

'He said,' said Benjamin, ' "When I grow up, I'm going to marry Miss Bickerton." '

'So?' She gave a throaty laugh. 'He has grown up. What are we waiting for?'

They sat in silence. House-martins chattered under the eaves. Bees were humming round the night-scented stocks. Sadly, she spoke of her brother, Reggie:

'We were all sorry for him. The leg, you remember? But he was a bad lot, really. Should have married the girl. She'd have been the making of him. And it was all my fault, you know?'

Often over the years, she had tried to make amends to Rosie, but the door of the cottage always slammed in her face.

There was another silence. The setting sun made a rim of gold around the ilex.

'My God!' she murmured. 'The guts of that woman!'

Only the week before, she had sat and watched her from the car — a bent, pigeon-toed figure in a knitted hat, knocking at the vicarage door to collect her weekly envelope of two five-pound notes. Only Nancy and the vicar knew where the envelope came from: she daren't increase the sum in case Rosie suspected.

'You must come again.' Nancy clutched each twin by the hand. 'It's been such fun. Now promise me you'll come!'

'And you'll come to us again?' said Benjamin.

'Oh but I will! I'll come next Sunday! And I'll bring my niece, Philippa! And you can have a good long natter about India.'

The tea-party for Philippa Townsend was a tremendous success.

Benjamin went to endless pains, meticulously followed his mother's recipe for cherry cake, and when he lifted the lid of the willow-pattern dish, the guest-of-honour clapped her hands and said, 'Gosh! Cinnamon toast!'

When the table was cleared, Lewis unwrapped Mary's Indian sketchbook, and Philippa turned its pages and called out the names of the subjects: 'That's Benares! There's Sarnath!...Do look! It's the Holi Festival. Look at all the lovely red powder!...Oh, what a beautiful punkah-wallah!'

She was a short and very courageous woman with laugh wrinkles at the edge of her slaty eyes, and silver hair cut in a fringe. She spent several months of each year riding alone round India on a bicycle. She turned the last page but one and stared, thunderstruck, at a watercolour of a pagoda-like structure, standing among some conifers with the Himalayas stacked up behind.

'I don't believe it,' she shouted at the top of her voice. 'I thought I was the only white woman to see that temple.' But Mary Latimer had seen it in the Nineties.

Philippa told them she was writing a book about English lady travellers of the nineteenth century. She asked if she could have the picture copied to use as an illustration.

'You can,' said Benjamin, who insisted on her taking it away.

Three weeks later, the sketchbook came back by registered mail. In the same parcel was a lovely colour-plate book, entitled *Splendours of the Raj*; and though neither of the twins was quite sure what they were looking at, it became one of the treasures of the household.

Every month or so, the Radnor Antiquarians held meetings in the Village Hall at Lurkenhope; and whenever there was a lantern-slide lecture, Nancy took her 'two favourite boy-friends' along. In the course of the year, they listened to a variety of topics — 'Early English Fonts in Herefordshire', 'The Pilgrimage to Santiago' — and when Philippa Townsend gave a talk on travellers in India, she told the audience of the 'fascinating sketchbook' at The Vision, while the twins sat beaming in the front row with identical red polyanthuses in their buttonholes.

Afterwards, refreshments were served at the back of the Hall and Lewis found himself being manoeuvred into a corner by a fleshy man in a purple-striped shirt. The man spoke very rapidly, slurring his words through a set of discoloured teeth, his eyes darting shiftily to and fro. He dipped his ginger-nut into his coffee, and sucked it.

Then he slipped Lewis a card on which was written, 'Vernon Cole — Pendragon Antiques, Ross-on-Wye,' and asked if he could pay them a call.

'Aye,' Lewis answered, assuming 'Antiques' and 'Antiquarian' were the same. 'We'd be pleased for you to come.'

Mr Cole came the very next day in a Volkswagen van.

It was drizzling and the hill was lost in cloud. The dogs kicked up a shindy as the stranger picked his way through the toffee-coloured puddles. Lewis and Benjamin were mucking out the cowshed, and resented the interruption; yet, out of politeness, they stuck their dung-forks in the steaming pile, and asked him to come indoors.

The antique dealer was entirely at his ease. He eyed the room up and down; turned a saucer over, and said, 'Doulton;' peered at the 'Red Indian' to make sure it was only a print; and wondered whether, by chance, they had any Apostle spoons.

Half an hour later, smearing strawberry jam over his bread-and-butter, he asked if they'd ever heard of Nostradamus:

'Never heard of the prophet Nostradamus? Well, I'm darned!'

Nostradamus, he went on, lived centuries ago, in France; yet he got Hitler 'spot on': his Antichrist was probably Colonel Gaddafi; and he'd predicted the End of the World for 1980.

'1980?' asked Benjamin.

'1980.'

The twins stared at the tea-things with crestfallen faces.

Mr Cole then rounded off his monologue, walked up to the piano, laid his hands on Mary's writing cabinet, and said, 'It's terrible!'

'Terrible?'

'Beautiful marquetry, like that! It's a sacrilege.'

The veneer on the lid had buckled and cracked, and one or two bits were missing.

'I mean, it's got to be repaired,' he continued. 'I've got just the man for it.'

The twins hated letting the cabinet leave the farm, but to think they'd neglected a relic of Mary's made them even more miserable.

'I'll tell you what,' he pattered on. 'I'll take it with me, and show him. And if he hasn't come in a week, I'll bring it straight back.'

He removed from his pocket a receipt-pad on which he scribbled something illegible:

'What...er...what figure shall we say then? Hundred quid?...Hundred and twenty! Better be on the safe side! Here, sign this, would you?'

Lewis signed. Benjamin signed. The man ripped off the bottom copy; grabbed his 'find'; bade them a very good afternoon, and left.

After two sleepless nights, the twins decided to send Kevin to recover the cabinet. Instead, a cheque – for £125 – arrived with the postman.

They felt dizzy and had to sit down.

Kevin borrowed a car and offered to drive them to Ross, but their courage failed. Nancy Bickerton offered to 'box the man's ears' but she was eighty-five. And when they called in on Lloyd the lawyer, he took the receipt, deciphered the words, 'One antique Sheraton writing-cabinet. For sale or return' – and shook his head.

He did, however, send a stiff solicitor's letter, but from Mr Cole's solicitor got a far stiffer letter by return: his client's professional integrity was being impugned, and he would sue.

There was nothing to be done.

Embittered and violated, the twins retreated back into their shells. To have lost the cabinet through theft or fire, that they could have borne. To have lost it through their own stupidity, to a man they had invited, who had sat at Mary's table and drunk from her teacups – the thought of it preyed on their minds and made them ill.

Benjamin had an attack of bronchitis. Lewis, with an

infection in his inner ear, took even longer to recover—if, indeed, he was ever the same again.

From then on, they lived in dread of being robbed. They barricaded the door at night; and Lewis bought a box of cartridges to set beside the old twelve-bore. One stormy night in December, they heard someone thumping on the door. They lay motionless under the bedclothes until the banging died down. At dawn next morning they found Meg the Rock asleep among the wellingtons inside the porch.

She was numb with cold. They led her to the firestool, and she sat with her hands on her cheeks, her legs ajar.

'And Jim's gone!' It was she who broke the silence.

'Aye,' she went on in a low monotone. 'His legs was all mossified and his hands was red as fire. And I put him a-bed and he slept. And I was woke in the night, and the dogs was yelpin', and Jim was out-a-bed, on the floor, like, and his head was all a-blooded where he fell. But him was livin' and talkin', mind, and I put him back up.

' "Well, cheerio!" he says. "Feed 'em!" he says. "Feed 'em yowes! An' chuck 'em a bit o' hay if you got any! Feed 'em! Fodder 'em! And give 'em ponies a bit o' cake if you got some o' that. An' don't let Sarah sell 'em! Them'll be all right with a bit o' feedin'...

' "An' tell 'em Jonesies there's plums up at Cock-a-loftie! Tell 'em to pick some plums! I see'd 'em...Beautiful yeller plums! An' the sun's up! The sun's a-shinin'! I see'd 'im! The sun's all a-shinin' through the plums..."

'That's what him said—as you was to 'ave some plums. And I felt his feet, and them was cold. And I felt him up, and him was all cold. And the dogs was a-howlin' and a-yowlin' and a-yowlpin' and a-rattlin' at the che-ains...and that's as I knew Jim was gone...!'

XLVI

A N HOUR AFTER Jim's funeral, the four principal mourners had wedged themselves in the Smoke Room of the Red Dragon, ordered soup and cottage pies, and were thawing out. The day was raw and drizzly. Their shoes were soaked from standing in the slush-covered graveyard. Manfred and Lizzie were dressed in shades of black and grey; Sarah wore slacks and a blue nylon parka; and Frank the haulier, a bulky man in a tweed suit several sizes too small, hung his head with embarrassment and stared at his crotch.

At the bar, a cider-drunk slammed down his tankard, belched and said, 'Aah! The wine o' the West!' A man and a girl were playing a computer game, and its electronic warbling filled the room. Manfred racked his brains to stave off a row between his wife and sister-in-law. He leaned across and asked the players, 'What do you call zis game?'

'Space Invaders,' the girl said glumly, and emptied a packet of peanuts down her throat.

Lizzie pursed her colourless lips and said nothing. But Sarah, her face already flushed from the fire, unzipped her parka and made up her mind to speak.

'Nice onion soup,' she said.

'French onion soup,' said the thinner woman.

There was a silence. A party of climbers came in and dumped their rucksacks in a heap. Frank refused to touch his soup and continued to stare at his crotch. His wife tried once again to make conversation.

She turned to a huge brown trout in a glass case above the mantelpiece, and said, 'I wonder who caught that fish.'

'I wonder,' Lizzie shrugged, and blew at her soupspoon.

The barman's girlfriend came with the cottage pies: 'Yes,' she said in broad Lancashire, 'that trout's quite a talking point. An American caught it in the Rosgoch Reseryoir. An airforce-man, he was. He'd have had a Welsh record if he hadn't gutted it. He left it here to be stuffed.'

'Quite some fish!' Manfred nodded.

'It's a hen,' the woman went on. 'You can tell from the

shape of the jaw. And a cannibal to boot! Has to be to reach that size! The taxidermist had a terrible time finding eyes big enough.'

'Yes,' said Sarah.

'And where there's one, there's two. That's what the fishermen say.'

'Another hen?' Sarah asked.

'A cock, I should imagine.'

Sarah glanced at her wristwatch and saw that it was almost two. In another half hour they had their appointment with Lloyd the lawyer. She had something else to say and gave a hard look at Lizzie.

'What about Meg?' she said.

'What about her?'

'Where's she going to live?'

'How should I know?'

'She's got to live somewhere.'

'Get her a living van and a few fowls and she'll be perfectly happy.'

'No,' Manfred interrupted, the colour invading his cheeks. 'She not be happy. You take her from The Rock and she go crazy.'

'Well, she can't go on living in that pigsty,' Lizzie snapped.

'Vy not? She live there all her life.'

'Because it's for sale!'

'I beg your pardon?' Sarah swivelled her head – and the quarrel flared out into the open.

Sarah believed The Rock should be hers. For twenty years she had bailed Jim out; and he had promised to leave her the property. Time and again, she'd gripped his arm: 'Now you have been to the lawyer, haven't you?' 'Aye, Sarah,' he used to say, 'I seed Lloyd the lawyer and I done what you said.'

She had counted on selling up the moment he died. Frank's haulage business had been doing badly and, besides, The Rock'd make a 'nice little nest-egg' for her teenage daughter Eileen. She even had a purchaser in mind – a business-man from London who wanted to put up Swedish-style chalets.

Lizzie, for her part, maintained The Rock was her home as

much as anyone's, and she was entitled to her fair share. The argument volleyed back and forth – and Sarah became quite weepy and hysterical, prattling on about the sacrifices she'd made, the money she'd spent, the times she'd battled through snowdrifts, the times she'd saved their lives – 'And for what? A kick in the teeth, that's all!'

Then Lizzie and Sarah started screaming and yelling, and though Manfred shouted, 'Pliss! Pliss!' and Frank snarled, 'Aw! Cut it, will you?' the pub lunch almost ended in a fist-fight.

The barman asked them to leave.

Frank paid the bill and they walked up Broad Street, picking their way through the lines of slush till they came to the lawyer's door. Both women blanched when Mr Lloyd lifted his spectacles and said, 'There is no will.' Furthermore, since neither Sarah nor Lizzie nor Meg were Jim's blood relatives, his estate would be passed to the Crown. Meg, Mr Lloyd added, had best claim on the place – for she was the incumbent and had lived there all her life.

So Meg lived on alone at The Rock. She said, 'I can't live for the dead 'uns. I got my own living to do.'

On frosty mornings she sat on an upturned bucket, warming her hands around a mug of tea while the tits and chaffinches perched on her shoulder. When a green woodpecker took some crumbs from her hand, she imagined the bird was a messenger from God and sang His Praises in doggerel all through the day.

After dark, she would huddle over the fire and fry up her bacon and potatoes. Then, when the candle guttered, she curled up on the box-bed with a black cat for company, a coat for a blanket, and a sack stuffed with fern for a pillow.

Having so little to separate the real world from the world of dreams, she imagined it was she who played with the badger cubs; she who soared with the hawks above the hill. One night, she dreamed of being attacked by strange men.

'I heard 'em,' she told Sarah. 'A young 'un and an old. Poonin' on the roof! Aye! And te-akin' off the tiles and comin' down in. So I lit me a candle and I shouted, "Git, yer buggers! I got me a gun in here and I'll blaow yer bloomin' heads off." That's as I said and I ain't heard nothing since!' — all of which went to confirm Sarah's opinion that Meg was 'losing her marbles'.

Sarah had arranged with Prothero's for Meg's groceries to be delivered to a disused oil-drum by the side of the lane. But this hiding place was soon found by Johnny the Van, a red-eyed rascal who lived in an old fairground waggon nearby. There were weeks when Meg almost fainted from hunger; and the dogs, without meat, howled all day and night.

When the spring came, both Sarah and Lizzie set out to curry favour with Meg. Each would arrive with cakes or a box of chocolates, but Meg saw through their blandishments and said, 'Thank you people very much, and I'll see you again next week.' Sometimes they tried to get her to sign a prepared statement: she simply stared at the pencil as if it were poisoned.

One day Sarah drove up with a trailer to fetch a pony which, so she claimed, was hers. She walked towards the beast-house with a halter, but Meg stood, arms folded, by the door.

'Aye, you can te-ake him,' she said. 'But what are you people going to do about them dogs?'

Jim had left thirteen sheepdogs; and these, cooped up in tin shanties, had grown so mangy and ravenous on a diet of bread and water that they were unsafe to be let off their chains.

'Them poor ol' dogs is mad,' Meg said. 'Them'll 'ave to be shot.'

'We could take 'em to the vet?' Sarah suggested, doubtfully.

'Nay,' Meg answered back. 'I'm not putting them dogs in no death-van! Get that Frank o' yours to come up with his gun, and I'll dig a hole and put 'em in the ground.'

The morning of the shooting was damp and misty. Meg gave the dogs their last feed and led them out, two by two, and chained them to a crab-apple in the pasture. At eleven, Frank gulped down a swig of whisky, tightened his cartridge belt, and walked out into the mist, in the direction of the tree.

Meg stopped her ears; Sarah stopped hers; and her daughter Eileen sat in the Land Rover listening to rock music through the headphones of her cassette-player. A whiff of gunpowder drifted downwind. There was one final whimper, one isolated shot; and then Frank came back, out of the mist, haggard and about to vomit.

'An' a good job,' said Meg, slinging a spade across her shoulder. 'Thank you people very much.'

Next morning she saw Lewis Jones driving along the skyline on his red International Harvester. She ran up to the hedge and he switched off the engine.

'So them come and shot the dogs,' she said, catching her breath. 'Poor ol' dogs what done no 'arm. Nor che-ased no sheep nor nobody. But what with them all a-hungered, and with the summer a-comin', and the heat a-comin', and the smell in them coops, and the che-ains'd bite into their necks, like...Aye! And bloody 'em! And then the flies'd come and lay eggs and there'd be worms in their necks. Poor ol' dogs! And that's why I 'ad 'em shot.'

Her eyes flashed. 'But I'm a-tellin' yer one thing, Mr Jones. It's the people not the dogs as should be punished...!'

Not long afterwards, Sarah ran into Lizzie outside the chemist's in Rhulen. They agreed to have a coffee in the Hafod Tearoom, each hoping the other would dispel a dreadful rumour: that Meg had a fancy man.

XLVII

THEO THE TENT was his name. He was the red-bearded giant whom Lewis Jones had met in the lane. He was known as 'The Tent' on account of a domed construction made of birch saplings and canvas, and pitched in a paddock on the Black Hill, where he lived alone with a mule called Max, and a donkey to keep Max company.

His real name was Theodoor. He came from a family of hard-nosed Afrikaners, who had a fruit farm in Orange Free State. He had quarrelled with his father over the eviction of some workers, quit South Africa, come to England, and 'dropped out'. At the Free Festival near Glastonbury, he met a group of Buddhists, and became one.

Following the Dharma at the Black Hill Monastery made him calm and happy for the first time in his life. He shouldered all the heavy labour; and he enjoyed the visits of a Tibetan Rinpoche who came, now and then, to give courses in higher meditation.

His appearance sometimes put people off. Only when they realized he was incapable of hurting a fly, did they take advantage of his gentle, trusting nature. He had a little money from his mother, to which the leaders of the commune helped themselves. During one financial crisis, they ordered him to collect his entire annual income from the bank, in cash.

On the way to Rhulen, he stopped by the pine plantation and stretched out on the grass. The sky was cloudless. Harebells rustled. A peacock butterfly winked its eyes on a warm stone – and, suddenly, everything about the monastery disgusted him. The purple walls, the smell of joss-sticks and patchouli, the garish mandalas and simpering images – all seemed so cheap and tawdry; and he realized that, no matter how hard he meditated, or studied the *Bardo Thodol*, he would never come, That Way, to Enlightenment.

He packed his few belongings and went away. Soon afterwards the other Buddhists sold up and left for the United States.

He bought his paddock, on a steep pitch overlooking the Wye, and there he made his tent – or rather his yurt – from a plan in a book on High Asia.

Year in, year out, he roamed the Radnor Hills, played his flute to the curlews, and memorized the tenets of the *Tao Tê Ching*. On rocks, on gate-posts and on tree stumps, he would carve the three-line *haikus* that came into his head.

He remembered, in Africa, seeing the Kalahari Bushmen

trekking through the desert, the mothers laughing, with their children on their backs. And he had come to believe that all men were meant to be wanderers, like them, like St Francis; and that by joining the Way of the Universe, you could find the Great Spirit everywhere – in the smell of bracken after rain, the buzz of a bee in the ear of a foxglove, or in the eyes of a mule, looking with love on the blundering movements of his master.

Sometimes, he felt that even his simple shelter was preventing him from following The Way.

One wild March day, standing on the screes above Craig-y-Fedw, he peered down and watched Meg's tiny figure, bent under a load of brushwood.

He decided to pay her a visit, unaware that Meg had already been watching him.

She had watched him winding his way over the mountain in the grey winter rain. She had watched him on the skyline with the clouds piled up behind. She was standing, arms folded in the doorway, as he tethered up the mule. Something told her he was not the kind of stranger to cringe from.

'I was wonderin' when you was a-comin',' she said. 'Tea's in the pot. So come on in and sit down.'

He could hardly see her face across the smoke-filled room.

'I tell you what I done,' she went on. 'I was up with the sun. I foddered the sheep. I gave hay to the horses. Ay! And a bit o' cake to the cows. I fed the fowl. I fetched up a load o' wood. And I was just havin' my cup-o'-tea and thinkin' to muck out the beast-house.'

'I'll help you,' said Theo.

The black cat jumped on to her lap, clawed at her breeches and scratched the bare patches of thigh.

'Ow! Ouch!' she cried. 'And where be you a-goin', little black man? What be you a che-asin', little darkie doll?' – squealing with laughter until the cat calmed down and started purring.

The beast-house had not been cleared for years; the layers of dung had risen four feet above the floor, and the heifers scraped their backs on the roofbeams. Meg and Theo set to work with fork and shovel and, by mid-afternoon, there was a big brown pile in the yard.

She showed not a trace of being tired. Now and then, as she pitched a forkful of muck through the door, the bows on her sweaters came undone. He could see that, underneath, she had a nice tidy body.

He said, 'You're a tough one, Meg.'

''Ave to be,' she grinned, and her eyes narrowed down to a pair of Mongolian slits.

Three days later, Theo came back to mend her window and rehang a door. She had found a few coins in Jim's pockets, and insisted on paying him a wage. In fact, whenever he did a job of work, she'd reach for a knotted sock, untie it, and hand him a ten-penny piece.

'Ain't much pie in it for you,' she'd say.

He took each one of these coins as if she were offering a fortune.

He borrowed a set of rods to clean her chimney. Halfway up, the brush snagged on something solid. He pushed, harder, and clods of soot came tumbling into the grate.

Meg chortled with laughter at the sight of his black face and beard: 'And I'd think you was the divil hi'self to look on.'

As long as her gentle giant was around she felt herself safe from Sarah, or Lizzie, or any outside threat. 'I'll not 'ave it,' she'd say. 'I'll not let 'em lay their 'ands on one o' m'chicks.'

If he stayed away a week, she began to look terribly dejected, imagining that 'men from the Ministry' were coming to take her away, or murder her. 'I know it,' she said gloomily. 'It'll be one o' them things in the papers.'

There were times when even Theo thought she was 'seeing things'.

'I see'd a couple o' townees' dogs,' she said. 'Black as sin! Coursin' down the dingle to buggery and che-asin' 'em little lambs! And I'd be gone out and find 'em dead and thinkin' 'em dead o' cold but them was dead o' fright o' the townees' dogs.'

She hated to think that he would, some day, go away.

For hours on end, he used to sit by the fire listening to the harsh and earthy music of her voice. She spoke of the weather, the birds and animals, the stars and phases of the moon. He felt there was something sacred about her rags and, in their honour, composed this poem:

> *Five green jerseys*
> *A thousand holes*
> *And the Lights of Heaven shining through.*

He brought her little luxuries from Rhulen – a chocolate cake or a packet of dates – and, to earn an extra pound or two, he hired himself out as a drystone waller.

One of his first jobs took him to The Vision, where Kevin had backed the tractor into a pigsty.

Kevin was out of favour with his uncles.

He was due to take possession of the farm in a year and a half; yet showed not the least inclination to take up farming.

He mixed with the 'county' set. He drank. He ran up debts; and when the bank manager refused him a loan, he demonstrated his disdain for life by joining a parachute club. Then, to compound the catalogue of his infamies, he got a girl into trouble.

Usually, his grin was so infectious that the twins forgave him everything: this time, he was white with apprehension. The girl, he confessed, was Sarah's daughter Eileen; and Benjamin banned him from the house.

Eileen was a pretty, purse-lipped girl of nineteen with a freckled nose and a head of bouncy russet curls. Her normal expression was a pout; yet, providing she wanted something, she could assume an air of saintlike simplicity. She was mad about horses, won trophies at gymkhanas and, like many horsy people, her financial needs were large.

She first met Kevin at the Lurkenhope Show.

The sight of his trim figure, perfectly balanced astride the bucking pony, brought her flesh out in goose-pimples. She felt a lump in her throat as he collected the prize. On learning that he was rich – or would be – she methodically laid her plans.

A week later, after flirting through a Country-and-Western evening at the Red Dragon, the pair crept into the back of Sarah's Land Rover. Another week went by, and he had promised to marry her.

Warning her to tread warily with his uncles, he brought her to The Vision as a prospective bride, and though her table-manners were excellent, though she studiously admired every knick-knack in the house, and though Lewis thought her 'quite a little piece', it made Benjamin far from happy to think she was one of the Watkinses.

One sweltering day in early September, she scandalized him by driving her car in a bikini, and blowing him a kiss as she passed. In December, on purpose or otherwise, she mistimed the pill.

Benjamin stayed away from the wedding, which, at Sarah's insistence, was held in an Anglican church. Lewis went alone, and came back from the reception tiddly, saying that even if it had been a 'shotgun wedding' – an expression he'd picked up from a fellow-guest – it was, all the same, a very nice wedding and the bride had looked lovely in white.

The couple went on honeymoon to the Canaries and, when they came back, brown and beautiful, Benjamin relented. She failed to charm him: he was immune to her kind of charm. What did impress him was her common sense, her grasp of money matters, and her promise to calm Kevin down.

The twins agreed to build a bungalow for the youngsters at Lower Brechfa.

In the meantime, Kevin moved in with his parents-in-law – who proceeded to run him off his feet. Either Frank's truck needed a spare part from Hereford, or Sarah's show-jumper had a sprain, or Eileen would have a sudden craving for kippers and send her husband off to the fishmonger.

As a result, in the last weeks of Eileen's pregnancy, Kevin hardly had a moment for The Vision; missed the sheep-drive, the shearing and the hay harvest; and because they were so short-handed, the twins employed Theo to help.

Theo was a magnificent worker, but because he was a strict

vegetarian he made a scene whenever they sent an animal for slaughter. He refused to drive a tractor or operate the simplest piece of machinery, and his opinion of the twentieth century made Benjamin feel quite modern.

One day, Lewis questioned the wisdom of living in a tent – whereupon the South African got extremely nettled and said that the God of Israel had lived in a tent; and if a tent was good enough for God, it was good enough for him.

'I expect,' Lewis nodded, doubtfully. 'Israel's a warm climate, isn't it?'

For all their differences, Theo and the twins were devoted to one another and on the first Sunday in August, he asked them over to lunch.

'Thank you very much,' Lewis said.

Coming up to the skyline above Craig-y-Fedw, the two old gentlemen paused to catch their breath and mop their foreheads.

A warm westerly breeze was combing through the grass-stems, skylarks hovered over their heads, and creamy clouds came floating out of Wales. Along the horizon, the hills were layered in lines of hazy blue; and they reflected how little had changed since they walked this way with their grandfather, over seventy years before.

A pair of jet fighters screamed low over the Wye, reminding them of a destructive world beyond. Yet as their weak eyes wandered over the network of fields, plotted and painted red or yellow or green, and the whitewashed farmhouses where their Welsh forbears had lived and died, they found it hard – if not impossible – to believe what Kevin said: that it would all go, any day, in a great big bang.

The gate into Theo's paddock was a mishmash of sticks and wire and string. He was waiting to greet them, in his homespun jerkin and leggings. His hat was crowned with honeysuckle, and he looked like Ancient Man.

Lewis had crammed his pockets with sugar-lumps to give to the mule and donkey.

Theo led the way downhill, past his vegetable patch, to

the entrance of the yurt.

'And you live in that?' The twins had spoken in one breath.

'Yes.'

'Fancy!'

They had never seen so strange a structure.

Two tarpaulins, a green one over a black, were lashed over a circular frame of birch branches, and weighted down with stones. A metal chimney poked from the centre: the fire was out.

Out of the wind, Theo's friend, a poet, was boiling water for rice, and some vegetables were sizzling in a pot.

'Come on in,' said Theo.

Squatting down, the twins crept through the entrance hole and were soon sitting, propped up on cushions, on a ragged blue carpet covered with Chinese characters. Pencils of sunlight filtered through the holes in the tarpaulin. A fly droned. It was all very tranquil, and there was a place for everything.

A yurt, Theo tried to explain, was an image of the Universe. On its south side, you kept the 'things of the body' — food, water, tools, clothing; on the north, the 'things of the mind'.

He showed them his celestial globe, his astronomical tables, a sand-glass, some reed pens and a bamboo flute. On a red-painted box sat a gilded statuette. This, he said, was Avalokitesvara, the bodhisattva of Infinite Mercy.

'Funny name,' said Benjamin.

On the sides of the box were some lines of poetry, stencilled on in white.

'What does it say now?' asked Lewis, 'I canna see a thing without my proper specs.'

Theo flicked his feet into the lotus position, half-crossed his eyes, and recited the verse in full:

> *Who doth ambition shun,*
> *And loves to live i' the sun,*
> *Seeking the food he eats,*
> *And pleas'd with what he gets,*
> *Come hither, come hither, come hither:*
> *Here shall he see*

> *No enemy*
> *But winter and rough weather.*

'Very nice,' Lewis said.

'*As You Like It*,' said Theo.

'I wouldn't like it for winter, either.'

Theo then reached for his bookstand and read his favourite poem. The poet, he said, was a Chinaman who also liked to roam around the mountains. His name was Li Po.

'Li Po,' they repeated, slowly. 'That's all?'

'All.'

Theo said the poem was about two friends who rarely saw one another and, whenever he read it, he remembered a friend in South Africa. There were lots more funny names in the poem and the twins made neither head nor tail of it till he came to the last few lines:

> *What is the use of talking, and there is no end of talking,*
> *There is no end of things in the heart.*
> *I call in the boy,*
> *Have him sit on his knees here*
>   *To seal this,*
> *And send it a thousand miles, thinking.*

And when Theo sighed, they sighed, as if they too were separated from somebody by thousands and thousands of miles.

They said the lunch was 'very tasty, thank you!' and, at three o'clock, Theo offered to walk them back to Cock-a-loftie. All three walked, in single file, along the sheep tracks. No one exchanged a word.

At the stile, Benjamin looked at the South African and anxiously bit his lip: 'He won't forget Friday, will he?'

'Kevin?'

Friday was their eightieth birthday.

'No,' Theo smiled from under his hat-brim. 'I know he hasn't forgotten.'

XLVIII

ON FRIDAY the 8th of August, the twins awoke to the sound of music.

Coming to the window in their nightshirts, they parted the lace curtains and peered at the people in the yard. The sun was up. Kevin was strumming at his guitar. Theo played the flute. Eileen, in maternity clothes, was clinging to her Jack Russell terrier, and the mule munched a rose-bush in the garden. Parked outside the barn was a red car.

Over breakfast, Theo gave the twins their present — a pair of Welsh love-spoons, linked with a wooden chain and carved by himself from a single piece of yew. The card read, 'Birthday Greetings from Theo the Tent! May you live three hundred years!'

'Thank you very much,' said Lewis.

Kevin's present had not yet arrived. It would be ready, he said, at ten, and it was an hour's drive away.

Benjamin blinked. 'And where would that be?'

'A surprise,' Kevin grinned at Theo. 'It's a mystery tour.'

'We canna go till we fed the animals.'

'The animals are fed,' he said; and Theo was staying behind to keep an eye on the place.

'Mystery tour' suggested a visit to a stately home; so the twins went upstairs and came down in starched white collars and their best brown suits. They checked their watches with Big Ben, and said they were ready to go.

'Whose is the car?' asked Benjamin, suspiciously.

'Borrowed,' said Kevin.

When Lewis got into the back seat, Eileen's terrier took a nip at his sleeve.

He said, 'Angry little tiddler, ain't he?' — and the car lurched off down the track.

They drove through Rhulen and then up among some stumpy hills where Benjamin pointed out the sign to Bryn-Draenog. He winced every time Kevin came to a corner. Then the hills were less rocky; the oak trees were larger, and there were half-timbered manors painted black and white. In Kington High Street, they got stuck behind a delivery van, but soon they were out among fields of red Hereford cattle; and, every mile or so, they passed the gates of a big red-brick country house.

'Is it Croft Castle we're going?' Benjamin asked.

'Perhaps,' said Kevin.

'Quite a distance, then?'

'Miles and miles,' he said and, half a mile further, turned off the main road. The car bounced down a stretch of bumpy tarmac. The first thing Lewis saw was an orange wind-sock: 'Oh my! It's an aerodrome!'

A black hangar came into view, then some Nissen huts, and then the runway.

Benjamin seemed to shrivel at the sight of it. He looked frail and old, and his lower lip was trembling: 'No. No. I'd not go in a plane.'

'But, Uncle, it's safer than driving a car...'

'Aye! With your driving, maybe! No, No...I'd never go in a plane.'

The car had scarcely stopped moving before Lewis had hopped out and was standing on the tarmac, stupefied.

Ranked on the grass were about thirty light aircraft – Cessnas mostly, belonging to members of the West Midlands Flying Club. Some were white. Some were brightly coloured. Some had stripes, and all of their wingtips quivered as if they were itching to be airborne.

The wind was freshening. Patches of shadow and sunlight raced one another down the runway. On the control tower, an anemometer whirled its little black cups. On the far side of the airfield was a line of swaying poplars.

'Breezy,' said Kevin, his hair blowing over his eyes.

A young man in jeans and a green bomber jacket shouted, 'Hi, Kev!' and strolled over, dragging his boot-heels across the asphalt.

'I'm your pilot.' He grasped Lewis by the hand. 'Alex Pitt.'

'Thank you very much.'

'Happy birthday!' he said, turning to Benjamin. 'Never too late to take up flying, eh?' Then, pointing to the Nissen huts,

237

he asked them to follow. 'One or two formalities,' he said, 'and we're off!'

'Aye, aye, sir!' said Lewis, thinking that was what you said to a pilot.

The first room was a cafeteria. Above the bar was a wooden propeller from the First World War: the walls were hung with coloured prints of the Battle of Britain. The airfield had once been a parachute-training centre — and still, in a sense, it was.

A party of young men, dressed for a 'drop', were drinking coffee. And on seeing Kevin, a beefy fellow got to his feet, slapped his hand on his friend's leather jacket, and asked if he was coming too.

'Not today,' Kevin said. 'I'm flying with my uncles.'

The pilot ushered them into the Briefing Room, where Lewis greedily examined the notice-board, the maps marked with airlanes, and a blackboard covered with an instructor's scribbles.

A black labrador then bounded out of the air-controller's office, and rested its paws on Benjamin's trousers. In the animal's appealing stare, he seemed to see a warning not to go. He felt dizzy, and had to sit down.

The pilot put three printed forms on the blue formica table — one...two...three...and asked the passengers to sign.

'Insurance!' he said. 'In case we land in a field and kill some old farmer's cow!'

Benjamin gave a start, and almost dropped the ball point pen.

'Don't you scare my uncles,' Kevin bantered.

'Nothing could scare your uncles,' said the pilot, and Benjamin was aware that he had signed.

Eileen and the terrier waved at the flying party as they walked across the grass towards the Cessna. There was a broad brown stripe down the length of the fuselage, and a much thinner stripe along the wheel-spats. The plane's registration number was G-BCTK.

'TK stands for Tango Kilo,' Alex said. 'That's its name.'

'Funny name,' said Lewis.

Alex then began the external checks, explaining each one in turn. Benjamin stood forlornly by the wingtip, and thought of all the crashes in Lewis's scrapbook.

But Lewis seemed to think he was Mr Lindbergh. He crouched down. He stood on tiptoe. His eyes were glued to the young man's every movement. He watched how to check the landing gear, to make sure of the flaps and ailerons, and how to test the warning horn that beeped if the plane was about to stall.

He noticed a slight dent in the tail-fin.

'Probably a bird,' said Alex.

'Oh!' said Benjamin.

His face fell even further when the time came to board. He sat in the back seat and, when Kevin fastened his safety-belt, he felt more trapped and miserable than ever.

Lewis sat on the pilot's right, trying to make sense of all the dials and gauges.

'And this one?' he ventured. 'Joystick, I suppose?'

The plane was a trainer and had dual controls.

Alex corrected him: 'We call it the control column nowadays. One for me and one for you if I faint.'

There was a hiccough from the back seat but Benjamin's voice was drowned by the rattle of the propeller. He closed his eyes as the plane taxied out to the holding-point.

'Tango Kilo checks completed,' the pilot radioed. Then, with a touch of throttle, the plane was on the runway.

'Tango Kilo leaving circuit to the west. Estimate return forty-five minutes. Repeat, forty-five minutes.'

'Roger, Tango Kilo,' a voice came back over the intercom.

'We take off at sixty!' Alex bawled into Lewis's ear — and the rattle rose to a roar.

By the time Benjamin opened his eyes again, the plane had climbed to 1,500 feet.

Down below there was a field of mustard in flower. A greenhouse flashed in the sun. The stream of white dust was a farmer fertilizing a field. Woods went by, a pond coated with duckweed, and a quarry with a team of yellow bulldozers. He thought a black car looked a bit like a beetle.

He still felt a little nauseous, but his fists were no longer clenched. On ahead was the Black Hill and clouds streaming low over the summit. Alex climbed the plane another thousand feet, and warned them to expect a bump or two. 'Turbulence,' he said.

The pines on Cefn Hill were blue-green and black-green in the varied light. The heather was purple. The sheep were the size and shape of maggots, and there were inky pools with rings of reed around them. The plane's shadow moved up on a herd of grazing ponies, which scattered in all directions.

For one terrible moment, the cliffs above Craig-y-Fedw came rushing up to meet them. But Alex veered off and eased down into the valley.

'Look!' cried Lewis. 'It's The Rock!'

And there it was – the rusty stockade, the pool, the broken roof, and Meg's white geese in a panic!

And there, on the left, was The Vision! And there was Theo!

'Aye! It's Theo all right!' Now it was Benjamin's turn to be excited. He pressed his nose against the window and peered down at the tiny brown figure, waving its hat in the orchard, as the plane flew low on its second circuit, and dipped its wings.

Five minutes later, they were out of the hills and Benjamin was definitely enjoying himself.

Alex then glanced over his shoulder at Kevin, who winked. He leaned across to Lewis and shouted, 'It's your turn.'

'My turn?' He frowned.

'To fly.'

Gingerly, Lewis laid his hands on the control column and strained, with his good ear, to catch each word of the instructor. He pulled towards him, and the nose lifted. He pushed, and it fell away. He pressed to the left, and the horizon tilted. Then he straightened up and pressed to the right.

'You're on your own now,' said Alex, calmly, and Lewis made the same manoeuvres, on his own.

And suddenly he felt – even if the engine failed, even if the plane took a nosedive and their souls flew up to Heaven – that all the frustrations of his cramped and frugal life now counted for nothing, because, for ten magnificent minutes, he had done what he wanted to do.

'Try a figure-of-eight,' Alex suggested. 'Down on the

left!...That's enough!...Now straighten up!...Now down on the right!...Easy does it!...Good!...Now another big loop and we'll call it a day.'

Not until he had handed back the controls did Lewis realize that he had written the figures eight and zero in the sky.

They were coming in to land. They saw the runway approaching, first as a rectangle, then a trapeze, then as a sawn-off pyramid, as the pilot radioed his 'finals' and the plane touched down.

'Thank you very much,' said Lewis, shyly smiling.

'It was my great pleasure,' Alex said, and helped the twins step down.

He was a professional photographer; and it was only ten days since Kevin had commissioned an aerial photograph of The Vision, in colour.

Mounted and framed, this was the second half of the twins' birthday present. They unwrapped it in the car park, and gave the young couple each a kiss.

The big question was where to hang it.

Plainly, it belonged on the wall of photographs in the kitchen. But nothing had been added since Amos's death, and the wallpaper, though faded in between the frames, was as fresh as new behind them.

For a whole week, the twins bickered and juggled and lifted uncles and cousins off hooks that had been theirs for sixty years. And finally, just as Lewis had given up and decided to hang it above the piano, with 'The Broad and Narrow Path', it was Benjamin who lit on the solution: that by shifting Uncle Eddie and the grizzly *up* one, and by shifting Hannah and Old Sam *along* one, there was just enough space for it to fit beside their parents' wedding-group.

XLIX

T HE DAYS WERE drawing in. Swallows chattered on the
electric cables, all set for the long journey south. A gale
blew in the night and they were gone. Around the time of the
first frost, the twins had a call from Mr Isaac Lewis, the
minister.

They went so seldom now to Chapel, but the Chapel was
on their conscience, and their visitor made them nervous.

He had walked all the way from Rhulen, over Cefn Hill. His
trouser bottoms were coated in mud and, though he scraped
his soles on the boot scraper, he left a trail on the kitchen floor.
A long forelock hung down between his eyebrows. His
bulging brown eyes, though glittering with the light of faith,
were none the less watering from the wind. He commented on
the unseasonable weather: 'Harsh for September, isn't it?'

'Harsh!' agreed Benjamin. 'Like as it's the first day of winter.'

'And the Lord's House deserted,' the minister went on
sombrely. 'And the People far from Him...Not counting the
cost...!'

He was a Welsh nationalist of extreme views. But he
expressed these views in so allusive a language that few of his
listeners had the least idea what he was talking about. It took
the twins twenty minutes to realize he was asking them for
money.

The finances of Maesyfelin Chapel were in disarray. In June,
while repairing some tiles, the roofer had uncovered a patch of
dry rot. The pre-war wiring had proved to be a fire hazard,
and the interior had been repainted, blue.

The minister was very red in the face, as much from
embarrassment as the heat of the fire. He sucked the air in
through his teeth, as if his whole life consisted of embarrassing
interviews. He spoke of materialism, and of an ungodly age.
Gradually, he hinted that Mr Tranter, the contractor, was
pressing him for payment.

'And have I not paid fifty pounds from my own pocket? But
what is the good of fifty pounds today, I ask you?'

'How much was the bill then?' Benjamin interrupted.

'Five hundred and eighty-six pounds,' he sighed, as if exhausted by prayer.

'And will I make the payment to Mr Tranter directly?'

'To him,' said the minister, too surprised to say anything else.

His eyes followed Benjamin's pen as it wrote out the cheque. This he folded meticulously and slipped into his wallet.

The wind was tossing the larches when he came to leave. He paused by the porch and reminded the twins of the Harvest Festival, at three o'clock on Friday.

'Indeed, a time for thanksgiving!' he said, and turned up the collar of his coat.

Early on Friday morning, Lewis drove his tractor to The Tump and asked Rosie Fifield to join them.

'To thank who for what?' she snapped and banged the door.

At half past two Kevin came to collect the twins by car. He was smartly turned out in a new grey suit. Eileen was expecting at any minute, and so stayed at home. Benjamin was limping with a touch of sciatica.

Outside the Chapel, farmers with fresh weatherbeaten faces were quietly moaning about Mrs Thatcher's government. Inside, children in white ankle-socks were playing hide-and-seek among the pews. Young Tom Griffiths was distributing the Harvest Hymn Sheet, and women were arranging their dahlias and chrysanthemums.

Betty Griffiths Cwm Cringlyn – the one they all call 'Fattie' – had baked a loaf in the shape of a wheatsheaf. Heaped on the communion table were apples and pears; pots of honey and chutney; ripe tomatoes and green tomatoes; green grapes and purple grapes; marrows, onions, cabbages and potatoes, and runner beans that were the size of sawblades.

Daisy Prothero brought in a basket labelled 'Fruits of the Field'. There were corn-dollies pinned to the pillars of the aisle, and the pulpit had been wreathed with old man's beard.

The 'other' Joneses came, Miss Sarah showing off as usual in her musquash coat and hat of parma violets. The Evan Bevans had come, Jack Williams the Vron, Sam the Bugle, all the remaining Morgans; and when Jack Haines Red Daren hobbled in on a stick, Lewis got up and shook his hand: it was the first time they had spoken since the murder of Mrs Musker.

There was a sudden silence when Theo came in with Meg.

Aside from her spell in hospital, she had never left Craig-y-Fedw in over thirty years: so her appearance in the world was an event. Shyly, in an overcoat down to her ankles, she took her place beside the giant South African. Shyly, she raised her eyes and, when she saw the rows of smiling faces, she screwed her own face into a smile.

Mr Isaac Lewis, in a suit of goose-shit green, was standing by the door to greet his flock. He had the odd habit of cupping his hands in front of his mouth, and gave the impression of wanting to catch his previous statement and cram it back between his teeth.

Bible in hand, he went up to Theo and asked him to read the Second Lesson – Chapter 21 of the Book of Revelation: 'I suggest you leave out verses 19 and 20. You might have some difficulty with the words.'

'No,' Theo stroked his beard. 'I know the stones of New Jerusalem.'

The first hymn – 'For the Beauty of the Earth' – got off to a shaky start with the singers and harmonium player at variance as to both tempo and tune. Only a few valiant voices struggled on to the end. Then the preacher read a chapter of Ecclesiastes:

'"A time to be born, and a time to die; a time to plant, and a time to pluck up that which is planted..."'

Lewis felt the heat of the radiator burning through his trousers. He smelled a whiff of singeing wool, and nudged his brother to move down the bench.

Benjamin stared at the black curls curling over the back of Kevin's collar.

'"A time to get, and a time to lose; a time to keep, and a time to cast away..."'

He glanced down at the Harvest Hymn Sheet, on which were printed pictures of the Holy Land – women with sickles, men sowing grain, fishermen by Galilee, and a herd of camels round a well.

He thought of his mother, Mary, remembering that she too had been in Galilee. And of how, next year, when the farm belonged to Kevin, it would be so much easier to slip through the needle's eye, and join her.

' "A time to love, and a time to hate; a time of war, and a time of peace..." '

On the back page was a caption reading 'All is Safely Gathered In' and, below it, a photo of some smiling crop-haired boys, with tin mugs in their hands and tents behind.

He read that these were the Palestinian Refugees, and thought how nice it would be to send them a Christmas present – not that they had Christmases over there, but they'd get their present all the same!

Outside, the sky was darkening. A clap of thunder sounded over the hill. Gusts shook the windows, and raindrops pecked against the leaded panes.

'Hymn Number Two,' said the preacher. ' "We plough the fields and scatter the good seed on the land..." '

The congregation rose and opened its mouth, but all the thin voices were silenced by one strident voice from the back.

The room was alive with the noise of Meg's singing and, when she came to the line, 'By Him the birds are fed,' a tear fell from Lewis's eyelid, and trickled down the crease of his cheek.

Then it was Theo's turn to hold the audience spellbound:

' "And I saw a new heaven and a new earth: for the first heaven and the first earth were passed away; and there was no more sea. And I John saw the holy city..." '

Theo moved through the text, listing the jasper and jacinth, the chrysoprase and chalcedony, without misplacing a syllable. The people facing the windows saw a rainbow arched over the valley, and a flock of black rooks beneath it.

When it was time for the sermon, the preacher got to his feet and thanked his 'brother in Christ' for so memorable a reading. Never in his experience had the Holy City seemed so real, so palpable. He, for one, had felt that he could reach out and touch it.

But this was not a city you could touch! It was not a city of brick or stone. Not a city like Rome or London or Babylon! Not a city of Canaan, for there was falsity in Canaan! This was the city that Abraham saw from afar, a mirage on the horizon, when he went to dwell in the wilderness, in tents and tabernacles...

At the word 'tent' Benjamin thought of Theo. Meanwhile, Mr Lewis had lost all trace of his ineloquence. His arms reached out to the roofbeams.

'Nor', he thundered, 'is it a city for the wealthy! Remember Abraham! Remember how Abraham returned his wealth to the King of Sodom! Remember! Not one thread, not one shoe-latchet would he take from the Kingdom of Sodom...!'

He paused for breath, and continued in a less emotional tone:

They had gathered in this humble chapel to thank the Lord for a sufficiency. The Lord had fed them, clothed them, and given the necessities of life. He was not a hard taskmaster. The message of Ecclesiastes was not a hard message. There was a time and a place for everything – a time to have fun, to laugh, to dance, to enjoy the beauty of the earth, these beautiful flowers in their season...

Yet they should also remember that wealth was a burden, that worldly goods would stop them travelling to the City of the Lamb...:

'For the City we seek is an Abiding City, a place in another country where we must find rest, or be restless for ever. Our life is a bubble. We are born. We float upwards. We are carried hither and thither by the breezes. We glitter in the sunshine. Then, all of a sudden, the bubble bursts and we fall to the earth as specks of moisture. We are as these dahlias, cut down by the first frosts of autumn...'

The morning of the 15th of November was bright and freezing hard. There was an inch of ice on the drinking-troughs. On the far side of the valley, twenty bullocks were waiting for their fodder.

After breakfast, Theo helped Lewis hitch the link-box to the International Harvester, and forked some hay-bales on to it. The tractor was slow to start. Lewis was wearing a blue knitted muffler. Another chill had gone to his inner ear, and he had complained of feeling giddy. Theo waved as the tractor lurched down the yard. Then he went indoors and chatted to Benjamin in the back-kitchen.

Benjamin had rolled up his shirtsleeves and was scouring egg-yolk from the plates. In the stone sink, rings of bacon fat had floated to the surface. He was very excited about Kevin's baby boy.

'Aye,' he smiled. 'Him be a perky little fellow.'

He squeezed out the dish-mop and dried his hands. A surge of pain shot through his chest. He fell to the floor.

'It be Lewis,' he croaked, as Theo helped him to a chair.

Theo rushed outside and looked across the valley at the frost-covered field. The oaks made long blue shadows in the slanting sunlight. Fieldfares were calling from the root crops. A pair of duck flew down the brook, and a vapour trail bisected the sky. He could not hear the noise of the tractor.

He could see the hay strewn over the field; but the bullocks had scattered, although one or two were beginning to edge back, in the direction of the hay.

He saw a muddy streak running vertically downhill along the line of the hedge. Below it was something red and black. It was the tractor lying on its side.

Benjamin had come out through the porch, hatless and shaking. 'Wait there!' said Theo, quietly, and ran.

Benjamin followed, limping down the path to the dingle. The tractor had slipped out of gear, and rolled. He heard Theo running on ahead. He heard the splash of water and, through the trees, he heard the seagulls shrieking.

The leaves had fallen from the birches along the brook. Points of frost sparkled on the purple twigs. The grass was stiff, and the water moved easily over the flat brown stones. He stood on the bank, unable to move.

Theo was walking towards him, slowly through the shining birch-trunks. 'You shouldn't see him,' he said. Then he folded his arms around the old man's shoulders, and held him.

L

B Y THE GATE into Maesyfelin graveyard there is an old yew-tree whose writhing roots have set the paving slabs askew. Rows of headstones flank the path, some carved with classical lettering, some with gothic, and all of them furred with lichen. The stone is soft; and on those that face the prevailing westerlies, the letters have almost worn away. Soon, no one will read the names of the dead and the tombs themselves will crumble into the soil.

By contrast, the more recent tombs have been cut from stone as hard as the stones of the Pharoahs. Their surfaces are polished by machine. The flowers placed upon them are plastic, and their surrounds are not of gravel, but green glass chips. The newest tomb is a block of shiny black granite, one half with an inscription, the other left blank.

Now and then, a tourist who happens to stray behind the Chapel will see, seated on the edge of the slab, an old hill farmer, in corduroys and gaiters, gazing at his reflection while the clouds pass by above.

Benjamin was so confused and helpless after the accident that he could hardly even button his shirt-front. For fear of upsetting him further, he was forbidden to go near the cemetery, and when Kevin moved his wife and baby into The Vision, he would stare straight through them as if they were strangers.

Last May, Eileen began to whisper that the uncle was 'going ga-ga' and that the proper place for him was the old people's home.

He had watched her sell the furniture piece by piece.

She sold the piano to pay for a washing machine, the four-poster for a new bedroom suite. She redecorated the kitchen in yellow, shoved the family photos into the attic, and replaced them with a picture of Princess Anne on a show-jumper. Most of Mary's linen went to a bring-and-buy sale. The Staffordshire spaniels vanished, then the grandfather clock; and the old iron range lay rusting in the farmyard among the docks and nettles.

One day last August, Benjamin walked from the house and, when he failed to return at nightfall, Kevin had to organize a search.

It was a warm night. They found him next morning, sitting on the tomb and calmly picking his teeth with a grass-stem.

Since then, Maesyfelin has become Benjamin's second home — perhaps his only home. He seems to be quite happy as long as he can spend an hour in the graveyard each day. Some afternoons, Nancy Bickerton sends her car to fetch him over for tea.

Theo has traded his South African passport for a British one, has sold his meadow, and gone off to India where he hopes to climb in the Himalayas.

No decision has been reached about The Rock: so Meg lives on there, alone.

Rosie Fifield, too, continues to live in her cottage. Because she is crippled with arthritis, her rooms have become very squalid, but when the District Health Officer suggested she move to an almshouse, she snapped, 'You'll have to drag me by the feet.'

For her eighty-second birthday her son gave her a pair of ex-Army binoculars and, at weekends, she likes to watch the hang-gliding off the summit of Bickerton's Knob — 'helicoptering' as she calls it — a stream of tiny pin-men, airborne on coloured wings, swooping, soaring in the upthrust, and then spiralling like ash-keys to the ground.

Already this year she has witnessed a fatal accident.